Obsessed – Until you're Mine
By Don Both and Maria O'Hara
First published in Germany 2019

Contact: https://www.facebook.com/DonBothMariaOHara/
Special thanks to Kerstin Patze and Nicole Zdroiek
Cover: Marie Grasshoff
Editing: buchuebersetzer.webs.com
Published by:
A.P.P.-Verlags GmbH
St. Gallerstraße 49
9100 Herisau
Schweiz
Mobi: 978-3-96115-635-1
E-Pub: 978-3-96115-636-8
Print: 978-3-96115-637-5

Don Both & Maria O'Hara

OBSESSED

Until you're mine

A.P.P.
Romance

For all women with the heart of a fighter.
For all single moms.
For all those who were so much in love that it left them devastated.
For all those who had to put up with crazy teachers, money problems, and prejudice.
For all Cinderellas who are still searching for their prince.
And for all those princes who let their Cinderellas go.
For all those who have lost often, only to get back up again and again.
This is for you.

Foreword

Dear readers,

A little warning upfront: This story is unlike any previous Don Both and Maria O'Hara publications. This time we allowed ourselves to be more daring. We became so engrossed with the story we had a difficult time ending it.

We would like to give our gratitude to the great author, Caroline Kepnes. It was her inspiration and motivation that made us approach a darker topic that we had denied ourselves for so long. Also, this time we wrote in the intense Present Tense, opening new doors for us.

Yes, we want YOU to feel personally addressed.

So that YOU immerse yourself in this world.

So YOU know what it means to be obsessed with Keaton J. Rush.

So YOU know what it means to immerse in the dark world of lust, desire, and total insanity.

But beware.

If you have problems with crude and crass language, prefer conventional lovey-dovey stories, and only tolerate sex in the missionary position, then you should set this book aside and seek more suitable reading material.

However, if you are willing to delve into the dark abysses of a relationship and become involved in an unconventional love story where you get a peek beyond the characters' facades, well then, this story is the right choice and we hope you enjoy it.

Don't say we didn't warn you...

Prologue

You don't see me, but I see you.

I always see you.

I'm always there — no matter what you do.

No matter if you're a lovely mother during the day or a debauched whore at night.

Are you presently reading to your child or wrapping your legs around a pole.

I see you rubbing your petite hot body against other men and serving guests in your chaste uniform.

I know how you think, who you are, and who you would like to be.

I know what you need and you will get it.

Soon.

Then you will be mine.

1. On the finishing line

Keaton

Again, you're wearing those ridiculous shoes that should be tossed in the trash. I have no idea why you don't spend 20 bucks for new sneakers. But even that would be not enough. You deserve the most expensive high heels.

And you are running late again because every morning you make the mistake of hitting the snooze button on your alarm clock, again and again, even though you should get your ass out of bed.

Every morning the same stress.

Your hair is messy.

Your clothes are put on haphazardly... I see more skin than is good for me or you. I can't focus when you show so much skin, Olivia. You'd almost think you're doing it on purpose.

You get a kick out of making the same mistakes. However, I will not be a mistake, sweetie. I will be the best thing that ever happened to you.

I'm rock hard again.

You want a sip of coffee while trying to comb your hair at the same time. I suppress a grin as some coffee spills and ruins the white blouse you just put on. You are so cute. I want you. I want to lick the coffee from your décolleté, whisper in your ear to knock it off or I'll fuck you right here propped up against the doorframe, and you can forget about getting to work on time. I want you to look me in the eye when you come and know to whom you belong.

Not too much longer now and my fantasies will become reality. I cannot take it anymore. I can't stay away from her any longer, not one more minute.

But it's time to leave for one should stop when things are at their best...

I am the hunter.

You are my prey — and I will get you.

Today.

2. Time

Olivia

There are so many wise sayings about time. How infinite and transient it is. How to make proper use of it while there is still time. It is impossible to turn back to undo things.

Now!

I consider time nothing more than pressure! Every morning – yet the funny thing is, I'm incapable of learning from it.

"MOMMY, LOOK!" roars Riley. "TODAY I GO AS A SUPERMAAAN!"

I sigh and try to entice Rosie, our bulldog lady, to eat her food. To claim that English bulldogs eat anything is a lie. Rosie is incredibly picky.

"Riley, baby, you cannot wear the Halloween Superman

costume. It's March! Come on, Rosie!" I whisper in the same breath and shove the bowl toward her. Rose has allergies and cannot eat everything. She just sits there, her beige and white fur shining in the sun, her fat rolls moving leisurely as she raises her wrinkled head with overbite and stares at me.

"Rosie!"

"OUCH!"

Groaning, I sternly look at the dog one last time, then head into the living room while attempting to blot the coffee stain from my one and only white blouse.

Riley is sitting on the floor. He is six, but sometimes I still see the baby in him, like now. His chocolate-brown curls stand up on all sides. He actually manages to squeeze into the Superman costume and rubs his cheek. There is something in his open hand. Rosie trudges past me to inspect the item.

"Mommy, I lost a tooth!"

Great!

I sigh – again – and hurry over to him. A drop of blood wets the corner of his mouth. He obviously has not rinsed the sleep from his dark eyes and has a baby tooth in his hand that Rosie apparently wants to eat. I roll my eyes – she wants it but not her expensive food.

"Wow, honey! Do you think the tooth fairy will come tonight, huh?" I am a little sad and wistful. Riley is growing up too fast. Considering his idiosyncrasies, adulthood will certainly not be easy for him.

I'm upset with myself for oversleeping. I have a job interview in half an hour. Rosie still has not done her business outside and the only white blouse I own has a stain.

"IT HURTS!" roars Riley as he stares at me with huge saucer eyes.

"Oh, baby," I mumble and place my hand on his, wrapping it around his tooth. "Soon, you'll be all grown up and will have forgotten about it." I kiss his hand and whisper conspiratorially, "I heard the Tooth Fairy pays top dollar for this tooth." It's his cuspid.

His eyes widen. "REALLY?"

"Yes, really! Place it under your pillow! Then go wash your face." He nods eagerly and jumps up, instantly hobbling while bracing himself against the wall before disappearing into his room, the only other room we have. I sleep on the sofa.

While Riley freshens up, I rush to the rod holding the few clothes I own and grab a dark gray sweater to wear over my blouse. It looks a bit conservative, but that's okay I guess just as long as no one can see the stain. The utility room has a common washing machine that costs a dollar per load, which adds up, especially when you have a child and...

"ROSIE NO!"...a dog soiling the apartment.

Rosie seems totally relaxed as she squats on my blanket that is still on the sofa and does her business.

I race over to her. "ROSIE!"

Startling her, she jumps down and tries to hide in the small open kitchen.

I sigh and shake my head. She did it again. I'm so frustrated and quickly remind myself why I have this dog. Rosie had been left to fend for herself when she was a little pup. I took her repeatedly to the nearby shelter, but she was so strong-willed, always managing to escape and hunt me down that I eventually gave up and adopted her.

"Listen, young lady," I admonish her while at the same time my heart grows weak as she lowers her head and gives me puppy dog eyes. "This is not for you to go on, lady! This is my bed, got that?"

She makes a strange noise as I quickly clean up her business, then peel off the blanket while keeping an eye on the clock the entire time – when the doorbell rings. It must be Penny, my neighbor and best friend. She always comes to my rescue. She's a nail technician who works under the table out of her apartment, thus always available to watch Rosie during the day or Riley at night when I pursue my secret second job.

Rosie is right on my heels as I dash to the door to let in my girlfriend. She wears a pink ADIDAS tracksuit and has a cigarette between her red-painted fingers, as usual, and despite her wanting to quit, all the while chewing gum. Her perm is out of style, the ends of her hair split. As always, she wears pink lipstick, which I think she even sleeps in.

Regardless, Penny's soul is gold, her heart a diamond.

"I have to run!" I greet her and grab the cup of cold coffee from the dresser for one last sip. "RILEY, LET'S GO!"

"No problem, sweetie."

"You'll have to take Rosie to do her business. She just had an accident on my blanket. RILEY!"

He comes hobbling while supporting himself on anything he can put his hands on. He is still wearing the Superman costume and I sigh – again – because there is no time to change clothes.

"AUNT PENNY, I LOST A TOOTH!" he yells.

I have a headache. Like every morning. It's way too early for all this.

"Where are your crutches, Riley?"

"Darling, you have to put it under your pillow," Penny says seriously, her blue eye shadow all shiny. She is a beautiful woman with no taste. Nevertheless, I don't care for I've long since learned that people with good taste are mostly superficial assholes.

"I DID THAT ALREADY! THE TOOTH FAIRY COMES LATER. MOMMY SAYS..."

"Where are your crutches, mister!" I cut him off.

"I don't want to use my crutches, Mommy! Nobody but me uses crutches, it makes me look stupid!"

I've been wearing my scuffed shoes for quite a while now and at the last moment, decide they are inappropriate for my job interview. "Honey, they're nothing special," I explain as I lsearch for the boots I bought some six years ago. "You're Superman, okay? You are special!"

He stares at me as if he doesn't believe me and I realize he is getting too old for my sweet nothings.

"Oh come on, cowboy," Penny attempts to sweet talk him while petting Rosie. "The crutches are your secret weapon, right? We talked about that!" He nods. "And no superhero faces his enemies without a secret weapon, right?" He nods again and grabs Penny's outstretched hand. "Come on, let's go get them together."

I love Penny.

Really.

* * *

Chicago, the windy city, an apt name. As soon as Riley and I stepped outside, icy wind blows around our ears. Thankfully, I was able to talk him into wearing his jacket over the costume, though I see he is slowly outgrowing it. He is growing up too fast.

I want to hold his hand like other mothers do when they walk their children to the school bus, but he needs to hold his crutches since his right leg is missing from the knee down. It breaks my heart that I can't carry him, can't give him my leg, and can't afford a prosthesis. It breaks my heart to see his scrawny arms supporting his weight while other children run and stumble around happily.

Despite running late, I keep pace with Riley.

"I'm cold," he says as he glances up at me. He is gorgeous. He looks like my dad when he was a child. I'm glad there are no similarities to his biological father. None whatsoever.

"Wait," I say and he stops. I get down on one knee and zip up his jacket.

"But no one can see my emblem anymore!" he complains.

I kiss him on the forehead. "No need, even closed everyone can tell you are a strong man."

He smiles and my heart melts. I get back up and we continue to the bus stop. Whenever Riley and I are walking, I push whatever terrible thoughts come to mind away as quickly as possible. Wallowing in self-pity doesn't do any good. I'm a fighter now, at least since I became a mom.

Next to the bus stop is a small cafe where many mothers enjoy a beverage as they wait for their little rascals to board the bus. And yes, all are rascals. Spoiled, ill-behaved, naughty, cruel rascals. Although I know Riley has problems with his classmates, I have to work nonstop with no time to hang around the bus stop or see his principle.

The bus stop is full of giggling children who are pushing each other around. Others are already constantly staring at their cell phones, which makes me appreciate my little one's modesty. Still, I can see the sadness in his eyes, wanting to be normal like the others.

To have two good legs.

"Okay, baby, Aunt Penny and Rosie will pick you up here when school is finished, okay?" I give him another peck on the forehead and ignore the whispering mothers. I know they are gossiping. Children might be cruel, but parents are much worse. They talk about my clothes, my upbringing, me being a single mom, that I never attend PTA meetings, and that I am not as good as they are.

I let it slide by me and my voluptuous butt, which is still plump despite my busy schedule. Unlike their asses, which are flabby from doing nothing but gossiping all day while their husbands work their asses off.

"Can't you wait with me?" Riley asks and I swallow.

"Baby, I really have to go. Maybe soon I'll have a great job that allows me to spend more time with you."

"Really?"

I nod. "You'd like that, wouldn't you?"

"OH, YES!"

"That's why I have to go now or my new boss will be angry, you understand, right?"

Bravely, he nods. I love him more than life itself.

"I love you," I say and give him a kiss on the cheek. "More than anything."

"Me too," he replies. I quickly hurry away so I won't hear the conniving mothers' nasty words.

3. Weird Eyes

Olivia

Miraculously, I arrive at the huge tower three minutes shy of eight o'clock. Its glassed walls glisten, creepily stretching into the gray sky and I already know I'll never make it on time. No way.

Nevertheless, I quickly join the mass of people and am pulled along through the glass doors. I finally make it to the lobby, stumbling extremely inelegant, and face three elevators.

I step up to the nearby white marble counter manned by a blonde, impeccably looking hussy in a business suit. Though she appears to be barely of legal age, she already has a haughty attitude, thinking she is better than everyone else. She gives my off-the-rack outfit, certainly not from an expensive boutique, a snooty once over, then more or less professionally asks, "How can I help you?" although you can tell I'm actually bothering her, for, 'Oh my God, what's this tramp want from me?' is literally written across her perfect forehead.

As I'm older and wiser, I simply ignore her bitchiness. I don't have the time to deal with another woman's insecurities when she looks at me for the first time and realizes I'm...beautiful, I'm competition.

Boo-hoo.

"I have an interview with Mr. Rush, department 587."

"Take the elevator to the sixth floor, you can't miss it."

"Thank you," I growl and go to the elevators. The doors of one are closing but I manage to stick my hand in between to make it open. The suits stare at me like I am a purple cow as I hurriedly enter while tugging the straps of my old handbag repeatedly over my shoulder. I think about mooing so they have reason to stare at my getup, but vehemently resisted. It would be embarrassing if one of the sheep is my potential employer. I don't think mooing would make a good first impression.

At one minute past eight, I stepped off the elevator and onto the floor that I will soon be in charge of providing all goes well. The corridor is unadorned and quite boring with its blue wall-to-wall carpeting and few pictures of cabins in the woods. The tiny reception desk is manned by a pretty Latina. She is no hussy like the receptionist on the ground floor, more like bull is written across her forehead, though considering her arrogance she is in no way inferior.

Did I mention I hate people?

"Yes?" she asks anything but polite. I make sure to maintain my composure and state my business.

"Ah, yes..." She quickly glances at the clock – now two past eight – then back to me in a more than reprimanding way. I barely keep from rolling my eyes. My goodness. A mere two minutes! TWO! Not twenty!

Asshole.

"Well then...have fun with Mr. Rush. He does not like tardiness," she announces, then nods at the three chairs lined up against the wall. Like a good little girl, I sit down on one. Killing time, I check out the nameplates next to the doors...

Montgomery Simmens.

Leila Harper.

Chester Parker...

Typical American names in an office that does not look like an office of the notorious FBI.

I'm sitting with a straight back, feeling as if I'm about to be called into the principal's office to be lectured because I was unruly in class or whatever. I believe the high school I went to back when, had these EXACT chairs that hurt your butt while you were waiting to get it chewed off. I grow increasingly more nervous since I cannot afford to mess this up. I want to improve my life. I have to improve my life, starting with winning the jackpot so I can pay for

Riley's prosthesis as well as a tour across Europe. One should keep one's dreams modest...

Penny got me this job interview — somehow, and I'm incredibly grateful. The pay is great and the working hours perfect for me! The work is not hard, at least not compared to what else I do... *God, please...should you exist, which I highly doubt, though that's another story, make them hire me! I'm not asking for much! As I've said, winning the jackpot, touring Europe, and this job! Fuck a hot guy, expensive jewelry, or a dream apartment... Men are nothing but trouble and who knows what Rosie would do to the dream home…*

I'm so lost in thought, I am unaware I'm being watched. It had to be for some time because eventually, my alarm bells go off and scream at me to look up. I am almost startled as I stare into...weird eyes. Although, I can't really say why I find them strange, I'm sure it will become clear to me soon.

He is standing there staring at me as if he had been doing so for some time and it's creepy. And hot. I have to admit.

He is tall.

Taller than most men with an athletic build. I can tell immediately. His face is beautiful and clean-shaven. His gaze his piercing. Oh, and his lips, my goodness, there should be a law against a man having such beautiful lips, especially when he doesn't kiss me.

He appears serious.

No smile on his face.

Even though he is leaning casually against the doorframe with his arms crossed in front of his chest, he is still tense. And, naturally, his suit is not off the rack. It takes me but a quick glance to see its tailor made and, together with a white shirt, fits his tall athletic body like a glove.

His intense gaze make the hairs on my arms, neck, and wherever else stand on end. Even my throat feels dry now and my head dizzy.

Fuck!

Like an imbecile, I have been holding my breath before finally filling my aching lungs with air.

I am captured by his intense gaze.

He literally takes my breath away. It is not until I glance at the ground and mumble, "Good morning, I'm...Miss Pierson," that I breathe normally again.

WOW!

I've never experienced such an intense first encounter.

I step toward him and force myself to look up into those weird eyes. They are blue, green...brown. Damn, quite an unusual eye color. His gaze is so piercing and intuitive, it is like he instantly sees every nuance of me, like who I am, really am, who I want to be, what I'm scared of, and what gives me pleasure. It is like he knows everything about me as well as this world.

He shakes my hand and it disappears in his. His strong fingers are dry. I hate nothing more than damp sticky hands, a limp handshake — and people. Naturally. He moves his eyebrows slightly as he squeezes my hand firmly but not too firm. Just right.

He holds my hand a little too long when he says, "My name is Mr. Rush... Nice to meet you, Miss Pierson." Once again I'm taken aback for I did not expect such a voice. It's cultivated, calm and yet quite...quite...alluring...as if he knows something I don't. His lips twitch as he greets me and I see a hint of a smile, which only makes his male face even more attractive.

Damn, what is this here?

I must be missing something!

As I'm so captivated by him, I pull my hand back much too late and stammer, "Yes, likewise...a pleasure!" DAMN YOU DUMMY! Pull yourself together! You are 26 with a child, no longer a little girl, Liv! Seriously!

He steps aside and I enter his office, again feeling a hot tingling on my neck and butt. Or am I simply imagining it because I want him to look at me like that, like a man ogles a woman, not like a boss observing a possible new employee.

His office is roomier than expected with a wonderful view of the Windy City. A bookshelf takes up one wall of the room. I'm intrigued and would like to peruse the book covers, but I refrain. Before it stands a black sofa, a coffee table, an armchair, and a counter with refreshments. Not one plant or picture. Also, an ancient recorder player and a large selection of albums are next to the sofa. Wow...his voice distracts me as I try to take a closer look.

"Please, take a seat."

I do as ask and sit on one of the two comfortable armchairs in front of a big mahogany desk. He sits down behind it, more like slides into his chair rather than plopping while holding his narrow dark tie in place. Clearly, the man has taste. The decor of his office shows it – even if it's typically masculine, minimalist, and impersonal – just like his clothes and modern haircut. Although his hair is a bit longer, it is neat, impeccably combed back, yet stays softly in place. It is dark, almost black, or is it brown? I'm unsure, his hair color is as hard to figure out as is the color of his eyes. Fascinating. Leaning back, he places his long fingers together and calmly looks at me. He does not say anything — I become nervous again.

Why doesn't he say anything, God? I hate small talk, so I force myself to smile professionally.

"Well, here I am..."

"Here you are." He continues staring at me. Fuck, what's wrong with the guy, I wonder. I cannot figure him out and continue to smile bravely, all the while, he makes me more and more nervous. The air seems too thick to breathe.

"Well..." I am at a loss for words and restlessly slide in my chair. I wish he would direct the conversation since I'm not good at that!

"You've applied for cleaning position." He finally puts me out of my misery, not looking at his papers or anywhere else but my face. Right into my eyes, into me. All the way to my soul.

I get goose bumps.

"Yes, I have." I swallow as his intense gaze becomes unbearable.

"I've received and looked at your references and I'd like to ask a few more questions. Please don't be alarmed, the questions might seem odd at first, but it is the standard FBI recruitment test."

"Uh... okay."

He leans forward, opens his black but quite ordinary notebook that's before him and picks up a pen that looks as if it might costs more than I pull in at the diner and my secondary job annually.

"Are you ready?"

"Uh, yes..."

Briefly, he grins.

"Please always reply with the first thing that comes to mind. Don't think about it." Am I seeing a therapist?

I nod, determined to get the job even if it takes — okay, I have limits.

The first question immediately confuses me.

"Black or white?"

"Black!" I reply as I suppress thinking about the answer. He smile a little wider as he neatly jots my answer in his notebook.

"Hot or cold?"

"Hot!"

"Sea or mountains?"

"Mountains!"

"Heaven or hell?" I'm sorry, I hesitate, he merely looks at me expectantly.

"Um..." Honestly, I actually lean more toward hell because I imagine heaven to be totally boring, everyone buzzing about in white gowns, playing the harp or whatnot...but who would answer hell?

"Heaven," I answer, he grins even wider...and jots something I cannot read.

"Tea or coffee?"

"Coffee of course!" I laugh, he does not. Perhaps he lacks humor, poor guy!

"Sports or couch?"

"Couch!"

"Reading or TV?"

"Reading!"

"Rock or pop?"

"Rock."

"Latex or satin?" Uh...he cannot be serious! Blazing red, I feel like asking if he has all his marbles. He continues looking at me seriously. I avert his eyes, glance downward, and timidly say, "Latex." I simply hate satin!

This cannot be a normal job interview! Something seems off! Honestly, another weird question like that and I'll ask him what his damn problem is. He is unaware of my dangerous mood and casually asks,

"Dog or cat?"

"Dog!" Though I also like cats, it's simply that my allergy stands in the way of getting a fluffy feline.

"Roses or orchids?"

"Roses," I reply not comprehending what all this has to do with a cleaning position. You would think I'm applying for a profiler job or whatever...

"Steak or fish?"

"Fish!"

"Pasta or rice?"

"Pasta!"

"Day or night?"

"Night." I've always been a night owl.

"Sugar or fat?" Now I'm completely taken aback.

"What does that…?"

"Just answer the question!"

His stern tone makes me flinch slightly and I mumble, "Sugar?" His mysterious smile throws me.

"Alcohol or drugs?"

"NEITHER, OF COURSE!" bursts from me way too quickly and hysterically. He just grins to himself. Dammit!

"Monogamy or..." He falls short and tilts his head. "I think we're done for now."

THANK GOD!

"That is it..." He abruptly closes his notebook.

"That's it?"

"Yup." Mr. Rush stands. "Please see Mrs. Rodriquez for your contract." I also rise, convinced I appear completely flabbergasted... I mean, we did not even talk about my pay expectations, work hours, or whatever. It's mindboggling.

"I've got the job?" I stare at him, still unable to

comprehend. This is the weirdest, quickest job interview ever. He elegantly – so damn elegantly – walks to the door and holds it open for me. Clearly, I am dismissed. At least for now...

"Yes." I step through the door. "And have a nice day, Miss Pierson." He closes the door right in front of my nose, no shaking hands, nothing at all...I'm even denied one last glance at his stirring eyes. From one moment to the next, I stand in middle of the corridor, still staring at the door and oh-so-slowly realize I have the job! I HAVE IT!

OH

MY

GOD!

4. My Holy Whore

Keaton

I have the boner of a lifetime and you're not here, Olivia.

Nobody can resist your cherry lips. Experience has taught me this, not to mention, I see how those fuckers look at you. Although you wear the most virginal impossible clothes, you are a feast for the eyes. The way you blush when embarrassed. The way your pupils dilate when you lie. Or your crystal clear green eyes, which betray too much suffering, too much grief. Or how you try to tame your unruly golden hair and I love when it is all disheveled and wild, just like your nature. You have no idea how much I want to bend you over this desk and fuck you until you scream my name!

However, I'm patient.

Good things come to those who wait.

And I have waited a long, very long time.

Your fragrance, that cheap perfume you buy in a drugstore, still lingers in the room, long after you've left. But it doesn't matter, Olivia, because you smell like heaven no matter what you're wearing. Soon you will bathe in Dior and be pampered with the most expensive oils. By me. All over your body.

You sensed how dangerous I am. Your posture betrayed you when you slid around insecurely, as did your puckered lips, dilated pupils, and your anxious and innocent looking wide eyes.

But then you're anything but innocent, aren't you?

And you stuck it out despite the alarm bells going off in your pretty little head. All because of the job? Possible. Because of your son? Also possible.

Or maybe also because you crave a little danger because you like leading a double life.

My saint. My little whore.

Now you will become mine.

5. Too late, as usual

Olivia

"…it just won't do, Mrs. Pierson!"

"MISS," annoyed, I correct her as I stumble off the bus and rush to the diner. "I'm not married, Mrs. Garvey." Riley's teacher, a strict Catholic, simply cannot handle me being unmarried and a young single mother.

"Whatever! Riley cannot come to school wearing a Halloween costume! What do you think will happen tomorrow?"

I grin. "Another Halloween party? Just let the kids have some fun!" Even though the sun is shining through the breaks in the clouds, I'm still cold. Spring might be approaching, but it is way too slow. Once summer is here, it'll be hard again on Riley when he wants to go to the pool and everyone ends up staring at him. Stupid people, I hate them. Since I have Riley, I realize how terrible this world is and how he deserves much better.

"Mrs. Pierson..."

"MISS!" I interrupt her as I shoulder open the heavy door of Jack's Diner while still keeping my old cell phone pressed to my ear. Jack is at his usual spot behind the counter. His lecherous gaze pointedly eyes the clock. Is today punctuality of particular importance or what?

I mouth a silent "Sorry".

"Whatever!" Mrs. Garvey hisses. "This is a school and..."

"I understand! Riley will come in regular clothes tomorrow. Is that it?"

She snorts, probably thinks I am a bad mother, yet I am working 16 hours a day so my child can have a somewhat decent life.

"You really should attend the PTA meeting..."

"Oh...Mrs. Garvey?" I interrupt, intentionally leaving out words as I walk into the back room and set down my bag. "I'm...tunnel...cannot...you..." I hang up, rolling my eyes, and tie my apron. It's orange like everything else in the diner. Only a man could pick such a shitty color. I'm annoyed, extremely annoyed, even though I should be celebrating for I got the job with Mr. Rush and my life is about to change. Granted, I'm 'just' the cleaning lady, but it allows me to give up my second job and the need to lead a double life. No more working until way past midnight, no more functioning on little sleep and rushing to the diner, and no more spending only little time with Riley! Mr. Rush gave me a one-year contract for now and the pay is substantial considering I'm only cleaning. Anyway, for my qualifications, I find 25 bucks an hour quite good! I've never earned such a high wage.

I go to the main part of the diner and greet Jack.

"You're late," he grumbles. Jack sports a beer belly, always wears a dirty shirt, and he sweats whether it's winter or summertime. I cannot help it, but he reminds me of a butcher. Then there is his thinning hair that is always plastered to his forehead. He also stinks of sweat and at times, alcohol, still, he is not short on patrons, probably because of me as I'm quite friendly to my customers. The bigger the tip the better.

"Lousy 20 minutes," I add and nod. "The bus was running late."

"You'll be staying 20 minutes longer today!"

I scrunch my forehead. I really don't have the time to stay past my regular shift. "You know I'm always pressed for time, Jack. I'll come in 20 minutes earlier tomorrow."

He tries to brush back the few sweaty hairs he has. "That'll work for me!"

I roll my eyes, like he has a say in it. If it weren't for me, he could declare bankruptcy. The orange tables and overall orange decor gives everyone a headache!

I'm tired and unfocused. Time and again, I drop something, get names of the regulars mixed up, and who is sitting at the bar drinking coffee. Today is simply a weird day. I'm still haunted by those intense eyes. I cannot help but repeatedly contemplate what that man might have exuded. What mesmerized me so much? Actually, he came across a bit scary. He has a side to him that I definitely don't want to know, still, I was not afraid. Especially not men, considering everything I've experienced. I'm not easily intimidated.

I work through the day without breaks to make up the 20 minutes. Jack does not mind. When my shift ends, I take a roasted chicken and two hot portions of French fires with me so Riley and I can have a warm meal. There is no time to shop and though Penny makes sure he eats something for lunch, he needs a proper meal for dinner. Granted, fried food is not exactly nutritious for a growing boy. I'd much rather feed him an organic casserole, but nowadays, organic products cost more than a sweater at Wal-Mart.

I'm rushing home, but I don't catch the first bus and run late again. Now I only have four hours to spend with Riley, talk to Penny, and freshen up. I have a long commute to get to my nighttime job. I would not do it nearby where I might be recognized and people started talking. Riley already is bullied because of me, no need to add to it.

The wind blows around my ears and I'm cold. It's hard to believe it is already March, to me it still feels like winter.

Impatiently, I wait for the next bus without noticing what is going on around me. How nice it would be to drive home in my own little car after my shift at the diner, then cook a homemade meal for supper, and a bedtime story for my child. To have more time for everything, even to take better care of myself and treat myself more often to facial masks or talking to Penny about serious important issues...however, that's not the case and I've long since made peace with my situation.

It's half past six in the evening by the time I make it home and the food is no longer hot. As soon as I open the door, Rosie comes trudging toward me, grunting and happy with her big butt swaying, knocking whatever is in its path down.

Her wet nose and drooling snout are glued to my leg, curiously taking in whatever smells are on my nylons.

"Hello, darling," I mumble as I pet her oversized head. She is so happy her butt hits the wall, startling her into running away.

I laugh.

Typical Rosie!

"MOMMYYYYYY!" Riley limps toward me while supporting himself against the wall. He hardly uses his crutches at home, simply refuses, but I gladly let him move about freely. At least at home he can. He has already showered – I just love Penny – and is in his pajamas.

"Sorry I'm late," I murmur as I hug him. I love the way he smells and how just holding him in my arms, feeling his purity perks me up, no matter how bad the day. He is innocent and pure-minded, unlike any of the people I associate with on a daily basis.

"Hi!" Penny appears behind Riley. She's still wearing the tracksuit, but now her hair is now tied back. She's chewing gum, as always, and I give her lots of credit for not smoking in front of Riley. She makes due with chewing gum until her cravings become too great and she goes outside for a smoke. Oftentimes, Penny takes Riley and Rosie upstairs to her apartment, but apparently not today.

"Hi," I greet as I set Riley down and pick up the bag. "I brought dinner."

"I'm stuffed!" Riley announces. "Aunt Penny and I cooked lots of food!"

Penny smiles and nods toward the kitchen. "We left you a plate."

I. Love. Penny.

I go to the kitchen and cut the chicken into pieces for Rosie. Her bowl is still full of the dry food the princess doesn't like. She's huffing, all hyper, impatient for me to set a bowl of chicken in front of her. She inhales it rather than eating it.

Riley starts babbling and even though my head is not up for that right now, I do enjoy his voice. It's warm in the apartment and Penny has tidied up. She usually has only two or three customers a day, which she takes care while Riley is at school. Penny does quite well. Granted, by no means is she rich – or she wouldn't live in this neighborhood – but she makes ends meet. She is alone and if she's really up a shit creek, as it happens from time to time, her sister helps out. She does not declare her manicure earnings and uses the cash for shopping.

I hear the TV in the background, one of the thousand children's series Riley loves so much. Penny reheats a bowl of stew for me and I eat it at our small kitchen table. Riley is so excited I'm home, he cannot sit still and is putting too much strain on his leg.

Penny joins me at the table and nods to Riley. He hops onto my lap. I hope he doesn't grow up too soon, where he finds it embarrassing.

"I have to leave again soon," I say to Penny.

"I'll put our little Superman to bed." Penny winks at Riley and he laughs, though his big wide eyes look up at me.

"Mommy, why can't you take me to bed?"

"Baby, you know I have to work." I have a spoonful of stew, it is delicious. "But the good news is that from next week on, Mommy will be home to tuck you into bed!"

Penny raises her eyebrows. "You got the job?"

Smiling, I nod. "Yes, I got the cleaning job!"

She claps her hands enthusiastically. "That's great, sweetie! Congratulations!"

"Thanks." I smile. "I have to be there at ten and clean for two hours. Every day. And they're paying twenty-five bucks an hour, can you believe it?"

Penny's eyes widen. "Holy shit!"

"You don't say shit!" Riley shouts.

"That's right, you don't say that, but I'm a grown woman," Penny explains and we all laugh. It's nice to feel relaxed and let go of the stress and weight.

It’s nice to have a family.

6. *Gods & Monsters*

Olivia

I'm running late again as I could not deny Riley and put him to bed myself. By the time he's happily asleep, I know for certain I won't get to work by nine. Though my shift starts at ten, I need time to prepare.

I quickly shower, don something loose, and tie my hair back. I'm still not made-up for usually I have enough time to do it at work.

I slip into my shoes while Penny leans against the wall in the hallway. I hear Rosie snoring, something playing on TV, and feel like lying down next to her. But I can't.

"Twenty-five bucks an hour is great, Liv. I mean, in your current job, you only make fifteen." Penny, like everyone else, thinks I'm cleaning offices at night, which is not true.

"Yes, I am so happy." I put on my jacket.

"Hey, I meant to talk to you about something else. It's about Riley."

"What about him?" I ask, fighting the zipper.

"He always tells me about a friend of his."

Now my ears perk up for I know Riley has no friends. Ignorant brats with a stick up their butts aren't friends with Riley.

"So?"

"He says his name is John and he always comes to his aid when other kids make fun of him." She scratches her temple. "I think he's imagining him."

I sigh. It was only a matter of time before Riley did that. "He is a loner who gets bullied. Most likely, he made up an imaginary superhero friend." Actually, I know it's quite common for little kids to have imaginary friends, but in Riley's case, I'm bothered for it tells me his situation is weighing on him and he needs someone to give him encouragement.

"Fuck, I'm running late," I curse. "Let's talk about it tomorrow, okay?"

She nods and gives me a peck on the cheek. "Okay."

* * *

I have no idea how I was only a few minutes late. Perhaps the bus running on time for once helped.

The bus stop I get off at is in the middle of nowhere. The place I work at is nearby, right along a highway, so we have a passing clientele. And that we have plenty of. Tonight is foggy and the street relatively quiet. I hold my jacket closed as I walk to the club since the zipper is now broken for good.

The red neon letters of the club, SATISFACTION, break the foggy darkness. The parking lot is already quite full and the music rich bass can be heard booming outside. I enter the club and feel like the atmosphere devours me. Every night it's the same — as soon as I'm in the door, I feel like another person. The interior smells of deception, power, and sex. Of lust.

Well, it's a strip club after all.

The lighting is kept dim so guests are hardly recognized, the fog machine adding to it. Along the entire length, from the facade to the club's rear wall runs a bar. Along the center of the open space is a stage or rather a catwalk with a pole on either end. Two of my colleagues are already pole dancing. We can decide how much skin we show. Then again, the more you show the more money you make, that's a no brainer. Only a few of my colleagues bare all, certainly not me, but I still show more skin than others. Dark blue and cool white spotlights oscillate across the stage. The clientele varies — from rich business suits to everyday husbands to truck drivers taking a break on their haul. All types of men.

But that is not my problem.

Without any close relationships with my colleagues as we generally are all in competition with each other is, we simply say hi and goodbye and occasionally team up to give private dances providing a customer asks for and pays according. That's as far as it goes.

I quickly disappear in the employees' only area and slip into my changing room. Every girl has their own, complete with nameplate. It's where I keep my makeup and outfits. I plan on talking to Pablo today, the owner of *Satisfaction*, to give my notice. I hope he won't give me a hard time and demand a notice period.

As I'm putting on my outfit, I tell myself it won't be for much longer, still, it's quite daring, a salacious piece. But I make double, unlike were I do not reveal as much. So I decide not to cover my breasts, just some pasties over my nipples.

Gone are my cotton panties, replaced by a sheer black thong, which actually consists of only a few strings that do not cover anything. My nipple pasties are same colored pads in the form of small crosses. To complete my ensemble, I step in front of my mirror and quickly put on makeup — a little eyeliner, a bit of rouge, strong perfume that attracts men, and red lipstick that matches my *underwear*. I only put on a little mascara. The men out there aren't interested in my face I admit to myself with an eye roll.

After I unbinding my hair and shaking it loose, I don a black skin-tight wraparound leather dress – after all, I have to take off something – and slip into my high heels.

It should do.

I leave my golden curls dangling whichever way. I know the cretins out there love disheveled hair.

As soon as I'm done, I hear my name announced — *Blossom.* It's my stage name, naturally, for no one here uses their real name. I'm not even sure if the owner's name is actually Pablo.

I take a deep breath and slip into the role I assume here. A good mother and waitress are not called for in this establishment. A different kind of personality is required.

I have to become the hot bitch...the femme fatale.

Once I'm ready, I step out of my changing room to cheering men. Although I'm nothing but a piece of meat to them, my assumed dark side rather likes it.

I step up onto the still dark stage and wait for my song to begin. As the dark tones of *Gods and Monsters* fills the room, I step forward when the first bass sounds and with it, the spotlight is turned on me. I grab the pole with one hand and let my body move to the rhythm with my eyes closed.

As I take a deep breath, I smell it.

Something seems off today.

There's something here that shouldn't be.

I pull on the string of the dress and it peels slowly off my body. The greedy lustful men almost drool as they lean forward trying to touch me. I'm in another dimension. I slowly slide down the pole and continue holding it as I feel the music, feel the words of the song that gives me goose bumps.

Something is different.

My legs wrap around the pole and I start rubbing against it as if my life depends on it, knowing a few already have a stiffy. Knowing they want me, my heart starts to beat faster.

Something is different.

I open my eyes and see what it is.

I'm losing my mind, overwhelmed by emotions, feeling the bass deep in my bones as I stare into those eyes that haunted me all day.

I see him!

He stands there all in black, his muscular arms stiffening as he stares absolutely lecherously, lustfully at me.

A groan escapes my lips as I swing around the pole and lower my head and upper body into the spotlight...

When I look back, he is gone. My eyes search for him and his scent.

He's a stranger.

He's always there.

Since seeing him in his office this morning, I cannot get him out of my head.

Now he is gone.

I get down on my knees, crawl to the edge of the stage, and toss my hair around. Presenting my ass to the viewers, I immediately feel hands on me, feel them tucking bills under the strings of my thong.

I scan the place but can't find him.

The situation is getting to me. I feel confused. It's like he's still there, like I can sense him.

Perhaps I am imagining it.

After all, I've been thinking about him since this morning.

I turn back around with my legs spread, dangling over the edge of the stage while running my fingers through my hair, smiling, seducing, enjoying teasing the men...though I still can't see him.

When the song ends, I'm completely spent.

Breathing heavily, I am confused and sweaty.

Boisterously, the men applaud as I grab the bills that fell out of my overstuffed thong and hurry back to my changing room.

What just happened?

7. Trips into Darkness

Keaton

You enjoy it here. You can act out a different persona when those spotlights are directed at you, presenting you like a piece of meat.

Oh, baby, you've no idea the places I'll take you once you're mine. But you already are, for just one look into my eyes was enough. We already connected, you can feel it deep inside you and it rattles you, right?

You are searching for me.

You want me.

And you love being treated like dirt. You must have low self-esteem, otherwise, you would not allow strangers to touch your ass and let their fingers glide over your sweet little pussy when the opportunity presents itself. But you love it, you love their attention.

During daytime, the good mother, at nighttime, the whore.

I know you're a whore.

I am aware of it and love it.

I'm watching you toss your long hair around while moving to the music. The way you wrap your body around the pole, like it's my cock. I can hardly wait to feel you, Olivia, to thrust into your wet little pussy, filling you until you roll your eyes ecstatically.

I'm looking at you while you're looking at me, just the way I want. Keep in mind, nothing happens unless I want it to happen. I want you to look at me, think only about me, nothing else.

You are aroused.

I can tell by your glazed eyes and the way you're raping the pole. You are excited you saw me. You want it. You want me. You want my attention, my hands. You want to feel it.

Oh, I'll let you feel it all right. Soon.

The song ends and you appear confused. I can tell by your big dazed eyes that you cannot wrap your head around what just happened.

Let me explain it to you, baby. *We* happened. We are a force of nature. Putting us in a room together will rattle the walls and create earthquakes.

You're connected to me — because that's what I want. Because it supposed to be like that. You are the one.

I'm following you. The commotion here makes it easy to get unobserved to your changing room. I don't care about the next whore dancing. The others don't feel it. They cannot compete with you.

You're breathing heavily as you stand in front of your Hollywood vanity mirror, eyeing yourself with your hands braced on the makeup table. I'm watching you, it's precisely what you want, or you would not have left the door ajar. However, I'm here to protect you, Olivia, in case a madman follows you! I have to take care of you. You are amazing.

The pasties do little to hide your hard nipples, which you now rip off your big round yet oh-so-nicely firm breasts. Your skin glistens from whatever cheap body lotion you used. The skimpily made thong is stuck between your plump ass cheeks and I can see your beautiful pussy shining through. The glaring neon light in your changing room makes me quickly realize you're wet.

If I came and fucked you, you would let me. But this is not the right moment, Olivia, despite my cock straining the seams of my pants. I want you so much. But it's up to *me* if I give in to lust. Not you.

You're brushing your fingertips over your cleavage and round breasts while you look yourself in the eyes. You're so hot for me, you're about to explode.

Just like I am.

But I won't succumb.

I'll just keep on watching you.

Still.

I quickly turn around, glad nobody else is in the back. I have to be careful not to attract attention.

Are you aware I'm watching you?

Are you putting on a show for me?

Resisting the overpowering urge to open the zipper of my pants and relieve myself, I resolutely grind my teeth as you pull your thong aside and plop onto the chair. I can see you in the mirror, Olivia. If anyone else witnessed this it might be fatal. You are careless.

You brush your fingers over your wet labia while biting your lower lip so no one hears you. Your breathing is rapid as you throw back your head and spread your legs further while massaging your little pearl. I feel my boner ooze drops of pleasure while my excitement increases with yours, my breathing as fast as yours. We're now connected and I cannot wait to get you out of here. Those fuckers who stare at, touch you, should see you belong to me. I will mark you for everyone to see. Soon. At a time I decide. Right now, I've decided to just stand here, enjoying your little private show.

You are so incredibly hot, baby. If we were together now, I would fill you all the way. I would fuck you from one orgasm to the next.

You slide two fingers inside you and start moving your hips.

It's embarrassing that I could come in my pants right now without even touching you, simply because you're the hottest thing I know, because your wet pussy is robbing me of my mind, because your bouncing tits mesmerize me.

You scream softly and cup your hand over your mouth so no one hears you climaxing.

You're mine, soon everyone will know.

8. No Longer Normal

Olivia

I just finished having a great hot intense orgasm. I almost felt as I wasn't alone when the door leading to the boss's office opens... Little skinny Pablo, as usual, with a gray three-day beard, greasy hair slicked back, wearing suspenders, and a cheap suit walks in and grins.

"Livi, my girl, how are you?" he asks pseudo-friendly. I straighten up and try to slow my breathing and wild beating heart, all the while, certain muscles continue contracting sporadically.

I swallow. "I'm fine, Pablo, thanks for asking!" I impede his hand as he trying to fondle me. He likes to grab and though, until now, I have always been able to endure it, it's time to put a stop to it. *Now.*

His milky blue eyes that are always red and clouded by alcohol and whatever drugs, flash a warning that I simply ignore.

"I'm quitting, Pablo."

His eyes widen as he throws his head back and laughs so that the stench of his nasty foul teeth assaults me. God, such a disgusting guy!

Why are all men in my vicinity so utterly disgusting, except one...

"Quit? You?" He can't stop laughing.

"Yes. I. Quit," I say with as much dignity as my nudity allows and start to dress, quickly slipping into my jeans. I will shower at home. I just want to get out of here. "You knew I would not work here forever, Pablo...and you have many..." I can't finish my sentence because he abruptly grabs my throat and shoves me against the wall. He's faster than I thought. His face with huge pores is as close to me as the knife he's pressing against my throat.

I swallow as my skin scrapes the old blade.

"You'll only do what I tell you to do!" he growls in my face, and unlike this afternoon, I'm not getting hot and cold at the same time. Neither do I have goose bumps. Or feel afraid. All I feel is scorn — deep inside me. Because I have no respect for this man, the same goes for most men I meet. Men are feeble creatures who have zero control of themselves and who succumb to their urges. I find them nothing but...pathetic. "I own you, you damn little..." I cut him off by ramming my knee full force into his crotch and immediately shove him back with both hands. I quickly grab my jacket and handbag and as icing on the cake, I ram my knee in his face on the way out my room, and he falls to the ground, holding his crotch, writhing in pain and insults. I would love to have a cool comeback like you hear in movies or TV shows, but of course can't think of anything. No matter how much I want to, it's always later on in bed when I think up something cool and powerful to say. Just like I'm a firm believer that saying things you wish for out loud will in principle nix them.

My brain is a mess as I rush out of my room into the dark corridor, leaving behind a trail of bills spilling out my purse when...I abruptly stop. Again, I'm overcome with an eerie feeling. Plus it smells too damn good, it never did before! Anyway! I have to get out of here and quickly put on my well-worn jacket, holding it together on my chest as I continue. Then it occurs to me how stupid I was not wait until the end of my shift, after I receive my money for the night, to quit. As the saying goes, hindsight…

***

Keaton

Just one second. I was just one second away from taking that greasy little bastard's life. But you surprised me by kneeing him, the only option available to you and the reason I dismissed the idea of intervening.

You have no idea how proud I am of you.

Plus, I'm relieved, it's not like I wanted to become a murderer — then again, for you I would do anything.

I would do anything for you, baby.

***

Olivia

Today was nerve-racking. Riley came home crying, which does not happen often. Penny comforted him, but he wouldn't tell either us what happened. He's quite sensitive, at the same time, he tries to be strong, *especially* for me so I won't be plagued by more worries, more fears. Regardless, I always worry about him. So I called Garvey for information on what happened, but naturally, she was clueless — no knowledge of anything that happened. God...sometimes I want to throw in the towel when everything becomes too much, when I feel drained, unable to handle it all.

This evening, I would have preferred to stay home, curl up on the couch with Rosie and a bag of Fritos, and watch some show. However, I have to make the best impression possible at my new job and hope the offices are empty as promised when I arrive at ten. This evening, a Tuesday, is the first time I actually tuck Riley into bed. I even read him a story out one of his favorite books, then kiss his forehead before he fell asleep, and check one last time that he is nicely tucked in.

I unlock the glass door with the key Miss Rodriquez-the-bitch gave me yesterday and all the security lights go off except the green emergency lights. I turn on the overhead lights for the long corridor as well as the reception desk, that way it's not as spooky. Outside, it is already dark and the windowpanes act like mirrors, making it seem as if I am alone in a parallel universe. Then again, I like solitude, not being watched, able to move freely while taking my time looking at everything. I can take all night if I want to, but I will only be paid for two. Today though, I'll take my time.

"Hi!" a voice behind me says. I am almost frighten to death, scream and whip around, flailing an arm into the face of a petite blonde.

"Ouch!" she yells, holding her cheek as her eyes flash me a look that could kill.

"Holy shit, you scared me!" I say in my defense, I mean, who sneaks up on someone from behind in darkness?

"Oh, I didn't mean to," she replies snappily. "You always slap people who startle you?"

I clutch my heart, take a deep breath, and give the little one some credit for she has no idea everything I've been through. It's a bad idea to sneak up on me.

"I'm sorry," I mumble. "It was reflex."

The blonde with legs like a supermodel and two beautiful symmetrically breasts like juicy melons winks at me with her thick heavily mascara eyelashes. "Whatever." She lightly moves her perfectly shaped jaw back and forth as if checking if it's broken. I refrain from rolling my eyes since I have no idea who's standing before me.

She gives me a once over. "You must be the new cleaning lady."

"No, I'm a burglar who is planning to steal top-secret documents."

For a moment, I actually think she believes me for her big blue eyes gaze stupidly at me, but as soon as I smile, she seems to relax.

"Yes, I'm the new cleaning lady." I hate being called a cleaning lady, it is degrading and makes me feel old.

"I've been waiting for you."

I raise an eyebrow. "I had no idea cleaning ladies receive a special welcome. So thanks for waiting. And, how can I help you?"

She looks down her nose at me, which, by the way, looks unnaturally perfect. "As you're new, I'm here to lend a hand and answer any questions you might have. I'm Pam, Mr. Rush's personal assistant."

AHA!

That explains it.

She is his *assistant*, perfect, blonde, with honey-melon sized breasts.

"Hello, Pam. I'm Olivia, Mr. Rush's new cleaning lady. Nice meeting you." She's younger than me, at the most, 21, thus I dispense with *formalites*. Honestly, I have no idea why this doll assumes a cleaning lady needs instructions. Anyone with a household should be capable of handling this, especially a person who does it professionally. But, okay, maybe she'll show me how to properly scrub a toilet and teach me a thing or two…

I can tell I annoy her. All day long she's subordinate to everyone else, the lowly secretary, and now she probably expects me to fall in line given I'm the lowly cleaning lady. Well, she's barking up the wrong tree. I never associate someone's position with status, be it high or low.

It's not a person's job that counts, it's their actions.

She clears her throat. "Care to follow me, please." Not waiting for a reply, she struts by me on her endless high heels. Her butt is as flat as a board. Perhaps she only eats one tic tac a day. She should use some of her breast tissue to pad her ass.

She stops in front of a small room and gestures inside. "You can change in there. Please don't open any drawers or cupboards, all top secret. Mr. Rush likes it neat and sterile. No sweet scents or whatever room freshener."

I tilt my head and my impetuousness gets the better of me, yet again. "But he puts up with your perfume?" Damn! Why can't I keep my mouth shut? When I'm supposed to make a witty comeback, I can't think of anything, yet when I should keep my mouth shut, some shit bursts out.

That's me!

She smiles condescendingly. "It's Armani and costs more than you make in a week. Mr. Rush appreciates a good high quality scent. Unlike cheap drugstore fragrances." She even sneers at me. "You should be careful with him, screw up once and you're gone. He does not like to be kept waiting, back talk, or shown no respect. Actually, he cannot stand other peoples' breathing."

"It seems you don't have much of anything good to say about him," I state, thinking he had to have hurt her pride or whatever.

"That's none of your business." She nods to the office across the corridor. "Please clean the entire floor and be thorough with his office. When you're finished, lock up. Don't tamper with locked cabinets or the alarm will go off. Have fun." She grabs her handbag, which must cost what I make in a year and toddles off on her stilts.

I roll my eyes. Women are poison.

I open the door to the changing room and turn on the light. I'm about to set down my bag when I notice a uniform and stop firmly in place, utterly flabbergasted.

What the hell?

Neatly folded on a chair is a housemaid uniform with a note on top. Skeptically, I pick it up and see my name written on it in immaculate handwriting. It's almost as if a calligrapher wrote it with great dedication. It's so beautiful, so perfect.

I recall the blonde doll's warning about Mr. Rush not liking back talk. I am put off.

Why should I clean in a uniform that barely covers my ass? Typical man! They imagine a woman cleaning, dressed sexily, and wiping sweat off her cleavage while waving around her duster...whereas I usually wear jogging pants and a tattered shirt. I also stink of sweat, get pissed off, get covered in dust and Rosie's shit, and curse worse than any dockworker

Not to mention, who would see me in this uniform!

I ignore the uniform, rolling my eyes, and search for my cleaning supplies. When I'm in the restroom filling a bucket with water, the lights suddenly go dark. Taken aback, I stay rooted in place and search the darkness. A power failure? Just now? I can't fathom it. I turn the water off, set the bucket down, and timidly step out of the room.

"Hello, is anyone there?" I call stupidly like the dumbasses in horror movies, as if a killer would bother replying sweetly, *Yes, it's me. You should hide!*

"Pam, are you still here?" I call out just to be sure.

Unexpectedly, the lights come on again and I feel a cold shiver run down my back. I have no idea why that is nor why my hairs are standing on end. A little anxious, I quickly turn around and jump. Now the uniform lies on the edge of the sink I just used to run water.

"How?" I whisper uncertain and call out, "WHO IS MESSING WITH ME?" But of course nobody answers. Or perhaps it was there all the time and my mind is playing tricks on me. What's happening?

Another cold shiver runs down my back. I want to go home, then again...I really need this shitty job. It must be Pam trying to unsettle me.

"Okay, Pam, very funny. Ha. Ha. Ha," I shout. "I haven't had this much fun in a long time!" It seems I have no choice and give in, grab the tight uniform and exchange outfits.

Shortly thereafter, I use the industrial vacuum cleaner and cruise through all the offices. Although it seems prehistoric, it does a great job and I finish all eight offices, the conference room, and lounge in one hour. I also tried to get an idea what exactly Mr. Rush does here as I vacuumed. However, his desk is absolutely impersonal, no photos, no snow globe, no small flower arrangement or card with some general motivational saying. It's easy to dust since I only have to lift a keyboard and monitor, otherwise, it's bare and totally impersonal. However, some of the desks in other offices have too much personal crap on them. One wall of the conference room is actually a pin board like you see in Hollywood movies. It must be where they pin clues when working cases, hunting down bad criminals. Perhaps Mr. Rush is a covert operative and outside the office, wears disguises such as dark sunglasses and a cigar clamped between his teeth to blend in with mobsters or whatever. Or he pretends to be a ring leader. I grin as I picture him wearing tattered biker clothes and a headscarf. It doesn't suit him. He is the *I-command-in-a-suit type*. Everything and everyone.

God, just thinking of him makes me shiver...

I'd like to ask him what he wears in his leisure time. And what exactly is his profession.

But of course I won't. Who knows if I'll even see him again considering I work late evenings when everyone is home, relaxing on their couches watching TV... Besides, he probably wouldn't cast a second look at the *cleaning lady* and has already completely forgotten about me... So, why can't I stop thinking about him?

I notice every room is equipped with a surveillance camera with a red light that comes on whenever I enter. It's eerie. Perhaps they're only dummies, as is the case in most places.

It takes me a good three hours until I'm done. Today, I've taken my time and was especially thorough so I only have routine cleaning to do in the coming days. Everything is sparkling clean now. It's one in the morning when I leave the building and walk to the nearby bus stop. Unfortunately, on the way, it starts to rain and of course, I did not bring my umbrella. My ancient sneakers are immediately drenched. I'm glad I don't have to wait long for the bus despite the late hour of the night. I board and sigh as I plop down on my seat.

God, it's nice to get off my feet! Oh, yes... I close my eyes, trying to relax, but my neck gets all tingly. I open my eyes again and look out at the rain.

A man is standing next to the street light and although he makes sure to stay in the shadows, I can tell his black trench coat is soaked. His face is but a black mask, his hands are in his jacket pockets, and he stands completely motionless. Staring at me!

I feel like I know him!

Before I can react, the bus takes off with a jerk. I shake my head, close my eyes, and start rubbing my temples, for all of a sudden, I have a headache, probably thanks to my sick brain.

First in the strip club!

Now here!

I see him everywhere!

I really am no longer normal!

9. I Am A Mess

Olivia

Today, I even arrive at the diner on time and start my shift not directly stressed out. For the first time in a long time, I slept well and feel rested. A burden I was unaware of before seems to have been lifted from my shoulders. No more undressing, no more strangers groping me, or lecherous eyes ogling me. No more being afraid of encountering a familiar face in the audience and worrying about Riley finding out. I feel liberated, reborn, fresh, and cheerful. I'm greeting my regular guests with newfound enthusiasm. I even hug Paul – a ninety-year-old grandfather – who picked and gave me the first daisy of the season. I display it on the counter in its own special shot glass. Carefree, I serve coffee as I make my way around the tables, dancing to the music and making my regular grampas laugh. Though I hate people, I like the elderly, they are just too cute, always lots to say about with their experiences. I love the wisdom in their eyes and the silky skin of their hands.

The sun is shining — in tune with my mood.

As I start to make a new round with a fresh pot of coffee, I freeze when I discover it.

My ruination.

It sits in a booth by the window in the form of an outrageously attractive man who is dressed in a perfectly fitting dark-blue suit, basking his face in the sunshine. As the agents of the FBI are known to do, he too wears sunglasses. His angular jaw is shaved and the sight of him makes my heart beat faster. I'm unable to move.

I feel like a trapped mouse.

I want to run away.

I want to rush him immediately.

I want to look especially good for him.

I want to hide...

I'm overcome by contradictory emotions when, eventually, my mind goes blank.

Don't flatter yourself, him sitting here waiting to order breakfast has nothing to do with you, babe, one of my many inner voices hisses. Yet another murmurs romantically, *It's fate!* and sighs dreamily.

I square my shoulders, raise my chin, take a deep breath, and continue my rounds... I put on my professional, noncommittal smile and approach him. He does not look up or in my direction, just continues reading his newspaper that he holds in his well-groomed fingers.

Holy shit.

Even when a guy is impassive, he has the charisma of a nuclear power plant and the attraction of a black hole.

Suddenly, I move as if controlled by a remote. It's so surreal, like an outer body experience where I watch everything from an elevated position.

One step.

Another.

One more.

I take the fourth and trip right in front of him...

The coffeepot sails out of my hands – its contents spilling, which thankfully is no longer hot coffee, but now lukewarm. As if in slow motion, I watch the brown liquid splash over his shiny white shirt, pants, the table... It's a mess, it's all over.

To top it off, I land inelegantly, uttering "FUCK!" A second later, I find myself kneeing before Mr. Rush himself, my face almost in his coffee-stained lap, right between his knees, as if planned by some really bad fate!

Well.

That's the story of my life, a never-ending series of embarrassing unstoppable events...that always happen when least needed.

I stare up at him.

Oh-so-slowly, he sets down his now soaking newspaper, folding it neatly, then he takes off his sunglasses before finally looking at me. One eyebrow raised, a small smile on his full lips.

"Well hello, Miss Pierson," he says in a cultured voice, obviously enjoying me being as red as a tomato, kneeling on the floor in front of him while all the other guests gawk — curse my life.

"Hi," I manage to utter and avert my eyes. Looking into his eyes is...is just too intense. As he laughs softly, not intrusively and boisterously, but in a smooth, silky soft feathery way that is caressing my skin, I shiver. Unexpectedly, I feel his hands under my armpits and before I know it, he lifts me up – like a doll – and puts me down on the table right in front of him.

Holy shit!

"You okay?" he asks, lifting my leg, slowly moving it, checking the knee. Feeling his hands on my bare skin makes me hot.

God!

The guy is SO hot!

"Are you hurt?" he also examines my other knee. Though the grip of his strong fingers around my ankle is firm, it's also pleasant. It is the grip of a man who's good with his hands. They can build a house as well as bring a woman to orgasm. I just know it.

I can only stare at him, it's like I'm hypnotized. Mesmerized. I crave his touch, to interact with him, but unfortunately, he releases my leg and keeps it that way.

Dammit…

However, now he smiles at me, his eyes sparkle — right now they seem more bluish. Not a bright blue, more like a dark stormy ocean blue.

"I think you'll survive," he jokes. I mentally kick myself.

"Barely." I smile at him and his smile widens. Fuck...the man even has perfect teeth!

"Yes, it was a close one," he agrees seriously, then sits back down again, resting one arm on the backrest of the booth, and looks at me as I sit in front of him, biting my lower lip while my panties are literally on fire.

"And, now what?" he asks lighthearted while covered in coffee, simply...incredible.

"Oh, right!" I suddenly remember my mishap and grab a few napkins from the dispenser on the table. "I hope I didn't burn you?" I say as I jump off the table and start dabbing and frantically rubbing his shirt... Damn! It seems to cost more than I make a day and appears completely ruined. "I'm so sorry. I'll pay for a new shirt. I have never been so clumsy..."

"It's all right, Miss Pierson... I meant to give it to Goodwill anyway."

"Why would you?" It seemed perfectly fine before I ruined it! My hand stops at his chest and he looks at me. He is so close, oh-so-close, I can smell his aftershave. Though it's unobtrusively beguiling, it's totally panty wetting — like the whole man.

Dior Homme. I'm familiar with it since I like to go to the perfumery and smell men's fragrances. Why? No idea. It's simply a little fetish.

"It has a little tear in the back, close to the hem."

"That's no reason to toss the shirt, I'm sure it can be mended!" I reply and snort. It's so typical for snobs. Really.

He grins.

"I'm not that good with needle and thread." Yet his eyes sparkle as if he meant to say, *Baby, undress and lie down on the table, I'll have you for breakfast*.

Crap!

Imagination!

STOP!

THIS INSTANT!

"If you'd like, I'll mend it for you," I exclaim before I can stop myself. And for the first time since I met him, he seems surprised.

"You would?" He raises an eyebrow doubtfully as he eyes my hands. Instinctively, I would like to hide them. They are cracked and callused from work, unlike his nice, perfectly manicured hands.

"Yes. I'm a good seamstress, if you must know." A single mother with limited money has little choice.

"Okay." He shrugs and looks around. "Should I leave it in my office?"

"Oh." What a shame. Here I was hoping he'd take it off now. The thought makes me grin.

"Okay." I'm still standing in front of him as if ordered,

not picked up, while watching the sun rays making his hair shimmer. Usual it seems rather black, though now it clearly has a brown sheen to it. Interesting. He raises an eyebrow and I quickly avert my gaze.

"I'll go get fresh coffee."

"Yes."

"Once again, I apologize, Mr...*Rush*." His last name comes out like an embarrassing breath. God, what's wrong with me? I'm well past teenager-crush years, really.

The sparkle in his eyes grows more intense. "No problem, Miss Pierson." His tongue seems to caress each syllable as if my hard nipple was in his mouth, ready to do the most beguiling things to me. I have to suppress a shiver and instead grin, before I walk away...all the while having a hard time catching my breath.

Eventually, this man will cause me to choke.

Really!

10. Let The Games Begin

Keaton

All went as planned when you slipped exactly on the spot I prepped and ended up on your knees right in front of me. You have no idea how long I've been longing to see you like that, Olivia. Though you are not naked now, it doesn't seem to matter as my cock is rock hard anyway.

Things go as planned.

Until you offered to mend my shirt.

I had not unexpected that. I know you like to take care of others, you have a giving personality, baby, whereas I'm a taker. We complement each other perfectly.

So I'll let you because I'm going to enjoy the thought of you having something of mine. I'm watching your little hot ass walk away, knowing you only sway like that for me.

You are purposefully swaying your hips provocatively since you want me to desire you.

Oh, I do.

You have no idea how much.

I force myself not to rearrange my cock because I know your regulars are watching me. They are suspicious of me for they sense something is not kosher.

***

Tonight is THE NIGHT. I'm pumped up just thinking about it. Tonight begins a new phase between us. I can hardly wait.

Olivia.

Your name is made for me.

You are made for me.

And you know it. You can feel it. It is what makes you so nervous. I take full advantage of it.

Another hour and I can finally get on my way. The time seems to pass much too slowly, like it is taunting me.

Thirty minutes.

Fifteen…

Ten.

Five.

I glance out the window and see you leaving your apartment building. Oh-so-typically, you're running late, baby, and hurry to the bus stop. You just make it. I look at the window one floor above you where Penny Leonardson lives — who takes care of your son and dog. She's watching one of those endless reruns of Friends while painting her fingernails. Riley Markus Pierson is blissfully asleep in her bed, seemingly snoring to himself.

Your apartment – one floor below – is dark.

Still, I bide my time to play it safe.

As always at half past ten, Penny Leonardson is so tired, she falls asleep on the couch.

I calmly leave my observation post and walk through the house I recently acquired. It smells of mold, the stairs creak, and the house rather resembles a pig sty. However, I did not buy it to live in it. For my purposes, it's just fine. That I'm standing here seems to be fate. Empty and abandoned and across from her apartment building, I immediately closed the deal. Now I open the squeaky front door and step out onto the street. There are no people on the road except for a junkie at the corner waiting for business. He always stare at you lecherously whenever you walk by.

I don't like it.

I'm still contemplating what to do with him.

So far, he seems harmless.

Rather pathetic.

However, he also has nothing to lose and people with nothing to lose are by far the most dangerous. Like me.

I cross the street to your fucked up five-story apartment building and ring someone's bell. The buzzer sounds without anyone asking who it is...typical. So, I enter and walk straight up to the second floor. It does not even take me a minute to crack the lock and open door. I almost moan as I enter her apartment.

Her kingdom.

Finally.

I set my backpack down, then close and lock the door. If Penny Leonardson comes to check on what's going on in here, I'll hear the lock. I turn on the light for I refuse to look around with a flashlight. Not to mention, using a flashlight creates attention, whereas turning on the light seems natural. Neighbors who are aware of your schedule will think you forgot to turn the lights off. Just like you often do, baby. Tsk, tsk! Nobody will think twice about it and merely think I'm a male friend who is staying over. Naturally, I'm wearing my leather gloves, though I'd much rather touch all the things you touch day in day out directly with my fingers.

First, I follow your small hallway and enter the kitchen. You had no time to do the dishes, food smeared plates are stacked in the sink. You had spaghetti Bolognese. And there are three glasses, one was yours, one Riley's, and one your girlfriend's. She is good for you. She is not a bad person. You may continue seeing her, baby. Don't worry. However, if she arouses my suspicion, we'll see what we do.

I open the fridge and see only unhealthy food.

Though I figured as much, I only shake my head.

I unpack the apples I brought and arrange them in the bowl that stands on the kitchen counter, forlorn and a bit dusty. The boy needs vitamins you can't afford. I continue my inspection, open cabinets and take pictures of whatever seems important to me. Also of the photos on your fridge, all of which are of you, your child, dog, and your girlfriend. It's clear you love your child and your dog — you're a good mother, a good person. It's what I like about you. The picture where you and your girlfriend make weird faces makes me smile. You are dressed as a giant pumpkin, your girlfriend a witch, and your little one Superman — presumably taken this past Halloween. You're so damn cute, baby...

I go to the small coffee table and leaf through the magazines I find on it. Most are about dog training and family. Next, I lie down on the hide-a-bed and take a long whiff of your sheets and pillow. I can smell you... My cock is growing hard... But I'm not here to jerk one off even if the idea is tempting. Quickly, I get back up and walk over to the wall where the TV is. Nothing special. I look in Riley's room, but only because you put away your clothes in the small closet. I open your underwear drawer and take pictures of each piece. You have selective underwear. Though they are not expensive, all items are naughty. Well, you simply are a little slutty – which also fascinates me about you.

I would like to cum on your underwear.

NOT YET, KEATON!

Restrain yourself! I reprimand myself and go to the bathroom. I run my fingers over your towels, then rearrange your little perfume bottles, and place to them what I bought you today.

A brooch.

It is a little inconspicuous item decorated with pearls, clearly not mass-produced and quite old, which brought us together. I'm sure you don't even remember, yet I recall it as if it was yesterday. Actually it was half a year ago.

It was autumn, naturally, it rained, I was on my way to the supermarket around the corner from work to buy something to drink when I saw you. You were browsing the vegetable department, illuminated by the cool tube lights. You seemed so pale, so small in your little red trench coat and scuffed boots. You had a red nose from being sick, busy getting ingredients for soup. Leek, carrots, parsley. Your fingernails were unpainted and short. You were wearing no makeup and appeared pretty tired. But your hair was radiant and your eyes, they had that shimmer to them... Your lips were full and rosy, though a bit a cracked... Clearly, you did not have enough liquids in you. You were...fascinating — regardless of being sick and broken. Maybe I felt that way because I initially saw you as fragile and quite defenseless. I immediately found you worth protecting. As you unintentionally and briefly locked eyes with me, I was a goner. I wanted more. More of your eye contact. More of that tingly feeling. More of you.

I wanted it all.

You had already continued on, whereas I was still standing in the same spot, unable to move, though I still heard your coughs or sneezes.

I heard your phone ringing and watched you rummage in your purse for it. You picked up all stressed as you continued to push your shopping cart around the corner to the next aisle and disappear. I walked over to where the item had fallen out of your purse as you searched for the phone. It lay inconspicuously on the floor.

A brooch.

I picked it up and rushed after you to give it to you...but I was distracted — again, when I saw the smile you gave the woman behind the meat counter. It was so radiant it lit up your whole face and your warmth captured everyone around you. Especially me.

I could not take my eyes off you as though I'd lose a part of myself if you left my sight. So, as if in a trance, I followed you.

First throughout the whole store.

Then outside.

All the way to your home.

Once you disappeared inside, I did not ring the bell to return your brooch, no, I decided to hold on to it and closed my fist around it.

Because it belongs to me.

As does your smile.

As do you.

Back in the here and now, I take a few photos of your chaotic little bathroom and stow the camera away.

Now to the actual work.

I unobtrusively install small cameras in each room. They are from work, the latest technology. Now while I can watch you no matter where you are, you will never be aware that every aspect of your life is filmed — including sound. You will not realize that from now, I'll be with you every second, baby. By the time you may become aware of anything, it will be too late, for you will already be mine. Completely. Unable to leave again.

But not yet.

Because the game has just started.

11. Me, Myself, and Him

Olivia

Luckily, I am spared Pam's presence today and actually had a pleasant work day. Mr. Rush's shirt is in my handbag, as he said, it is neatly folded on the chair in the small chamber. On top of the shirt is a perfume bottle. *Swarovski.* I don't even want to know how expensive it is... A handwritten note, in his fine penmanship, is next to it: *A little token of my appreciation.*

I want to put the bottle on his desk and flip him off even if he can't see it, but then I make the mistake of removing the top and smelling it... I should mention, I actually spend hours in the perfumery searching for *just the right* fragrance for me. On men, I find many fragrances wonderful. On me, I have yet to find the right one. Until now. And it had to be an expensive one at that.

But this...is *my* scent. It's perfect. I can't return the token of appreciation, I would be crazy! Especially since I cannot afford it, I don't want to know how much exactly it costs. In return, I decide to offer my services to Mr. Rush, mending or even washing other items of his when needed, primarily because I don't like owing people and would rather work it off. Finally, I head home.

I arrive home completely exhausted, but satisfied and smelling like a queen. Like every night, Rosie obediently follows me down the stairs as I carry Riley – I can still carry him as long as his arms are around my neck like a monkey with one leg clamped around me – and quickly put the half-sleeping child to bed. I stroke his hair again and kiss his forehead. He looks so innocent...I wish he would stay like that his entire life. Unfortunately, no human on earth is granted this, right?

Smiling, I go straight to the bathroom, discard my clothes in the middle of the room, and hop under the shower. It takes forever for the hot water to flow out of the prehistoric showerhead and, as usual, the shower curtain sticks to me. What sadistic ass invented shower curtains, huh? Once the hot water cascades over me, I moan. After work, there is nothing better in the world than a nice hot shower. Well, I would prefer a bath, but of course this place has no tub. I force myself not to stand too long under the water – considering the costs involved – and quickly shampoo my hair and body. It is an all in one shampoo —

simply cheaper. I rinse and step out into the chilly bathroom.

Hastily, I towel off and wrap it around my body. Before I approach the fogged mirror, I open the door to the hallway so I can see myself. I grab the comb and am about to run it through my hair when my eyes fall on my collection of cheap perfumes...because in between...all shiny and innocent looking like when Riley is asleep…

My grandmother's brooch!

It is the brooch I've been searching for like crazy for half a year now.

Here I thought I had lost it.

Now it lies here in the warm bathroom light as if never misplaced, and my heart warms at the sight. Okay, it is a bit eerie too...I frown, look around, but whatever, so I grab it cautiously. It feels good between my fingers. I have no idea how it got here. Maybe the ghost of my grandma placed it here... Maybe Riley or Penny found it between the couch cushions... It feels good to hold the brooch in my hands again, I thought I had lost it for good.

Tears come to my eyes as a sequence of images flash through my mind; grandma smiling, her smell, her wrinkled hand holding mine while the other is stroking my hair. Thanks to her, I love old people. As suddenly as the images appeared they stop and I feel no longer connected to her. I am standing alone in my old bathroom with its disgusting dark green tiles, holding the pin. I look at myself in the mirror and smile.

A little bit later, as I'm lying in bed – okay, on the couch – I still have to smile. I am quite wired and replay the crazy day in my mind. Starting with this morning, when I landed on my knees before him and the sweet way he took care of me. Actually, it's a bit funny, during the interview, I did not believe him capable of such behavior. Then, while I was serving other patrons, I felt his eyes on me. When other people do that it makes me uncomfortable and I have to ask myself what they find so interesting, yet with him, I liked it. He was in the diner exactly a half hour, drinking only coffee with nothing to eat. I went to the backroom and when I returned, he was gone. Too bad, but he left me a large tip. Again and again, I feel his fingers on my leg, his skin on my skin, which is not as rough and cracked as mine. The way he gazed at my legs, his ocean blue eyes...that little cheeky grin that previously, I did not think him capable of either. As is my habit when I'm wired and unable to sleep, I slide my hand down my belly, straight into my panties and stroke my clit. Tenderly, yet it electrifies me so much so that I moan. I'm wet – actually have been the all day long – which is his fault and the naughty fantasies he awakens in me.

I imagine him kissing me right there at the table by the front window, in front of all the patrons — in front of my regulars and whatever passersby, and he whispers in my ear that he has wanted me since the first time he laid eyes on me. I imagine how he fucks me in front of everybody, the way his cock rubs against me, preferably without any obstructing material, and how his entire length slowly enters me. All the while, he's grasping my hair, my eyes, my heart, my everything... I imagine him stretching me as he enters me inch by inch and how I greedily embrace him as he presses his lips against mine again and forcefully thrusts all the way into me, when I already come. I never take long when I masturbate. Never more than five minutes and I quickly bite my lower lip to stifle my outcry, which would have sounded like, "Oh my God, Mr. Rush!" I'm rotating my hips as spasms of sweet salvation course through my body and flood my wired mind.

Then I lie unmoving in the dark, catching my breath. Though my heart is racing...I feel more balanced. I'm completely relaxed...grin and whisper, "Thank you, Mr. Rush..." Then I turn on my side and pretty quickly drift off into a good night's sleep.

12. A Normal Morning

Keaton

I have no need for an alarm clock – I've trained my mind to wake me every morning at six. The same happens this morning and I immediately think of you.

You.

The way you lolled under the sheets last night, as shamelessly as you are, did yourself in the darkness.

The way you moaned.

And once you finished, hearing you thanking me.

Well it was my pleasure, baby. Very much so.

Slowly but surely, my cook feels it's about to burst, but I ignore my morning boner. I go to the adjacent pigsty of a bathroom and try to pee with a hard on. I am successful...thanks to years of practice. Afterward, I shower

– and mourn a bit my luxury shower in my luxury penthouse and of course, the pool, in which I usually swim laps every morning. But my morning ritual will have to be put on hold for a while, for right now I have a new one. I need to be close to you. My place across town is too far. So, I'm camping out here on a mattress on the floor like a junkie, happy water, not brown ooze, comes out of the pipes as I wet my toothbrush. I brush my teeth as I walk to the second room on this floor, my command center. It houses a powerful surveillance unit that runs nonstop and a widescreen monitor. I click through the different cameras and find you snoring in your fold-out couch.

You are cute, drooling in your sleep. So far, everything is well. I put on a jogging suit and sneakers for a morning run for at least half an hour. My body is longing to exercise, to feel the burning in the muscles and heart racing. I don't feel well-balanced without it. Still, I reluctantly take my eyes off the screen and leave the house shortly after with the hoodie pull low over my face and make a round, jogging through the pretty landscaped park. But I cut my 20 minute run in half since I know you'll be waking soon and I don't want to miss it.

I'm as excited as a kid at Christmas when I get back to my command center with a hot coffee, croissant, and today's newspaper. I plop down on my office chair and take a sip of coffee, then a bite of my croissant. At last, I no longer have to peep through your windows like some pervert. While others read the newspaper as morning routine, I am watching you – for quite a while – as you push the *Snooze* time and time again until you're pressed for time and force yourself to leave the warm sheets while the drooling monstrosity you call a dog – Rosie – slobbers all over your face. That is really disgusting, Olivia.

You take the dog outside. She does not do anything. She'll probably relieve herself later on in the apartment again. You really are a poor wretch.

You shuffle back inside and make yourself coffee, then get Riley ready for school. He does not look too happy about going back to the loony bin where all those little lunatics run around.

I sympathize, little buddy.

I too hated school.

Though in your presence, he's trying to hide what's *really* going on and what's *really* going on could soon become a little problem.

A child's soul can only withstand so much meanness before it is lost forever. And his is close to it.

Thus, weeks ago, I lowered myself into doing something that *was not at all* part of my plan and which could lead to my doom.

I simply could not help it.

I like the little pale boy.

Most likely because he's a part of you, thus, it is impossible for me not to like him. Unfortunately, I have to leave or my whole plan is messed up. I quickly finish my light breakfast and get ready for the office.

Shortly thereafter, I'm sitting in my Maserati, which I keep parked a few blocks away so it does not to attract attention and drive to the small cafe in the city center. I love sitting there watching people. Even as a little kid, I loved watching people. Today is the first sunny, really nice warm day and decide to sit outside, near the bus stop. I don't have to wait long until I see you hurrying along. You give the little one another kiss. I can tell you hate all those present, so much so...you would like to accompany and defend him like a lioness. *But you cannot, you have to go work. But I'm here, baby, I'll watch over him.*

You're rushing off and I watch you for a few seconds before my gaze travels to the kid and...his to me.

He grins when he discovers me.

I smile in return — honestly. Seeing him grin makes me feel strange things...things I haven't felt for quite some time. Next, he hobbles over on his crutches, so brave, so admirable. Like every day, he's having a hard time sitting. I consider giving him a hand, but I don't, he's a strong boy and it's important for him to get around by himself. Finally, he succeeds and, as always, is a bit proud of himself. He cheerfully greets me, "Good morning, John..." Every time he joins me at my table, he is happy and beaming. I love how well behaved he is as well as his company and the things he talks about to me. He lets me see the world through his eyes and it fascinates me. Meanwhile, to be honest, our morning get-togethers have become the highlight of my day.

Smiling, I say, "Good morning, Riley," while pushing his beloved hot chocolate over to him, and, of course, his chocolate donut, like I would forget.

13. Toads

Keaton

He is intelligent, Olivia. I'm aware he got that from you, not his degenerate father whom, quite naturally, I investigated. I watch him woof down his donut and hot chocolate. I feel liberated just watching him, the way he enjoys sweets, like his life depends on it. It's so easy to make him happy. We could learn a thing or two from him.

"You're late today," I say.

He raises his head, looks at me with his big eyes, still chewing, and then swallows. "Mom overslept. She always gets up late."

I smile. "Why don't you wake her then?"

Conspiratorially, he leans toward me and whispers, "Because then I can also sleep a little longer!" I laugh. He is smart, without a mean bone in him, not like the other kids. I see the looks they give him and how the other mothers look down on you, Olivia. They have contempt for you, but only because they envy you, understand? They cannot handle it that you manage everything by yourself. They have husbands and cannot get a handle on their lives. Yet here you are, earning your own money and you don't have to answer to a man. You are also a single parent, not to mention quite beautiful — in a natural way. You look better than they ever did, even in their best years.

As a few kids laugh, he turns partially around. I glance at the assembled mothers who are supposed to look after their children, yet mostly stare in my direction. They see Riley and me sitting here together every morning, Olivia, though nobody has informed you that your child is hanging out with a stranger on a daily basis. They want to see you hurt. They are evil.

Their toads are close by. I know you call them that when you talk with Penny about them. They stare at Riley and giggle in a hateful way. One is purposefully imitating Riley's limp.

"What's their problem?" I ask calmly, though I'm furious on the inside.

Riley looks at me, he's obviously sad, though he has gotten used to not saying anything. He shrugs his tiny shoulders. "They're having fun."

"At your expense!" I point out skeptically.

He swallows. "I..."

The snooty blond boy is still limping about and I've had enough. I get up and determinedly approach the mother of that nasty little shit. She's smoking a cigarette, appears to have money, although is wearing an imitation designer label.

"Hi!" I brusquely interrupt her conversation with another mother.

She gives me the once over and I can tell she wouldn't mind getting fucked in the restroom of the little cafe behind me, but she's disgusting, Olivia. She is not pure, innocent, and feminine. She is dominant, mean, and looks used and abused.

"Hi," she coos and blows smoke in the air.

I step up closer, lean down, and quietly, though with emphasis say, "If your son bullies, bugs or so much as give that little boy over there a nasty look, I'll see to it that *he* needs crutches."

She didn't expect that.

She cringes and her eyes widen, the other mothers who overheard looked just as startled, which I don't care about whatsoever. Yes, that was a threat. She is welcome to inform the police, I would still have no qualms about breaking the boy's legs if he so much as harasses Riley again.

"Excuse me?" she hisses. "Who do you think…"

"This is my first and only warning. Get a handle on that little shit of yours!" and I turn away again just in time as the bus pulls up.

Riley is still sitting at the table and stares at me wide-eyed. I kneel in front of him and look into his innocent child's eyes. "Don't take any crap from those children," I say. "And if they tease you again like that, you tell me, okay?"

He nods, perplexed.

"You are the hero in the story. These kids are only mean because they got it from their parents. Do you understand that? But you are well mannered, Riley. Don't stoop to their level."

Another nod.

Smiling, I wink at him before I get up. "See you tomorrow."

Again, all I get is another shocked nod.

14. John

Olivia

Riley is not yet asleep by the time I get home. I chat briefly with Penny, who tells me he did his homework and afterward, they took Rosie for a walk in the park. Today, apparently, Riley talked a lot about his imaginary friend John, which worries me more and more. I take his hand and we go downstairs to our apartment. Rosie trots behind us and grunts. I am tired, my feet hurt, as does my head, and later on, I still have to clean for Mr. Rush. Usually, when such a situation arises, I leave Riley with Penny as she has to look after him later anyway, but since I'm a bit worried now, I decide to spend some alone time with Riley. When it's time for me to go to my next job and Riley is in bed sleeping, Penny will come down and watch TV in our place.

Rosie immediately trots to her sleeping place when I open our apartment door. It's already dark outside for the way home was a disaster. Practically every bus was running late. Now it is still raining, but at least it's not so cold anymore since we're approaching spring.

Riley does not use his crutches as he hobbles into the kitchen while using the wall for support.

"Are you hungry?" I ask just in case, for Penny told me they already ate.

As I slip out of my shoes and Rosie makes wearisome noises, Riley reaches for something on the counter. I walk over to him and frown.

"What do you have there?"

He turns to me as he takes a big bite out of a juicy red apple and sits down at the kitchen table. It's already past eight and I don't have much time left. Though Riley should already be in bed, talking to him is more important. Way more important than anything else.

"An apple," he says, smacking his lips.

I also sit down at the table and try to remember when I bought apples. Honestly, I can't remember doing it. Penny must have put them there. Every now and then, when she buys groceries for herself, she brings us small things...well, that's not important now.

"How was your day?" I ask lightly and see his eyes are already reddened. He must be tired and I should put him to bed and read to him before Penny comes to replace me.

However, this thing with his friend John bugs me.

He nods. "It was good, Mom! I ate a donut with John this morning!"

"Is that so?"

"YES! And then he really laid into Gared, Mommy, you should have seen it!"

I frown. Gared is that blond toad that always picks on Riley, among others. He comes from a nouveau riche family who became wealthy practically overnight, but of course, almost just as fast, pissed the money way like most do.

"Is that so?"

"Yesss! Gared was teasing me again and John told his mom he would break Gared's legs if he bugged me again!" He laughs and his eyes sparkle. "You know, that really scared Mrs. Ruffsteen and Gared actually left me alone today, I liked that!"

I blink as if a child could make up such a story. It seems a bit...too realistic, doesn't it? Then again, would an adult threaten a child in that way?

"Riley, this John...what does he look like?"

"Oh, he's very tall and super strong! And he always smiles when he sees me."

To a kid, most adults appear tall and super strong, so I keep at him. "So, you see him at the bus stop every morning?"

"YES! He's always there waiting for me, just ask Mrs. Ruffsteen!"

I don't think I'll engage in a conversation with Mrs. Ruffsteeen-butt-fuck. I hate her and her toad. Yet I don't recall seeing a man at the cafe.

"Riley, I thought I taught you not to talk to strangers, right, baby?"

Now he seems guilt-ridden and lowers his eyes. I sigh. The half-eaten apple is on the table in front of him. He blinks and says, "But John's different."

"It doesn't matter, baby. John is still a stranger. Clearly, he's nice, but many times such people are only nice to you to win your trust and then take you somewhere. They see how special you are and want you for themselves, do you understand?"

His head shoots up and his eyes pop open while my heart starts beating faster than normal. I am scared. Perhaps John is a real person and I did not take it seriously enough. The world is full of perverts!

"No, John's not like that," he mumbles, though I see fear in his eyes. I did not mean to scare him, on the contrary. Then again, I would die if anything happened to him. So, I have no choice but to go later to the diner and wait with Riley for the bus. Immediately, I have a bad conscience and feel like a bad mother for not having enough time for Riley. I feel like crying but restrain myself and instead, reach for his small, sticky with apple-juice fingers.

"You are everything to me, baby. I love you more than life itself. So, if someone hurt you, I'd feel terrible, understand?"

He nods and swallows.

"Promise me you won't talk to strangers anymore, okay?"

He whispers, "I promise."

* * *

The next morning, I'm tense when I take Riley to the bus stop. It is a warm day in windy Chicago. Spring is finally here. Everything appears so harmless; buds are sprouting, the sun warms my face, and people seem to be in a much better mood than on a freezing morning. Not even our neighborhood in Fuller Park looks as threatening as it usually does. The petty crooks loitering in corners appear to be young men who simply cannot be taken seriously — until they pull a knife. The street bums look like they're sunbathing. The threatening looking towering blockhouses across town seem rather peaceful compare to my rough neighborhood. Even the trash, cigarette butts, and needles littering the streets, which I always kick aside so Rosie or Riley won't encounter them, no longer appear so dangerous in the sun.

Riley braces himself on his crutches and I watch him limp laboriously. I carry his backpack. I let him wear the denim jacket Penny gave him for his last birthday. It is stylish and looks good on him. I know Riley will be a very handsome man despite his anomaly. I don't want something so superficial to ruin him.

With every step we take, my chest increasingly tightens. It's like someone is squeezing my ribcage together. I don't know what or whom to expect at the bus stop on Elm Street, though clearly I have a bad feeling, even though the sun is shining and birds are chirping and the morning seems so harmless. The pressure I feel inside increases.

"We should visit your grandma again, soon," I say louder than necessary to distract myself from my thoughts, besides, I think a little break, even for only a weekend, would be good for both of us.

"Oh, yes!" Riley's eyes glow. I smile. He loves his grandparents as I do and I miss them terribly. I'm not that old yet, just in my late twenties and, at times, like now, when everything becomes too much for me to handle, I would love to hide out in my old childhood room, pull the blanket over my head — then my mother would come with milk and cookies and comfort me. But for years now, I have been a mother myself and had to learn to stay strong, for to love someone more than any ideals or perceptions beats everything.

You might think I'm in my current situation because I grew up in a not so harmonious family home, but that wasn't the case. My parents were affectionate toward me...as well as with my five siblings.

We were a big household that was full of life, something was always going on. But there wasn't a single day when my mother was so overwhelmed that her hand slipped or that she left the house. We were four girls, two boys, and my parents. It wasn't always easy and we never had much money, but I learned other values along the way, which are more important than all the money in the world. Respect, love, sympathy. Each of us kids have gone our own way. To name them in sequence, there is Keisha – who works nowadays as a nurse in Philly, Richard – has two kids and works in a bank, Louisa – she's single and lives in New York, Trisha – now married and a mother to a nasty brat that I cannot stand to be in the same room with for more than three minutes, Daniel – who quit his studies, kind of lives the life I live and every day sees someone else, and then there's me. I'm the youngest and thus, Daddy's favorite, which always bugged my siblings.

At 16, when I dated a boy my parents disapproved of; I left home. At the time, Riley's dad was going to the university and actually was too old for me, but I thought I was in love with him and followed him everywhere. I fucked up greatly, quit high school, and watched him cheat on me, lie to me, and deceive me. However, for some reason, I could never bring myself to leave him. But when I became pregnant with Riley, his father, Dexter, panicked, saying he had so much to look forward to in his life, that I forced a child on him — all the crap I had to listen to. Once Riley was born, everything went downhill. Dexter is a fuckwad, the only good that came out of dating him was my little man.

I wanted to break it off with him, but he wouldn't allow it. He claimed I already messed up his life and he certainly would not let me leave him just like that. One night, when Riley was still small and Dexter had passed out from too much booze, we snuck out the door for good! I held his hand as we dashed out of the cramped apartment. When Dexter heard us and woke, he came after us. He chased us down in his car, drunk and swerving... That was how my baby lost his leg.

Since that incident, I have never heard from him again. I'm sure he'll never dare knock on my door again.

So, despite everything that happened, my parents always had an open ear for me. They forgave me, helped me with Riley, and made sure I kept it together. I owe them so much —- and here I have not visited them in such a long time, not since...

"MOMMY?"

I jump and blink. I was so deep in thought, I was unaware we had already arrived at the bus stop.

"Sorry, baby. What did you say?"

Riley looks at me and smiles. "Don't worry about it."

As always, the gang of mothers, who think so highly of themselves, is already gathered in their usual place. They're smoking and chatting, not paying attention to their toads, who are pushing each other on the street, which is pretty dangerous with the traffic here. Though today, I don't pay them any attention because I'm searching for a man with my arm around Riley's shoulders as if to protect him from their stares.

I see no man.

"Do you see John?" I ask without looking at Riley.

"No." He sounds disappointed and I glance down at him. He seems sad, which makes my heart constrict even more. I cannot help but wonder about John. "He's not here."

I'm relieved and breathe out, when I see Ruffsteen-butt-fuck coming toward me. Yes, yes, I may be a mother and don't show it for Riley's sake, but on the inside, I'm fucking furious.

She gives me the once over and I wonder how she can keep her eyes open with so much mascara. "Good morning, darling!"

My God, I'm already bored. "What's up, Ruth?" I mean, Ruth Ruffsteen. The woman's name is punishment that lasts a lifetime.

Her blond hair is held in place with so much hair spray that it appears greasy and the clunker on her ring finger does not reflect in the sunlight. Thus, not a real diamond, contrary to what she wants everyone to believe. "How nice to finally see you keep your son company while waiting for the bus!" she says in such a friendly way, you might believe we have plans together this afternoon.

I roll my eyes. "Well, I'm working two jobs. I won't be dependent on a man like most women are, understand?"

She smiles haughtily and nods. "Oh, yes, that's so admirable! I couldn't do it. I am so happy to have Harry! He's not one who shies away from responsibility...like other men do." Though she doesn't know anything about me, it seems she made up her own story. I see no need to set her straight as I don't care what she thinks.

"I mean, I would not let *my* son hand out with a stranger every morning..."

"I'm aware of what's going on!" I groan. "I'm here to take care of it!"

"How nice," she murmurs. I sigh. I realize I should not let pride get in the way. It seems Ruth might have some useful information for me.

"Have you seen him?" I ask reluctantly.

"Oh, yes." She nods. "He's an incredibly attractive man; tall, well-built, a striking face, and dark hair." Great, she's describing every romance novel's fictional character or actors, heck, every tenth guy on the street.

"And his name is John?"

"Obviously."

"Anything else?"

"He wears expensive clothes. Obviously likes to threaten kids." She says *obviously* a lot. Maybe it makes her feel smarter. "Usually, he sits at that cafe's outside table and chats with Riley."

I become angry and snort. That stupid bitch! "Meaning, you observed this a few times, yet *never once* told me about it. Or did you approach him and ask who he is?" The hand lying on Riley's shoulder clenches into a fist. How can she be so incredibly disgusting? I hate society! I hate these mothers! And I hate these teachers!

"Oh, darling!" she says, laughing. "But *you're* his mother, *you* should keep an eye on him, not me. It's not my fault you care more about other things than taking care of your child." I would love to punch her, but I restrain myself for Riley's sake. What a stupid chick! She doesn't know shit about me!

God...this day is off to a shitty start, who knows how it'll end. Even shittier?

"Besides, I'm telling you now, right?"

The bus pulls up and she turns away with her nose in the air.

She's lucky because my fingers are trembling with rage. I turn to Riley, who has been watching us intently, and bend down to him. "Listen, sweetheart," I say urgently while I stare into his eyes. "Don't let them get you. Not even one of them! Remember, they are merely jealous! And...don't talk to anyone, do you hear?" He nods. I kiss his forehead. "I love you!" I say and watch him climb awkwardly into the bus.

Life is shit.

15. And Then Everything Changes

Olivia

The shift in the diner is quite uneventful, unfortunately, for I really could use a little distraction. It takes me two hours to calm down after dealing with the little toads and their toad mothers. But then a group of Chinese tourists storm the diner and start up lively conversations with the regulars, which finally does the trick. I discontinue thinking about the previous escapade and concentrate on the here and now. Must concentrate...

By the time my shift is over, I'm totally exhausted, but thanks to Penny, who is picking up Riley today and taking him to his weekly physiotherapy, I have two hours to myself now. I always do the same thing during those two hours, namely, visit the library. The old one downtown, which no longer receives new editions, but it is located in city hall and rich with history. I love this place and almost feel my grandma's firm hand with its silky skin holding my little hand. Whatever vacation, I spent with her, either walking through the park for hours or down along the Bridgewood River where we fed ducks or strolling through the venerable aisles and indulging in our greatest passion, reading. Unfortunately, at this stage in my life, I hardly have time for it. What little time I have is not enough to submerge myself into the world of fiction that is brought to us by such talented people and it breaks my heart a bit. When I was little, I left this place with a stack of ten books to read for the week. From King, Rushdie, Orwell, Kundera, Tolkien, Rowling, Follett, to Gordon, I like them all. I've read every single one of their books, a few even several times. Whenever I was at my grandmother's and someone was looking for me, I could always be found in the attic on the ancient sofa that had springs popping out with a book in hand, only illuminated by a small table lamp. It was the reason I ruined my eyes and needed glasses, which, for some time now, I've replaced with contact lenses. No guy wants a stripper who wears glasses on stage...though some of my regulars enjoyed a lap dance with strict buns and glasses.

Speaking of...I remind myself to do what I've been delaying for some time now. The sooner the better!

Since I cannot put it off any longer, I spontaneously decide to get it over and done with this evening, after working for Mr. Rush. I finally got around to his shirt, washed it thoroughly — luckily all the stains came out, then sewed, even ironed it, and placed it neatly folded on his desk. I still wasted lots of time because I didn't want to go, but there was no way around it.

So I hop on the bus that fortunately pulls up as I step outside into the cold night, sigh and plopped down on a seat. My soles burn like I was running on hot coals, my eyes are weary... I made good time cleaning the offices, even managed not to think too much about Mister I'm-too-sexy Rush, although the box of assorted Band-Aids lying on my uniform took me a bit by surprise. My gaze automatically went to the cut I gave myself when I was stressed out earlier at the diner slicing bread and my hand slipped on the hard crust. I shuddered and glanced around...nothing to see but the blinking red light of the camera directly above me.

Is someone watching me? Maybe, even...HIM?

The thought made me grin.

You're such an idiot, my inner prudish voice scolds me, *now get your little butt to work, you're not here to daydream about a man who is so far out of your league as the distance between Earth and Jupiter!*

Sighing, I put a band-aid over my cut and get to work...

Now on the bus, I look at the box of assorted Band-Aids again. They are waterproof so they won't get soak when I handle dirty cleaning water and protect my wound. It has been the first time in years that anyone showed sympathy toward me. Okay, obviously, Penny always feeds me chicken soup whenever I allow myself to get sick, as well as she takes Riley and Rosie up to her apartment so I can recuperate in peace. This here, however, is entirely different.

Because *he* made the gesture.

Dreamily, I smile and almost stroke the stupid thing when all the secret personalities in my head roll their eyes.

Damn, I'm so fucked up!

***

The parking lot in front of the club is not all that crowded. I only see five cars, four rusty old vehicles and a sleek black Maserati. *Hot...*

It is raining again and I hustle the few steps from the bus stop to the entrance. I jump over several puddles that reflect the neon red letters from the club along the way and I again curse myself for *always* forgetting my umbrella. By the time I make it to the entrance, my hair is soaked. I remind myself that I should really look for a new jacket and sneakers for what I'm wearing no longer repels liquid. My socks are wet and I ignore that disgusting smacking sound as I enter the club and my eyes adjust to the dim lighting. It is still early since I finished the offices quickly today. I only see Celeste contorting herself on the main stage, which is surrounded by a few rather bored looking men who are brooding over their beers, probably contemplating their shitty lives. I mean, seriously, for someone to visit a strip club on a regular basis, they must have serious complexes they are compensating for!

Most of the time, the guys have little wieners in their pants, are butt ugly, or were not breastfed often enough, or whatever...

Anyway, I nod to Jerry the bartender and he gives me a wide grin so that his teeth glow a brilliant white in the black light. Scary...

I head to the back to the changing rooms. I'm lucky, none of the uber-bitches is getting ready for their show, and Celeste can't leave until a replacement arrives. So, I calmly unlock my locker and breathe a sigh of relief when I find it still inside...

I grab it and am delighted as I feel the ring snugly around my finger. I turn around, expecting to have my peace and quiet, but of course, no such luck.

Just then, Pablo opens and steps through the door, wearing a big nasty grin on his face with Karl – his bouncer – in pursuit. Fucking crap, now I'm really in a bind!

16. Change of Pace

Olivia

I hold my breath and my stomach knots up, almost painfully, when Pablo closes the door behind him and Karl positions himself with his arms crossed right next to him. Karl is huge. His arms look like tree trunks and he knows no mercy. He's a really fucked up guy. He takes care of Pablo's dirty work and the fact that he came along sets my alarm bells off.

Dammit!

I should not have come! I simply couldn't stand the thought of losing the ring. Apart from the brooch, it's the only thing I have left from my grandmother. Usually, I wear it on the ring finger as a deterrent for whatever creeps, of course, when I go on stage, I lock away it in my locker...

"Hi," Pablo whispers.

I grin. "And, everything okay in the crotch area?" I know I shouldn't provoke him, at least not too far, but showing fear right now would be even worse. Guys like him love timid women. It turns them on. He really is sick.

"I didn't think I'd see your bitch face in here again, it makes things so much easier for me."

I raise one brow.

"You still owe me money!" he snaps. I frown and take a step back. I gauge the distance to the window and try to gauge if I would be fast enough to open it and slip out. It might be the second floor, but in the back, there are some shrubs to break my fall, better than being in Karl's arms!

"I owe you nothing!"

"You up and left, your show was a bust. I lost money because of that!"

I roll my eyes and tell myself it would be better to play along even though he's full of shit. So I take out my purse and ask, "Okay, you have a point. How much?"

"Three thousand bucks!" My fingers stop and I glance up, straight into his wide grinning, ugly face.

"I never make that much in one evening!"

"Call it a no notice fee!" he grumbles and I grab my purse, raise my chin in defiance, and say, "Kiss my ass!"

"Oh, I was hoping you'd say that!" He gestures to Karl to step up and I retreat farther... All blood leaves me and my knees weaken as the giant with the expressionless face trudges toward me. Dammit!

I simply want to get away and instinctively jump to the side — toward the window. But he grabs my arm and hurls me so forcefully against the bare brick wall that I see stars and hear angels sing. But not Hallelujah!

OUCH!

I gasp, then search my purse for my pepper spray but I am not fast enough. I scream as Karl grabs my hair with one huge paw while the other twists my arm back so far, I believe I hear it crack. It burns like hell as he presses my face against the wall.

I have no way to defend myself against such a strong brute. I am helpless, my bag holding the spray lies uselessly at my soaked feet. Hot blood runs from my nose, down over my mouth and chin.

My heart is beating so fiercely, I'm afraid it might burst out of chest.

Dammit!

I should never have gotten involved with him! I should never have started working here for I've seen that with other girls, once on the payroll there was no turning back...

Never!

Again!

But now it's too late, I kind of fucked myself.

"Well...of course there are other ways you can make it up to me, like making you completely mine." Pablo lights one of his cheap disgusting cigars and sits on the edge of the makeup table next to me.

I try to spit in his face but only hit the wall and some

saliva runs down my chin — how embarrassing.

I won't belong to anyone!

No way!

Pablo grins, his eyes are bloodshot, and the bags are as huge as his pupils.

"What a pity, I thought you had more brains..." He nods at Karl again, who grabs my jeans and I know he will tear them from my body with brute force. The realization of what is about to happen turns my stomach. I start to scream and summon all of my strength, ready to fight...really fight. I'm ready to scratch their fucking eyes out and kick their balls...when a voice echoes through the room. Not calmly or quietly, but as hard as a whip.

"No!"

***

Even though his voice sounds as icy as the breath of death and his shoulders are tense under the white shirt, his expression is completely serene. He seems totally at ease...though his dark blue eyes glow intensely as he stares at Karl — and no one else.

"Who the hell are *you*?" Pablo asks snidely. "Fuck off, the entertainment takes place up front!"

He ignores the thug on the dressing table. "Let. Go. Of. Her."

Just four words, but those four words even give me the heebie jeebies. All at once, there is such tension in the air, I swear I feel static. Karl snorts and provocatively grabs the back of my pants.

I close my eyes as tears burn them! Tears! I haven't shed tears in so long. I cannot believe it!

And in front of him!

What is he doing here?

Please, just get out of here! I plead silently since I don't want anything to happen to him. But then I hear a scream echoing through the room and I rip open my eyes to see what's going on... Pablo is screaming, kneeling on the floor holding his hand. His fingers are at odd angles. My brain cannot process what I'm seeing. In the next moment, he is next to Karl and I feel his iron grip that is holding me captive, loosening. Next, I hear Karl roaring and watch as he flys against the wall next to me, immediately passing out – at least I hope so – and collapsing to the ground.

Shit!

Gently, very gently, compared to the way I was just manhandled, he grabs my arm and spins me around. My breath is so rapid, I'm almost panting. He, on the other hand, at first glance, seems completely calm. However, taking a closer look at eyes, I see they are full of rage, they downright sparkle with rage like two glaciers in the sun.

But he keeps himself in check. Absolutely.

He hands me his handkerchief. With trembling fingers, I take it and press it against my nose. Then he gives me a car key.

"Black Maserati! Get in and wait for me!" and turns away from me and confronts Pablo, who is sitting on the floor, holding his hand, howling like a baby and rocking back and forth.

Not hesitating for a damn second, I turn around and stagger out of the room without looking back. I catch myself on the wall and leave a bloody handprint behind, probably from my nose. I don't care and continue stumbling forward, past the bar and straight out into the rain... The icy drops feel good on my face, although, as I look up, everything goes black and I quickly grab the railing.

The car is right there. It's so close, yet so far away. It would have been better if had he carried me...

God, you're so stupid! KEEP GOING! one of my inner voices screams at me and I start to put one foot in front of the other...while trying to focus on my goal. But my vision remains blurry, but not due to the steadily increasing rainfall.

*You have a concussion...*one of my inner voices informs me dryly. *Considering the force you were slammed against the wall, I hope that shitty ring was worth it!*

I push the button on the remote and almost sob – almost – as I open the door and fall onto the passenger seat. I try to relax, but I don't close my eyes no matter how great the urge for that could be fatal with a concussion. Since the handkerchief is completely soaked with my blood, I use my shirt and press it against my nose to stem the flow and look around at the interior of the vehicle to distract myself and organize my thoughts.

The car is spick-and-span, not a speck of dust on its dark fixtures, leather seats, simply nowhere. It figures…

What is he doing here?

Was he checking out the strip club?

Why did he come to the back and enter the locker room just in time?

Before I can form my next thought, the driver's door opens and he swings absolutely elegantly into the narrow space, bringing along his scent and smelling of rain (unfortunately, all of which I'm presently unable to smell), starts the engine and turns on the dome light. My handbag, which he must have picked up, lands on my lap...

The light blinds me, my eyes are quite sensitive. "Keep your hands down!" He commands curtly and I let drop them. They're trembling and I curl my fingers in my lap. He gently examines my nose and is so damn close to me...I can see the gold sparks in his eyes. Now they don't look dark blue, more like a rich teal...

I peer at him, at his drenched hair, the shimmering drops in his eyelashes and on his lips, his white shirt...clearly showing red splashes, and frown. "You didn't kill him, did you?" I again immediately exclaim my first thought.

He snorts, then his eyes, which just now were on my nose and mesmerized me again, look me directly in the eye while he smirks coldly and makes me nervous. There is something in them, something dark, something dangerous

— yet also so attractive that I shiver.

"When did you become so informal, Olivia?" Oh my God! I'm such an ass! Here I just went through shit, about to faint, yet the only thing on my mind is the way he pronounced my name. No one ever said it like he did, nor did I ever feel this way when I heard someone say my name. I am completely flustered, at a loss for words. Once again. I am so embarrassed! God!

"Your nose is not broken," he announces, grabs the steering wheel and backs out of the parking lot. His right arm is on the headrest of my seat so that I can look closer look at his now expressionless face.

So devastating in its beauty.

So damn perfect...

Yet also dangerous-looking.

I smile and...finally pass out even though it is exactly what I tried to avoid.

"HEY!" He flicks his fingers in front of my face, so I open my eyes.

"Yes?" I ask, completely confused.

"No falling asleep!" he snaps, and I become aware that he is behaving quite differently than yesterday morning in the diner. He is tense, somber...and for some reason, he still seems pretty...pissed off. He opens the passenger window and cold rain smacks my face. I start yelling. As I curse, he grins and closes it again. Well, mission accomplished, I'm wide-awake again and the painful throbbing in my nose lessens more and more...just like the blood stream. Luckily.

But the butterflies in my stomach flutter again like crazy, actually, it's almost unbearable.

***

Two more times he opens the passenger window when he sees me drifting off and I'm startled awake by assaulting raindrops. When it happens the third time, I cannot restrain myself and cuss him out like crazy. I'm using words I would never say in Riley's presence. I'm sure Mister Rush has never heard a woman say that. But I just can't help it. He chuckles softly. An honest laugh...it reminds me of someone else.

RILEY!

I'm sure by now they're worrying, wondering what's keeping me, at least Penny is since Riley should already be asleep. So I rummage for my phone and text her:

Hey sweetie, I will be home later, do not worry!

I quickly press send before I can change my mind, lean back and close my eyes.

"Don't you dare!" I growl as I hear the window slide down a bit...then it shuts again as I watch with one eye. I look at him, he's totally focused on the empty road ahead while his hands clutch the steering wheel much too tightly and his lips are pressed together into a narrow line. It seems he's put off by something. I wonder if I should start a conversation, if I should thank him. I'm in the process of opening my mouth when my cell phone hums and shows I have a new message. It's from Penny of course. It starts with a shocked smiley, making me laugh, then comes...*Did you meet someone?*

Grinning, I roll my eyes...though I feel my cheeks blush and unobtrusively eye him from the corner of an eye. He's still looking straight ahead and in no position to make out what I'm typing.

I think so! Again, my heart almost bursts out of my chest.

Her reply is instant. *OMG. I want to know everything!*

I grin wider and simply reply, *Tomorrow!* then put my phone back in my handbag and look forward.

Since he makes no effort to start a conversation, I also keep quiet and enjoy the luxuries surrounding me as well as being near the driver. No matter how long it lasts, whatever it is.

I only know I want as much of it as possible.

17. What You Really Want

Keaton

You think you're safe now, Olivia.

The danger has just begun.

But now it's out of my hands. And it's your fault. My plan was scheduled differently, it was not to progress this quickly. The game was just beginning to become interesting — I don't want it to end yet. I don't want to be at that stage already. But you forced my hand because you were stupid and naive. Because you waltzed right into danger when any normal human would have stayed far away.

I would have retrieved that damned ring for you, Olivia.

I already had it planned.

Black on white.

In my notebook.

But you're not into making plans, right, pretty one? You don't like to abide by rules, guidelines, or common sense. You simply march right into the lion's den. Like a gentle, beautiful gazelle straight into the predator's mouth.

You were lucky there was an even more dangerous predator lurking in the shadows. You forced another hunter to leave his blind and take action. I would have never allowed them to hurt you seriously. The manhandling was already excessive. I really had to force myself to maintain my composure for it would have been easy to put those degenerates out of their misery. However, I prefer other methods, darling, some more subtle, much better than a quick death.

The way you've asked me if I killed them made me smile. One side of you is very naive, yet the other sees right through me.

Isn't that so, baby?

You sense the danger that emanates from me — and you love it.

You don't run away from it, you yearn for it.

You're a bad girl who has been playing with fire for years.

Be careful you don't get burned.

You are so *different* than me. One might think the perfect counterpart.

But we will never really know...

Unfortunately.

You're still not protesting as I pull into the underground garage of the tower where I live, you just go along with me. To the home of strange man! If it were not me, what would you do then, Olivia?

Would you do the same?

Just like that?

The thought makes me furious, something I don't want to be in your presence... I distract myself by staring at your legs, damn perfect butt in tight jeans, and narrow waistline as you enter the elevator ahead of me. On the ride up to my penthouse, I must stop looking at you since you're driving me out of my mind, that will, in the end, cause me to lose control, ruining everything... No woman has ever had that effect on me.

It's sad it will be over between us again tomorrow.

So sad.

***

Olivia

Seeing the way he lives, I can only say WOW! We walk toward an all glass elevator and pass the concierge on the way, who even at this late hour, is wide-awake and gives Mister Rush a friendly greeting. He acknowledges him with an equally friendly, "Good evening, Mr. Henson," which I like. Mister Rush – gosh, the name alone makes my body hot – is not an asshole. He does not treat someone of lower standing condescendingly, which I know about from my job interview.

Once we are in the small space of the elevator, I can no longer think straight with him so near for I can smell again and his scent surrounds me. He smells clean and fresh, like he just stepped out of the shower and has not been on his feet all day. His shirt has tiny speckles of blood on it that I should shy away from, but don't. I can't. Not with him.

The elevator opens directly into his penthouse — naturally. The lights come on automatically, illuminating expensive marble flooring that opens up to an immensely huge living and dining room slash kitchen... I cannot help but stand there with my mouth gaping. The entire kitchen, furniture and all, is high gloss white. The place is pristine, like no one lives here — no stains on light switches from years of use, no dirty dishes in the sink that still need to be washed. No bowls with knick-knacks like a coupons, shopping receipts, or keys. No withered plants — only huge, white, well-attended orchids. The large windows offer a wonderful view. A few doors lead off the hallway, presumably to the bedroom, den, bathroom, and who knows what a bachelor craves. And there is a staircase leading down.

How can he afford this place?

It's sheer luxury, like only really wealthy people can enjoy.

Oh, and the panoramic view, it simply is magnificent and draws me like a moth to light. I move close to the pane and barely resist placing a hand on it. His place is so sterile. I imagine he does not appreciate fingerprints on the glass. The clouds break apart, as if offering me this spectacular view of a starry night sky over the city and crescent moon.

Absolutely beautiful. He opens his shirt's top two buttons and rotates his head in all directions as if to stretch and relax his neck. From the living room, he walks around the dividing counter to enter the kitchen. He opens the doors of a couple of glossy white cabinets and returns with utensils and another shirt.

"I'm sure you'd like to change, perhaps freshen up first, the bathroom is downstairs." He nods in the direction of the staircase while opening a bottle of wine — filling two glasses. But he does not hand one to me or so much as look in my direction. He appears tense. His whole body seems to tremble from tension.

"Okay...um, thanks," I stutter. Barely able to resist sniffing the white T-shirt he gave me, not wanting to ruin it with my blood, I go downstairs to the bathroom – once again, I'm taken aback. It is as big as my whole apartment.

Madness! And again, everything is in white, even the marble is white. His and her sinks, even though he lives alone, and a walk-in shower, big enough to accommodate four people. Looking at the big mirror, the soft LED lighting makes my skin appear cleaner.

Quickly, I wash the blood off my face and watch the red liquid go down the drain. I take off my bloodstained top and wash off my smeared makeup. I cannot see anything personal down here; it's like a window display — creepy. Then again...someone who can afford such a place certainly has a cleaning lady!

I run my fingers through my disheveled hair so it won't look so chaotic, then rinse my mouth twice to get rid of the metallic taste... I already feel much better and slip into his T-shirt. Okay, my black bra shines through, but that can't be helped right now.

What the heck are you doing here anyway? Go home! One of my inner voices, the cautious one, the one that is ALWAYS afraid, begs me. I merely snort...

Oh hell no! I won't give up an opportunity to find out more about the oh-so- mysterious Mister Rush!

He won't kill me!

***

When I return, the faux-fireplace is on and he's sitting in one of the three oversized dark leather couches. He's still wearing his black trousers, though no longer the blood-spattered shirt, but a clean, black turtleneck sweater that snuggly hugs his athletic upper body. The shirt's sleeves are rolled up and his tanned muscular skin and Rolex distract me. A strand falls over his forehead. I want to brush it away and roll my eyes at myself.

I have to remind myself he's my boss.

I should not even be here.

Yet I accept the silent invitation, sit next to him on the beige couch – a bit too hard, but then expensive designer furniture such as this, most often are uncomfortable and more for the eye rather actual use –– and take the offered glass of wine. I need liquid courage — yes, I do. His gaze then travels from the fire he's been staring at to me.

Again, I feel like a butterfly that's pierced and displayed in a box. Immobile for eternity just to please its owner.

However, I manage not to flinch.

He says nothing, just stares at me. I clear my throat before I finally say, "The wine is good."

"Yes," he replies. Clearly, small talk is not one of his strengths...

He seems entirely focused on me. Like the only thing in the world is me. I like it. Way too much.

Or maybe he was waiting for me to leave, maybe he does not want me here at all, he merely feels obligated to take care of me after what I've been through.

Yet here I sit, making a dent in the upholstery, whereas he might want to be asleep already. He's simply polite!

Dammit Liv! Get a fucking move on! NOW!

I swallow, silently begging, *Give me a sign, some...something... SAY SOMETHING!* Yet he just sits there with one arm casually resting on couch back, taking a sip and looking at me over the rim of the glass with that look that confuses me. He does not say one word... And makes me swallow.

I still don't make a move.

"So...this is where you live..."

"I do."

"The view is spectacular."

"Yes it is!" Does he find me amusing? His sparkling eyes certainly appear amused, though otherwise *nothing*. I'm uncomfortable and feel like squirming, but instead, take another sip, when I feel the heat rising in me because I'm not used to drinking much alcohol. I know I should not drink more, or talk — preferable both, but I want to find out more about him! This is my chance!

"What were you doing in that strip club?" Again, I blurt out the first thing that comes to mind, I blame the alcohol! I sound...somewhat jealous and a total idiot. But, to be honest, the idea of him watching half-naked women gets to me. If only he knew what show *I* could give him, well, he would never set foot in such a cheap establishment. Never again.

Now he smirks obviously, as far as Mr. Rush even smirks

"I could ask you the same, Miss Pierson." I instantly blush as my question boomerangs to bite me in the ass. He might be using an FBI interrogation technique. I narrow my eyes and cross my arms in front of my chest.

Oh no, you won't.

"I asked first!" It might sound childish, but I don't care, especially seeing he's really amused now, somewhat looser.

"Very well, you're correct. I was there to meet a friend who needed spiritual help, Miss Pierson."

Oh.

Not there to ogle hot women?

Not there to rub one off in the dark?

The relief I feel shocks me.

"So, you usually don't frequent strip clubs?" I ask. He answers casually — with that damned superior smirk, like something is *really* amusing him. "No, usually not. How about you, Miss Pierson?" Now he's grinning again in that way that tells me he knows something that I'm unaware of and that he's enjoying withholding knowledge from me.

"I... I was there because…" Oh shit! Tell the truth or lie? Tell my new boss that before he hired me, I was stripper? A man who I apparently find hot? Although, like with other people, I want to lie, but I tell him the truth. Perhaps because I'm already tipsy.

"I worked there." I raise my chin, my pride won't let me feel ashamed! I had to earn a living, I never went against my principles, I have no reason to be ashamed! And he does not look down on me, on the contrary, he seems...impressed.

"Okay," he says and takes another sip.

"Okay? That's it?" I'm completely flabbergasted. No suggestive remark? No questioning why I did something so horrible? Not surprised at all, or YOU BETTER LEAVE MY APARTMENT THIS INSTANT, YOU CHEAP WHORE?

"How would you like me to react?"

"Shocked?"

"Why?"

"Because, I'm…"

"Because you earn money for a living? That's supposed to shock me?"

"I make money taking off my clothes in front of strange men!"

"And, you enjoyed it?"

Wow... I would have never expected that question and feel moved. I mean, what person would see it like that? Most would think about the fun part of the business, not the actual money aspect, right? But not him, no, Mr. Rush is a special kind of person — though I already knew that... It's what fascinates me about him in the first place. He is absolutely unpredictable and has that mystical, somewhat dangerous vibe to him that us women – unfortunately – are drawn to. Not to mention, he seems to have very little scruples. I swallow...dig down deep and again answer truthfully, like I never have before to anyone in this world. Then again, he's quite different compared to the people I have met so far. "Yes."

"So, all is well." He finishes his glass and refills it, as well as mine... I should not drink more, I already cannot think straight, oh who cares.

"You're funny, Mr. Rush."

"How so?"

"Because you're not shocked or make me feel ashamed."

"A person should never be ashamed doing what they love, Miss Pierson."

"So, what is it you love?" I burst out again without thinking. Oh God, what am I doing here? For a moment, he no longer is sitting elegantly as he runs a hand through his hair, messing it up, before catching himself.

"This and that!"

"Oh, come on!" I feel quite brave, sitting next to him on his couch. "I was truthful with you, now it's your turn!" He regards me, smiling, with his eyes glowing and a gentle expression like I've never seen. Almost...a little...fascinated. Here, I'm sitting in front of him, telling him what he should do. I don't think many people would even dare that.

"You think so, Miss Pierson?"

"Yep!" I take another sip. I have almost had two glasses now, *I really should* stop, but he refills it, leans back, and says, "Well..." His hand is directly behind me on the backrest. It almost touches my hair and I wish so very much that he would do it, but he merely looks at me with his head tilted and says, "What I love, Miss Pierson?"

His eyes make my skin tingly as they slowly roam my body with relish...obviously becoming ravenous. Urgent. Lustful. My insides pull together. Never before has a man looked at me with such voracity, I feel at his mercy. He makes eye contact again and I know my gaze is as urgent as his.

"Yes?" I ask. My voice trembles a bit.

"I love sincere people. People who stay true to themselves, who don't follow the mainstream or whatever popular fashion, people who do not abide by social constraints simply because everyone else does. I love people who present themselves as who they are. No pretense."

"Okay." Why does it seem he is taking about me? I'm getting very hot, hotter than the wine already made me feel, and I cling to the stem like I am drowning. "And, what else?"

"You're not at all pushy, are you, Olivia?" There he said it again! My name! Spoken with his sensual mouth. At some point, when he says my name, I might collapse and die.

"Like you are not!" I reply defiantly and take another sip. My head feels dizzy...*weeee...*

He takes the glass out of my hands and sets it on the table, like he decided I have had enough. "Am I?" he asks softly...and all of a sudden his fingers are delicately stroking my hair, playing with it, letting strands slide between his fingertip, thus overcoming the first hurdle.

I hold my breath.

And gaze into his sparkling eyes.

"Now you tell me what you love, Miss Pierson."

Mysterious, handsome men who pull me under their spell, I would love to say, but won't. Even though I just had a sip, my throat is dry.

"I love chocolate!"

"What woman doesn't?" His fingertips oh-so-gently slide over my neck, like the wings of a butterfly, I shiver...

They slide down...and back up again. I am distracted.

"I love feeling your fingers!" I burst out again, not thinking, almost squeakily.

"Really?" he says and brushes along my jaw – down my throat. It seems dangerous and tingles.

I close my eyes and slightly lean my head back.

"YES!" Damn. What's he doing to me? I'm biting my lower lip in anticipation...for once a hurdle is defeated, I want more, I want *it all*.

E

V

E

R

Y

T

H

I

N

G!

And much more…

"You're one of the most sensual people I've come across, Olivia Pierson." His voice is low and controlled, although a little hoarse that tells me he is not unfazed by this situation either. "What should my fingers do to you?" OH GOD!

His fingers brush over my chin, then two over my lower lip. I automatically pout a little and nestle my flesh on his slightly rough fingertips.

Hot...

I feel so hot...

The fire in me is blazing so hot, I know I'll end up burned...but I cannot stop. Although, I'm not even doing anything.

This situation is so intense...and he is merely touching me with his fingertips.

Madness.

I've never experienced anything like it.

Never...

"Whatever you want," I whisper and his fingers falter. I open my eyes and look at him, at his burning gaze.

"I can do whatever I want to you, Miss Pierson?"

"Yes!" I breathe.

"Your offer could put you in danger."

"I know!" Unblinking, I hold his gaze.

His expression is void of any humor.

He is so handsome.

The handsomest I've ever seen.

Slowly and cautiously, as if approaching a wild predator with no idea its reaction, I raise a hand and grasp his... As I pull it away from my face, I notice him clenching his teeth, presumably thinking I'm turning him down right now...but I could not do that, even if my life depended on it. His pupils widen as I entwine our fingers...and doing it feels right. Like the last two pieces find their place in a puzzle, one that is my life. I slowly rise. He allows me to sit on his lap. With our interlocked hands between us, I do the same with our other hands and steady myself with them as I slowly and with relish, move around on him. I circle my pelvis and immediately feel him reacting.

His gaze darkens...his nostrils puff out.

"What would you like to do to me, Mister Rush?" I ask while looking up at him from under my eyelashes, then bite my lower lip and snuggle up closer to him...

Oh, the way he looks at me now. It's the most greedy intense look I've ever been eyed with. I can tell he's fighting for control. The realization makes me smile...

Though he doesn't reply verbally, he shows me.

His hand releases mine and he leaps up and grabs my chin so firmly that I cannot move my head. Next, his lips abruptly crash against mine while his other arm hugs my butt in a vice grip and I cannot escape – even if I wanted to – and he hugs me so tight, no sheet of paper fits between us.

And I am lost.

18. Rush

Olivia

One moment, I'm still sitting on top of him, thinking I'm in control, yet in the next, I find myself on the floor in front of the couch with him towering over me. He's interlocking our fingers again as he pushes them to the cold floor, while my lower body is on the soft carpet, nestled against his lower body.

He does not say anything, simply keeps me like this...in his power. Defenseless.

His cock is hard and ready.

My panties are dripping wet like Niagara Falls.

I refrain from begging as he holds me there like this, so close, yet what I want most of his right now is still out of reach...

I raise and rub my pelvis against him.

He pushes his crotch forward and me with it, hard against the ground.

OH GOD!

I feel his entire length right next to my jeans, wishing I was naked...or at least out of the damn jeans...

It's not enough!

But I understand the message.

He has full control.

Not me.

So for now...I allow it.

For whatever reason, after all, that's not my style.

The men I meet in my life, I would never trust with control. But the way he holds me so firmly while looking at me warningly feels natural — then, still not saying a word, he takes his hands off me.

I stay in the same position, dare not move, even though my heart is beating like crazy and I'm panting.

Contentedly He grins briefly, then leans forward and kisses my neck. I would love to lift and snake my arms around him, pull him down...to do something, but I remain completely passive and enjoy what he gives me. His lips are so soft, so tender and his breath hot as they wander down my neck.

"Oh, Olivia, all that I will to do you," he whispers huskily into my ear while opening the button of my jeans.

The lust within me seems to explode into a thousand little pieces...

He pulls the zipper down while kissing my neck down to hem of my T-shirt...then pulls the shirt up over my breasts. I love the way his eyes darken with more lust as the fabric moves over my already hard nipples. They are literally aching to be touched and he seems to accommodate me...as he leans on one arm and with his free hand pulls the flimsy bra down just enough to expose my nipples. The sight makes him moan and I threaten to explode again.

He grins sexily and I whimper quietly... Honestly, I've *never* made that sound before. And I'm not ashamed as he leans forward and gently sucks on one nipple. His mouth is so hot, his tongue so soft.

I scream "Mister Rush!" as I arch my back and feel his broad grin on my overly sensitive skin...

"Call me Keaton!" he states patronizingly, then devotes himself to the other nipple.

"GOD!" I can no longer resist and dig my hands into his hair.

"That works too." His mouth disappears, then he does. Confused, I look up and see him standing over me. Her legs wide apart, his hands clenched, like a fallen angel...his well-defined chest quickly heaving under the thin sweater, his dark shiny hair disheveled, lips swollen, while the licking flames of the fireplace illuminate his face. Not to mention, there's something hard and huge in his pants.

My stomach contracts from lust. I want him. A lot. And he wants me too, though he restrains himself.

Madness...

This man is madness in all respects.

"Take off your jeans!" he orders a bit hoarsely, otherwise, he seems completely calm, in control, unlike me and my *inner* raging inferno. I want to rise, though he urges me to do it right there... I frown and stay on the ground. He's tall and powerful as a giant, whereas I'm small and vulnerable as an ant. That's exactly how I feel. Like one move from him could crush me. Deep down I know he would never do that. He pulls the rough fabric down my legs and I kick it off, now lying only in black panties in front of him. Okay, plus his shirt and my bra, which is still pushed below my breasts...shit...

"The shirt too!" With one hand, he pulls his sweater over his head and tosses it aside, then settles on the couch behind him, bare-chested... I swallow...

Open mouthed.

So stupid.

Because, honestly...I was under the impression men like him existed only on glossy magazine covers or in movies. Basically, it should be forbidden to give such a body to someone with a face like that. A specimen like that does not exist in reality, yet here one sits right in front of me, with his clearly defined chest, slightly toned six-pack, broad shoulders, and sexy V...as if he just *stepped* out of *Pinterest*. I like muscular, athletic, manly men, not bodies like bodybuilders. It feels like I created him from my wettest, dirtiest fantasies...as if he's only here to fulfill them. His skin seems pale in the candlelight, absolutely perfect, not a tattoo — or blemish in sight.

My nipples grow even harder and seem to strain the fabric so I reach to open my bra, when he says, "It stays on, only take the panties off..." I take it off and squeeze my legs together. I cannot help it.

He raises one brow admonishingly and I spread them...my cheeks glow and heat courses through my whole body.

I give myself to him like no other man. It takes so much more courage to strip just for him instead of a horde of hooting men.

"Touch yourself, Olivia!" he says softly. I close my eyes. "No, continue looking at me!" he says somewhat demandingly, so I open my eyes. Touching myself in front of a stranger, really now, that's too...intimate? It's really not easy, though I reach down and timidly brush over my clit. It way too sensitive... I flinch as lust immediately bursts into an inferno deep inside me, setting everything aflame again. I gaze into his eyes as I gather up all my courage and present this stranger with a show that no one else before has ever seen.

He makes it easy for me to let my naughty, slutty side out because I know he won't judge me. No matter what I do. My intuition tells me this and so...I let lust take over and guide my fingers. As if I am alone...I slightly move my pelvis and feel everything inside me longing for him to fill me. Braced on one elbow, I fully enjoy the moment and let my head fall back. I moan...close my eyes and feel my hair brushing the floor.

"STOP!" he says and rips me out of the maelstrom of ever-increasing lust... I stop all movement, pop open my eyes and look at him...though my gaze is somewhat blurry.

He's still sitting on the sofa.

He's still breathing rapidly — perhaps even more so than before.

His lips are open a crack.

His pants are open.

His cock is in his hand.

I freeze.

His cock is huge!

"Come here!" he demands hoarsely, no longer sounding that controlled.

I obey and crawl toward him...and lick my lower lip. I want to lick away the drop of pleasure on his fat gland. I want to feel it thrusting into me, stretching and filling me...

I place my hand in the one that's reaching for me, again feeling like putty, and allow him to pull me up. Now I'm straddling him... Our eyes are interwoven as I slowly lower myself onto his huge cock as I hold it in position with one hand. One cheek twitches as he pushes against me and fights the slight resistance. I lower myself oh-so-slowly, almost agonizingly, so that we feel every inch of each other. He's only halfway inside me and I think that's enough. The last time was a while ago, I'm too tight and he's too big. I want to move up as the sudden intensity of this union, of the moment, of his gaze and the closeness of his body is overwhelming me.

But he growls, "Too late!" And just thrusts all the way into me. It's like he's tearing me apart. I scream as I throw my head back... I must get used to his size first, but he doesn't give me time.

He's not gentle.

In no way.

"*Now* you're mine!" he growls, whirls me around, and throws me on my back onto the couch before thrusting into me again.

Now there is no stopping him.

And I understand.

He allowed me to go this far.

He even needed me to do so.

That I come to him.

Take his hand.

That I unite with him.

That I take control one last time...before completely giving into him.

19. Out of Control

Keaton

I had you, Olivia.

I had you in all the ways others had you – yet also in so many more ways.

No one ever did you like I did.

I know, for I not only fucked your body, I fucked your entire being.

You showed me your shy good side and your dirty nasty one.

Now they're all mine.

The good saint.

And the nasty whore.

It's the crack of dawn and I'm sitting on the edge of the bed right next to you, knowing the time has come. It is time to let you go. You have to disappear from my life forever, like all the others before you.

I'm sated.

The hunt was worth it, you were exquisite.

But now the thrill has run its course.

The night is over.

All secrets are revealed.

Now I know your taste.

Even the ones in the most forbidden places.

I also know the sounds you make when you come.

I also know how you feel inside and felt your contractions.

The way your eyes glaze over shortly before.

The way you say my name while moaning, screaming, gasping, or whimpering lustfully.

We didn't get much sleep.

We conversed even less.

And yet now I know everything I needed to know.

It is time to move on.

I should wake you now, show you to the door, and on the way, tell you you're fired, maybe even give you severance pay. I no longer have use for you. Yet here I am, still sitting on the edge of the bed next to you, watching the first rays of sunlight slowly creep over your skin, your perfect skin.

I catch myself lifting a hand and lightly touching your cheek, feeling your warmth, I even lean forward and smell your hair, inhale your scent deeply, and become aware of a certainty.

A certainty I have never felt with another woman.

I cannot let you go.

Never again.

***

Olivia

I wake up and immediately know I'm alone in bed. I also immediately recall every dirty little detail of what we did last night.

Oh my God!

I'm blushing, even now that it's over.

But last night...no, not last night.

I have done, said, and groaned things I never thought would come from my lips.

First on the couch.

Then in the shower ...

But especially in this bed.

Oh yes, especially here.

I bury my face in the pillows as I recall everything we did last night all at once. It is as devastating as it is powerful and it changes everything.

This man really managed to unsettle me and my world so that I will never be like I was before meeting him.

Keaton Rush swept over me and took everything, leaving only behind sweet devastation.

Yes, I'm devastated, my body is devastated. I'm sore in the most impossible places! And muscles ache that I had no idea I had before.

I am beet red and lift my head to look outside. The sun shines directly in my face. I moan laboriously. Then I remember it's early morning and I...should not be here!

I jump up naked as I am and immediately moan in pain before I continue hurrying out of the bedroom into the living room and down the hallway to my bag. I grab my cell phone and glance at the clock.

"Shit!" I curse, spin around, and dash back into the living room. I gather up my things that are still strewn about on the ground while attempting to *repress* what he did to me here... First, from above...then again from behind that gave me such a phenomenally intense orgasm, it left me spent. He took me deeply from behind while holding my hair in a fist... I try not to think about how it felt when his pelvis kept slamming against my butt and he ordered me to give into the moment, asking if I wanted to come again...if it felt good when he thrust harder and even deeper into me.

As if that had been even possible...

I cannot stop a nice gentle shiver from coursing through me as I recall everything — then I open my eyes when I hear him clear his throat. The sound comes from the direction of the dining area, where I see him sitting now fully dressed. He's wearing elegant dark gray trousers, a black belt, black shoes, and a white shirt. His hair is still damp, on his nose rests a pair of really hot stylish glasses. He's looking up from the laptop in front of him and eyes me with one brow raised as I hop around with one leg in the jeans, dreaming to myself.

His gaze causes a more intense shiver and again, it seems as if time stands still. I recall the way he looked at me last night when he was inside me, *devoured* me.

"I called in sick for you at the diner. I told whoever was in charge that you caught a really bad flu," he says and his voice...God...I still hear him ordering me around, orders that shook me to the core and which made me go beyond my limits. Shameless, unscrupulous, hard. The way he ordered me to jerk him off under the roaring water of the shower...and to swallow every drop when he came.

I still see myself kneeling in front of him, following through.

Then he grabbed me, wet as I was, set me on the carpet in his bathroom and pleasured me orally.

Oh, how great he was.

My God, this man is so talented with his tongue, fingers, words, cock... He's so vulgar — and I thought men like that only existed in books.

I'm getting wet again and stammer, "Okay." I don't know what to think of him deciding to let me sleep and calling in sick for me at work, but I guess it's better than a no show, no call, isn't it?

Spontaneously, I step into the other jeans' leg and pull up my pants. I'm still incredibly sensitive and flinch, though I don't let it show. I still have yet to find my panties. It seems to have grown legs and disappeared, just like my bra. The denim is rough on my private parts. I look around, see his shirt, and put it on. And…again I don't know what to do. My entire being is drawn to him, to feel one last time his mouth on mine, to be reassured last night was real and not only one of my absolutely hot fantasies with the sex god in front of me. The aforementioned leans back with his arms crossed in front of his chest and angles his head. His face is unreadable. Like the man himself.

"So, um...thank you for the night..." I say, step into my shoe, at least the one I see. He doesn't say anything, though his eyes are piercing. "I... I think I have bothered you long enough." I search for the other shoe in vain. Finally, I go down on all fours and peer under the couch. Luckily, I find it and put it on.

Now I'm ready to go...unfortunately.

But as I stand, out of nowhere, he's behind me and my heart skips a few beats. He abruptly pulls me against him...his strong muscular arms hold me tightly against his rock-hard body — his mouth and nose nuzzle my hair.

"You really think after last night I'll simply let you go like that, Miss Pierson," he whispers against my skin and I feel him growing hard against my back.

I close my eyebrows resignedly before I reply, "I was hoping you'd say that, Mr. Rush." It's weird to be informal with him while in his arms and his lips on my neck, feeling him grow a hard cock on my ass. Though it's weird, it's also absolutely perfect.

He turns me around, grabs my chin with two strong fingers, and bends my head back. His eyes are burning again as he looks at me. Strong greens captivate me as he says, "I'll tell you one more time, though I don't like having to constantly repeat myself, You. Are. Mine. Now!"

He kisses me, briefly but passionately while pushing me back against the couch. My legs catch, I lose my balance and fall...landing softly...and already he's kneeling between my legs. I'm breathless as he opens my recently zipped jeans and pushes his hand inside, massaging my throbbing pussy while his forehead is leaning against mine. "You still have two hours and thirteen minutes before you must leave..." He shoves two fingers inside me.

"Yes..." I gasp and urgently push my crotch toward him, wanting more. I want whatever he's ready to give me again.

"And we'll make use of every single minute, Olivia. What do you say?" He moves his fingers as much as the confines of my tight jeans allow him to while at the same time, he lowers his head and nibbles on my neck.

"That's a great idea," I barely manage to say and dig a hand into his dark hair, feel him grinning on my skin. Today he has more stubble, probably hasn't shaved yet, which tickles me as he kisses up my neck to my ear.

"Who do you belong to?"

"To you."

"What do you want from me?" He pulls his hand back,

which is all wet, then pushes it under my shirt and massages my breast as his tongue pushes into my mouth and explores. God, the guy is so hot! So demanding! So dominant! Exactly what I need!

"Your cock!" I gasp in his mouth. He grins again and pulls my jeans off my legs along with my shoes. And already he's back on his knees in front of me, pushing himself against my dripping wet privates. Unfortunately, he still has his pants on, how *annoying*. He briefly kisses me again before asking, "Where do you want my cock, Olivia?"

"Inside me!" I murmur, reaching down and unfastening his jingling belt. He lets it happen and I kiss him more urgently. Yes, I'm sore, yes, everything hurts, but damn, yes, I want him to take me again. This time harder. As hard as possible... I'm a slut, his slut.

"So take him then!" he says and moans softly as I open his pants and touch it. I get it out and run my fingernails over his shaft, making him twitch and in delight, he closes his eyes for a few seconds. It's so big, I can barely get my hand around it, but I manage and push my crotch toward him... "You little hot slut!" He gasps as I prop my feet up on the couch and assume a position where I can rub his gland between my labia.

I have no idea who I'm torturing more.

Though I enjoy seeing him clench his teeth and flex every muscle on his upper body.

"Stop toying with me!" he snaps and grabs my butt, holding it relentlessly in place. He holds me as if I am as light as a feather and I love the way his biceps tense and bulge under his shirt.

Then he thrusts into me...

Relentlessly.

Typical for him.

And it's what I need.

For a few minutes, I forget who I should be and just am...

It is awesome.

***

Time and time again, he thrusts into me as his mouth ravishes mine. His breath is inside my mouth, tastes so delicious, his body is as hard...as his thrusts. I'm already coming. He does not care and continues. Like last night. The man's stamina and strength is incredible.

He's fucking me as I orgasm and only pulls back once I'm finished, coming directly on my pubis, then demands harshly, "That stays there!" and gets up and walks away.

To who knows where, I couldn't care less...

He leaves me behind on the couch, totally spent and in seventh heaven. My muscles are trembling and my entire body is sweaty. I could shower again...I'm so happy, feel so free...

I've never experienced anything close to it.

Never…

And yes, he does not care for cuddling, kind words, or touching after sex. But right now I only need this dirty rough sex from him. I don't want more!

Or?

I'm certainly not here because I'm looking for a prince to ride off with into the sunset. After all, I know such men don't exist. I once thought I had that type, I really wanted it to work... though what did it get me, a child who cannot walk without crutches.

There's no room in our life for a man. And I only trust Penny to be near Riley. That's the truth ...I don't want him around a man!

This here is only a sexual arrangement!

I knew that from the onset and that's a good thing! I'm not like other women, who immediately fall head over heels for the guy who provided them with a great orgasm. I have no need for love, after all, love is a myth. When it comes down to it, every human being is selfish and thinks only of themselves. That's the ugly truth.

Yet right now, I want nothing more than to be with him. Maybe test what would happen if I were to snuggle up close to him. I want to find out if he can touch me other than in a rough demanding way. I want to know if he can kiss me gently, not only passionately. I want to find out if his eyes can sparkle with something other than lust.

But that would be playing with fire.

So I use the opportunity to do what's right while he's in the bathroom, quickly clean myself, put on my jeans, slip into my shoes, then grab my purse and disappear!

I'm running away from him, but more so...from my own treacherous feelings!

20. Saturday Morning

Olivia

Even as I get off the bus and hurry home, my heart is still racing. Oh, what happened last night? It's a bit of a cliché, but seriously, the man has turned my world upside down. OH YEAH! Shaken! He made me quake every second I felt him inside me. During the entire bus ride, images popped into my mind that I tried to suppress: His hands on my butt, his lips on my neck, the glass shower screen that gave a little as he abruptly pushed me hard against it, his scent in my nose, our skin pressed so firmly against each other, not even sheet of paper fit in between. My crotch is on fire. I can't help myself, but as I rush home through the drizzle, I again feel tingling in my stomach and the desire to feel him inside overwhelms me even though I'm sore.

Stop it, fool! the rational voice inside my head admonishes me. Better focus on not walking around aimlessly or you'll end up hitting a tree.

I shake my head to regain my senses. It was good I ran away even though everything inside me wanted to stay with him. I would still like to lie in his strong arms. Okay, we did not cuddle, but he held me while he did me from behind... Then when he floated over me and stared lustfully into my eyes, I clawed at his skin. No matter how much I tried, I didn't have the strength to break eye contact. It was simply...legendary. Maybe it's for the best to leave it at that. At one beautiful night that either of us can remember whenever we desire. I have no room for a man in my life and, from the looks of it, I'm sure Mr. Sexy-Rush is also not exactly interested in a relationship. I don't even believe the block of ice is capable of feeling anything other than his super sexiness.

I blink. The humidity frizzed my hair at the temples and I realize I walked right past my front door. So much for 'walking around with a stupid grin on my face'. Rolling my eyes, I turn back, open the ancient door, and make my way upstairs.

My legs are tired and I'm sore, so a short climb up the stairs feels like an extreme sport. Once I arrive at the top, I gasp and run a hand through my damp hair. Yes, it has gotten warmer, though the rain is driving me crazy, especially since it always comes on so suddenly.

I unlock the door, enter, and immediately jump because

Penny is suddenly standing in front of me. She is wearing black leggings and an oversized, thin, white sweater. Her perm is a mess and of course she is chewing gum again. Her eyes tell me exactly what she wants from me, but at the moment, I'm not ready.

"Why are you down here?' I asked nonchalantly and relaxed, as if last night nothing exciting happened.

"Oh, we spent the evening at my place, but we didn't want to miss you coming home." She winks conspiratorially and I already know I have to spill the beans.

"I should have known," I murmur and wonder how much I should tell Penny so she won't go ahead and make wedding plans. I know how much she wants for me to find Mr. Right, but even though the night with Keaton Rush was simply incredibly good, he is surely not the one for me...besides, even if he were, I would never find out since I only have love for Riley.

I shut the door and lower my bag to the floor. Penny is extremely excited, she might be trying not to show it, but I know her too well acting like she is — keen to hear information she can analyze with me down to the smallest detail. Analyze...analyze...anal...anal sex. Oh, my God! Now what's going on? I mean, such a thing hasn't even happened, so why am even thinking about it? I shake my head vigorously, Penny frowns.

"You okay?" she asks. "I mean, you seem worn out...but in a good way, which makes it the first time since I've known you." Now she's waggling her eyebrows suggestively, I sigh as I recall every dirty detail, of course, about what Mr. Rush did to me last night...

"Oh, my God, you're blushing!"

I actually flinch again. "Any chance I can grab a coffee first?"

"Of course!" She grins. "A hard night like you had first requires a moment of contemplation, I understand!" Amused yet also partly annoyed, I follow her into the kitchen from where I can see into the living room. Riley is sitting on the couch, apparently oblivious to my homecoming, which is no wonder since the typical Saturday morning cartoons are on TV. He's still in his pajamas, which is fine for Saturday mornings. One pant leg is cut off and sown closed so it won't swing around and in the way. His big eyes are glued to the screen while he nibbles on his thumbnail.

I smile when I realize I've missed him like crazy the past few hours. "Hey, baby, not even a hello for your mom?" I ask and his head whips around to me so fast, his too-long hair fans out. His eyes glow. He's so cute when he's surprised. Just like he looks on Christmas morning!

"MOM!" he shouts and tries to get up awkwardly when I beat him to it and hurriedly hug and kiss him on the cheek.

"Where were you?" he asks. His eyes appear reproachful like an adult's, almost making me laugh.

"I had to work longer, sweetheart."

"Until this morning?" he asks skeptically. "Aunt Penny said you were so tired, you slept in a hotel." Wow, I think and almost laugh. A stupid excuse, but fortunately, a child doesn't question too many things, taking what is said as truth.

"Yes, because I had to work so long," I say and nudge his nose with my index finger. Something isn't right. Riley is warmer than usual and only now do I realize he's pale. I peer at him intently. "Do you feel all right?"

"Come have breakfast!" Penny calls out. I hear dishes clatter and smell freshly brewed coffee, my stomach growls.

He shrugs. "I don't know, Mommy."

"Are you in pain?" I ask, thinking he might have the flu.

"A little," he says, pointing to the duck on his pajamas, under which is his stomach. "Here!"

I rub his stomach and kiss his warm forehead. Though it does not feel feverish, he definitely has an elevated temperature. "Let's eat something and afterward, it's back to bed!"

I help him up and we go sit at the wonderfully set table. I stare at the wide selection. "Did you go shopping?" I ask, puzzled.

Penny shakes her head. "The majority was in your fridge." My eyes fall on the sliced apples Penny added to the yoghurt. For the life of me, I cannot remember buying them! Then I think it might be because of a lack of sleep.

I'm glad Riley is sitting at the table and Penny cannot pester me anymore. For a while, I enjoy the homey atmosphere while sipping my coffee and listening to Penny tell me about their evening, how she and Riley played board games. All the while, my son is listlessly poking his food and even before I can ask if he is all right, he opens his eyes wide and I instinctively know what will happen next.

I'm on my feet and by his side in one leap, quickly reach under his arms and pull him over to the sink.

Just in time for him to throw up his entire stomach contents.

Dammit!

21. Chance is a Rumor

Olivia

Hello, bad conscience!

I was waiting for you to make an appearance.

I rushed down our street with my arms crossed in front of my chest. Between Madame Chloè's Bakery – which sounds fancier than it is – and the kiosk that sells vodka to juveniles, is the pharmacy where I need to buy something for Riley. According to Penny, he was fine last night, and, from experience, I know my little one catches the stomach flu easily. Now that he has vomited, he has a higher fever, so Penny is looking after him while I buy medication. I don't like pills, but of course I'm aware I need something for his nausea. Okay, yes, it would be best to go see a doctor, but I don't have the cash, so I'm hoping the medication, lots of tea, and leg compresses will do the trick.

I feel bad that I had fun all night while Riley was getting sick. I'm angry with myself for if I was home, I would have noticed the signs yesterday. And at Mr. Rush for taking me to his luxurious penthouse and fucking me senseless, literally, all I could think about was the Mr. Rush in his pants.

Fortunately, it stopped raining, though it's still a gray day. My hair is tied back, but it's still sticking out on all sides. I ignore the bums and drug dealers that are loitering everywhere. They know me, they know Riley, and I know them. The secret is friendliness. Many times, I am quite friendly and Riley is his usual cute self, so they leave us alone. Thankfully.

The little bell over the door jingles as I enter the pharmacy. The place is empty and smells of chamomile tea. I know Mr. Baker, the owner, is barely able to keep the store afloat. Nowadays, pharmacies are outdated, everyone gets their shit from everywhere else, even online, people have grown way too lazy.

"Hello, Liv!" the old man says when he sees me and smiles cheerfully.

"Hi." I wipe my forehead and look around. Most items are dusty. Nobody buys the stuff at the cash register or the overpriced apothecary tea on the shelves.

"How can I help you?"

"Riley has the stomach flu."

"Oh!" His brown eyes look really sad! "Wait a sec, I'll

get what you need." He disappears into the back and I stand there, impatiently tapping my foot while repeatedly glancing at my cell phone. I almost expect Penny to call to tell me he's getting worse and that we need to go to the hospital. One moment, I'm relieved she does not call, then in the next, I believe it isn't a good sign that I don't hear from her.

I look impatiently in the back and finally see Mr. Baker returning. He sets a few packages in front of me on the counter and explains that they're the best for reducing fever and stomach discomfort and controlling diarrhea in children.

"Okay, okay, I take them all!"

He smiles and scans the packages at the cash register. I see the amount and suppress a swallow, 45 bucks for a few OTC meds!

As Mr. Baker is packing my things in a bag, I pull my wallet out of my handbag. The artificial leather is cracked and peeling at the edges and is no longer beige but almost black because my handbag bled. It's cheaply made.

I only have 20 on me and think about what to do next when Mr. Baker finishes packing my things and looks at me expectantly, which really embarrasses me. Then I hear the tiny bell by the door again and grow even more embarrassed.

I swallow.

"Well...uh...you see, Mr. Baker..." I lower my voice so the new customer cannot overhear me. "Momentarily, I'm a bit strapped...” Even before I can finish explaining – perfectly knowing Mr. Baker would not give me credit, given he himself is low on cash – I suddenly feel a presence behind me that makes me freeze. I cannot say anything, immediately smell him, feel him even though he isn’t touching me, and my heart somersaults. I don’t have to see him to know it’s his big wonderful hand flitting passed my waist, placing a 50-dollar bill on the counter. I shudder.

“Keep the change!” I hear his deep voice in my ear and feel his breath. Oh, my God! Shakily, I exhale.

Mr. Baker looks at me confused. I’m tongue tied and cannot react, so he shrugs, thanks him, and takes the cash. Since I’m still frozen, he pushes the bag into Keaton’s hand.

“Thanks,” he says. My throat feels dry. “Olivia?” OH, MY GOD! He has to stop saying my name!

Since I still cannot move, he sighs, takes me by the arm, and leads me out of the shop. Once outside in fresh air, my senses return and I blink. Slowly, I look up and am faced with those eyes that are a mixture of all the pretty colors nature has to offer. His prominent jawbone is still covered by bristle and long eyelashes frame sparkling eyes, eyes like I’ve never seen before. He’s dressed all in black. A trench coat covers his thin turtleneck and pants. He looks absolutely stunning.

“You took off.” *What*?

I try to collect myself. “Please take the money out of my pay, Mr. Rush!” I make it a point to sound utterly dismissive despite the fact I know my voice is trembling. His presence, his aura is so strong, it makes me feel a bit small even though I'm not the type of woman who quickly feels small or who lets herself be made to feel small.

He does not give away any emotion whatsoever. "Consider it a gift, Miss Pierson." Oh, I can distinctly hear that he's pissed off.

"I don't like to be gifted out of the blue."

He raises an eyebrow. "Then regard it as an investment. I cannot afford you getting sick and perhaps missing a day. I have no replacement for you."

OUCH! That's putting me in my place. But I square my shoulders and jut out my chin. Hold on a second, I thought both of us had a wonderful night? Why so hostile?

Oh, yes...I left this morning, simply left him sitting there and no woman dares treat Mr. Sexy-Rush that way.

"The pills are not for me!" He does not know about Riley, which I intend to leave it that way. My son is nobody's concern, not my boss', or a one-night stand!

"So?" He looks at me expectantly.

"Well...my girlfriend is sick!"

He regards me intently for so long, I fear he is on to me, but then he shrugs. "Okay. Whatever. I'm not here to talk about your girlfriend."

Only now do I realize he is in a part of town he has no business in and it is me who is raising her eyebrows. "Are you following me?"

It makes him smile, like I missed an inside joke and I realize he does this quite often actually and it drives me a bit crazy.

"In that regard, yes. I find coincidences hearsay. You simply left. I'm not used to being just left alone. So, I had to catch up with you."

I narrow my eyes. "You followed me?"

"No, but I do know where you live."

"You were…"

"I was not in your apartment! I just caught up with you! And *you*'re not the one who's asking the questions, understand?" His harsh tone makes me flinch. I am speechless. He is not loud, simply authoritative. He closes in. Immediately, he takes my breath anyway with his scent and his miraculous eyes that sparkle only inches from mine, sending my emotions on a roller coaster ride.

"I told you you're mine now, Olivia. Run away again like that and you'll regret it. Do you understand?"

Wide-eyed, I stare at him. I am outraged at myself for being turned on by his clearly provocative threat! God, what is wrong with me? I'm turned on when he's bossy and mean to me! What does that say about me?

I've no idea, now get undress and rub yourself all over him, my libido yells and I sway my hips.

God!

"Did you threaten me?" I ask with my arms crossed in front of my chest.

"Did you understand what I said?" he asks directly

against my lips. I hold my breath as I automatically nod slowly.

"Good." He reaches for my hand, opens it, and hangs the bag on it. He promisingly brushes his mouth over my lips and whispers, "I'll let you go because you have a sick patient at home. But next time, you won't get off so easily, Miss Pierson." And before I can blink he's gone. Just leaves me standing there watching his broad back.

22. Detective Penny

Olivia

Riley is already asleep in the early evening. At least the medication helped lower his fever a bit and stopped him from having to go to the toilet every 20 minutes or throwing up in a bucket. Though he's still warm after the leg compresses and his meds, he's no longer glowing. I don't want him to be in pain, so I'm glad he's sleeping soundly. Sleep is known to be the best medicine.

I finally had time to hop in the shower and put on my nice fluffy bathrobe. Penny and I sit on my sofa drinking tea. Riley's door is ajar so I can hear him in case he wakes up.

Penny also went home and changed, her curls just held haphazardly together. Without makeup she looks so much nicer, though I leave her alone since she loves to paint her face for hours.

The TV is silent in the background and we turned on the small floor lamp in the hallway. The sofa is already folded out and my bed made, so we are nicely cuddled up. I know I can no longer avoid talking about Mr. Rush. Funnily, I don't want to, I need to share it all with my best friend. Since I saw him, only my concern for Riley ousts him from my head, but now that he's sleeping, it is as if thoughts of Keaton are beating like drums in my head.

Penny is comfy, sipping her tea and peering over the edge of the Disney cup. She is waiting. I have no intention of keeping her waiting any longer.

"Mr. Rush," I say dryly. She almost spits out the tea, swallows wrong, and has a coughing fit, her eyes wide. I pat her on the back in amusement until she calms.

"Really?" She immediately knows I'm referring to last night and not to some raise Mr. Rush gave me. Though Penny has never seen him, she naturally knows his name for a friend of hers told her about the job.

"Yeah, really." I told her about my fucked-up evening and how Keaton came to my rescue. About how he has mesmerized me from the first time I laid eyes on him and that I basically had no choice.

"So he took you to his penthouse?" She gasps, now kneeling on the folded out couch with her eyes wide with excitement.

I shrug and cling to my cup. Recalling last night or what he said earlier, makes my insides contract. Again, I feel like jumping into his arms — or onto his hips, but then I think of something else. He has that certain something about him, I can't really put a name to it, but...I know I like it. The way he stands over me like an avenging angel who wants to punish me! I also like to submit, not having to be the tough young mother, but the young woman who simply enjoys the moment. That side of me that is trying to come to the forefront...is simply beautiful!

"His penthouse is impressive, but it didn't really interest me."

"I know you're not into material shit." I didn't grow up worshipping things, nor will I ever. Matters of the heart are more important. "Now tell me already! Did you have sex?"

The word alone almost makes me float. "Oh, yes," I say and nod. "We did."

"OH, MY GOD, FINALLY!" Penny exclaims exuberantly.

"Hush!" I hiss.

"How long has it been since you've slept with a man? I was worried you turned asexual."

I roll my eyes. "Hilarious."

"And? How was it?" Her expression equals the thousand question marks that she would have put down if she had asked in writing.

"Indescribable, Penny. Really. It was...holy shit. First, and I swear to you, he has an absolutely perfect, huge...huge..."

"*Cock!*" she interrupts impatiently. "Go on!"

I grin. "Oh, yeah! Huge and bent in a way so it reaches..."

"*The right places!*" she impatiently bursts out again and winks at me. The mere memory of *the places* he reached makes me blush, my goodness! So far, I believed it merely a rumor that a guy could satisfies me *like that* with his cock. Well, Mr. Rush has opened my eyes... I swallow and wiggle a bit, like I can feel him inside me again, and try to remember what I was talking about.

"And he's...so dominant somehow. I...I never thought I would like that, but it was so exciting and hot to completely give myself to him!"

She tilts her head a bit. "SM is not my thing."

"No!" I say a little too loud and quickly lower my voice. "Not SM. It's the way he looks at me. The way he holds me. The way he tells me what he'll do to... You know, I'm not one of those women, but the experience was...wow."

She laughs, though her eyes betray her seriousness. "As long as you only let yourself be controlled in bed and not in real life..."

"Never!" I reassure her.

Satisfied, she nods. "And? Will you see him again? I mean, he's really hot!"

Her statement confuses me. "How would you know what he looks like?"

Penny lifts her phone and waves it in front of my face. "Hellooo? Social media?" Oh, right! I stay away from it because I don't want Riley's dad to be able to make contact in any way. I'm not on the run, but I don't want to give him an opportunity...

"I just saw him in the pharmacy," I admit.

"What?" Penny's eyebrow slips up so fast, watching it almost makes me dizzy. "Coincidence, or what?"

"Not a coincidence, no. He caught up with me because I up and left his place this morning, which he didn't care for."

Penny is quiet for quite some time while the sparkle of excitement in her eyes disappears. She blinks and I know what I did wrong! But it's too late to take the words back.

"Is he stalking you? You know, stalking is no joke! Did you not watch the show with that totally crazy guy?" Her ex stalked her for a long time, quite intensely so, until he was arrested for violating the restraining order. It was a difficult time and I can understand that it is a sensitive subject for Penny.

"No, he just caught up with me to confront me."

"Hmm..." she remarks thoughtfully. I hate the way she keeps eyeing me. "Still, it's a bit weird he didn't do it over the phone or wait until Monday. It's a bit eerie for him to show up at Mr. Baker's, isn't it?"

I roll my eyes. "Penny, not everyone is like Hank. Forget that scumbag already."

She sighs deeply and lowers her eyes. "I know, I'm

sorry. I'm probably over reacting." She says something else but my phone hums and I'm distracted. Instinctively, I know who it is and my heart is pounding as my suspicion is confirmed. A message.

Mr. Rush.

Come outside. Now!

23. *Punishments*

Keaton

Of course you immediately come outside, just like I want, Olivia. But then I didn't expect anything else. I stand in your filthy hallway and hear all kinds of noises or voices coming from every apartment, none of which interests me. I'm only interested in you. You with your long golden blonde hair hanging wet over your shoulders. Your small, luscious pouty mouth, which is made for my cock. You and your big oh-so-innocent eyes. They might seem innocent at first, but I see the fire dancing in them.

You have on a white thick bathrobe. I know you're naked underneath. I watched you take a shower. I watched you soap your body. I watched you sit next to Riley, worrying while you were petting him to sleep. You don't want me to know about him because part of you still does not trust me. But then it's all the other people around you who you should not trust, Olivia. I'm the last person who means you harm.

Except now.

I'm still fucking angry and since your son is fast asleep now with the worst over, I can't control myself any longer. You have no idea what I wanted to do to you earlier in that alley next to the pharmacy. So I'll do it now, especially since you told Penny about us and raved about my big cock. Yes, my cock is big and yes, I know exactly what to do with it and yes, he's ready for you. I did not hide cameras in your apartment for nothing, Olivia. I heard every word. And I'm rock hard.

"Keaton?" you ask. It is another three hours before you have to clean my office, at which point, it is back to calling me Mr. Rush. I'll let it go this time, but I cannot excuse what you did this morning.

I see uncertainty in your eyes as you nibble on your lower lip with your arms crossed in front of your chest. Are you afraid of me, Olivia? Well, by now, you should be.

"I've changed my mind," I say and notice how curt my voice sounds. I'll give you a moment to analyze what I said and see confusion in your eyes. Not knowing what I'm referring to messes with your head. Nobody leaves me sitting like that, Olivia. Besides, I might have thought our game was over once we had sex, but I have to admit, you have your charm and I'm not yet ready to let you go. And as long as I'm not ready, it will not happen.

Therefore, it is advisable that you to obey me from now on.

Your arms drop and you tilt your head. I could fuck you right here outside on the street in front of all the junkies and you would let me because you're totally addicted to me. Yes, you certainly are. You're as obsessed with me as I am of you. "Meaning?"

I grab your chin and warm air hisses out of your sweet lips. "You will not run away again, understand?"

Your eyes don't reflect fear or uneasiness and stare straight into mine. I see the struggle in you, Olivia. Like a little lioness fighting whether or not to send me to hell. Though we both know you won't do that. Finally, you nod and I smile.

"Good girl." You probably think I'll kiss you now, get romantic, but I push you to your knees. But that's not it. You need to feel what you've done. Only then will you learn your lesson, Olivia.

You don't defend yourself, you never would with me. You love to submit to me, just like last night. You love portraying the little defenseless one, simply love it when I do whatever I damn well please with you.

Your wide eyes look up at me while your breath comes quickly. I bet you're already dripping wet even though I haven't even touched you, not really. Not in the way you want me to touch right now.

You lift your hands and reach to open my belt, but that's

not how it works, babe. I grab your wrists, push them back down, and open my pants myself. I set the pace. You have no fucking shit to say right now. Your eyes are glued as I unpack my rock hard cock. You don't even feel ashamed, you little slut, you merely stare at him unabashedly. You even lick greedily over your lip, as if you had a glob of juicy warm chocolate cake on it.

"Open your mouth," I sneer. You actually obey and with a jerk I push all the way into your small wet mouth, down your throat.

You gag.

I moan.

I roughly grab your damp hair in my fist. You're trying to touch me, trying to help my along by massaging me with your tiny hands. Again, I push your hands away and curtly order, "Cross them behind your back!" You don't react fast enough and I growl warningly, "NOW." You do as ordered, just like that...and I almost come right then.

You're so perfect, baby.

You sense I'm willing to resort to more drastic means. If you had not done it voluntarily, I would have helped you with my handcuffs.

My gaze stays on you as I grit my teeth and you stare up at me. You're killing me, Olivia. But just wait until I'm through with you, you'll feel much worse.

Repeatedly, I thrust deeply into your mouth while your tongue plays with me. You moan enthusiastically so that I feel your hot breath. You like that right, babe? You want to be treated just like that.

I admit, you feel fantastic, baby. No matter how or where I do you, it's always perfect. I knew from the second I laid eyes on you that there was a little whore inside of you, which I simply love to bring out. To see you kneeling in front of me with my cock in your mouth and gazing up at me with that devoted look as if I was your god, as if I was EVERYTHING to you...is more than I wanted. I look at it as the perfect picture. I want to see it more and more and I feel it won't take much longer before I come inside you. But not in your mouth, rather in your tight wet pussy. That's why I pull you back onto your feet and roughly open your bathrobe, not giving you any time to grasp the situation. All the while, I'm aware someone could step outside at any time and catch us. Although it's dark outside, it's too well lit to hide from strangers' eyes. You have to live with that, baby. Next time, you might use your head first before you pull shit like you did. I'm hoping you get the message.

Your lips open and your eyes widen as I expose your wonderful body and rip the fabric from your body. Your nipples are hard and although I cannot see it, I know you are dripping wet between your legs. Your chaotic hair fans out wildly over your shoulders and as much as I want to look at you, it won't happen today.

"Keaton," you whisper, obviously worried, but I don't give a damn.

Wordlessly, I turn you around, roughly pin your face against the wall and press my cock against your tailbone. You feel so warm, Olivia, so soft. You hiss air as I whisper in your ear, "Shut up." You grit your teeth. You hate following orders, but then you also want to feel me inside you. Conflicted, right? Soon you won't have such feelings anymore because I will make you realize that I'm everything you want and need.

I grab your hips and pull your ass toward me so you must bend over even more and since you're my little slut, you arch your back perfectly and spread your legs, unashamed to show me your little pussy. But I won't provide you with salvation, Olivia, you will have to take care of that yourself later.

I brush my cock over your wet slit and you moan, so I cover your mouth with my hand. "I told you to be quiet!" You breathe against my palm and I thrust into you, neither gently nor slowly. I linger a few seconds since you feel better than I recall. I want you, Olivia, being inside you is not enough.

You moan, though cautiously and quietly, probably because you don't want to bear the consequences or do you?

Again, I grab your hair and pull your head back while I fuck you. I no longer care if someone catches us and sees you exposed. I want to take you rough and fast.

Now you even brace your hands against the dirty wall and urgently push your ass in my direction. I take a swing and slap your left ass cheek. You moan louder. You really are a little whore.

"Hold still!" I order. You have a difficult time but make an effort.

I'm not happy with your effort and slap your ass again.

This time you get it.

Your muscles start contracting around me and you can no longer control your moaning, I know you're close to climaxing.

"Don't you dare," I growl. "Hold back!" You whimper as you tense. I know it's hard what I'm asking you to do, but you have to do it. Or I'll punish you again.

"Oh, God," I hear you say sensually.

"Olivia?" Penny is calling your name from inside the apartment. I'm not even thinking about stopping, not even for a second and just keep fucking you even though I feel you are distracted at the moment.

"YESSS!" You reply much too loudly as you again start to contract around my cock.

"Don't. You. Dare!" With each word, I thrust hard into you. You hang your head and your hair falls in your face.

"I'm coming soon!" You call to Penny, but I know it's meant for me. I know it. But I won't allow it. It makes me smile as you strive to follow my orders, how hard it is for you not to come, not to betray yourself to Penny. How difficult it is for you to restrain yourself.

As you can no longer hold back, I allow myself to come. Though I can control it, at that moment, it seems right, so I thrust deeply, hold still, and ejaculate.

It is better than anything else.

Once I finish, I pull out, breathing heavily. You quickly whip around, totally sweaty and your legs trembling from being fucked by me.

Your eyes look on in disbelief and then horror as I close my pants.

"What…"

I press you against the wall with my body one last time and slide my fingers between your legs where it's dripping wet. I brush two fingers over your clit to your entrance and you moan.

"It stays inside," I whisper against your lips as my fingertips slide inside you, making you throw your head back and close your eyes. "From now on, you play by my rules."

As quickly as I appeared, I leave you standing there alone again, naked, hoping for your sake that you've learned your lesson.

24. What the Fuck?

Olivia

Oh, my God!

I'm still standing there bare-ass-naked and stare after him like an idiot. Slowly, I regain my senses and realize what just happened. I look around frantically, see no one, and quickly reach for my bathrobe. I put it on, tie the belt around my stomach more tightly than necessary, and try to compose myself before going back into the apartment. What just happened? God, he really didn't let me come! I cannot believe it! That was the hottest sex in my life, though here I am, still unsatisfied because he forced me to hold back my orgasm...and as soon as came, he took off! How dare he! I consider throwing a shoe after him but I realize he's long gone and I'm standing here like a fool, staring in front of me. I really can't wrap my head around it.

He punished me for leaving him like that this morning and now again while he fucked me. I should be pissed off, but somehow I feel like I'm on drugs.

Still totally intoxicated, confused, and quite sore, I go to the door and knock. Of course, in my rush, I forgot to grab the key. My first thought was that he wanted to talk about something important or whatnot; I certainly didn't expect what happened.

Penny opens. "Where the heck were you?" she asks. I'm afraid she might have overheard something or she would have come out looking for me, right?

"I...eh...Mr. Rush stopped by for a moment. I mean, Keaton."

She closes the door once I'm inside. "And?"

"He needed to discuss something with me."

I look at her searchingly and can tell by her eyes that she doesn't believe me. I know what Penny will think if I tell her what actually happened. I mean, my child is sick in bed and here I do something like that even though I knew Penny was looking after him and that he was safe!

"Is that so?" she says sarcastically and slaps her forehead like Keaton did my ass earlier, which still burns. Holy shit! With him it's unbelievable... "Forgot your cell phone and didn't have a homing pigeon."

I roll my eyes and go to the kitchen for a drink. I feel like I'm being...watched, like I'm not alone, excluding

Penny. It must be because I've grown so addicted to that man that I'm constantly thinking about him. "Hilarious," I say. Actually, I'm in no mood to joke around. I'm still too confused and turned on.

"Whatever! I'll go upstairs until you have to go to work," I hear her call out and become aware she sounds a bit pissed off, which I ignore.

"See you later," I mumble and take a sip from the water bottle.

* * *

It is raining again and my shoes are soaked by the time I make it to the office. *I really should buy new shoes*. I make a mental note as I pull off my wet socks to exchange for the dry ones I keep in my handbag. I open the door to the small chamber in which I always change and where the cleaning supplies are kept and think I'm struck by lightning. On the chair on which he places whatever is another item...

A classy-looking little package. Though I have no idea what it is, my heart is pounding fiercely.

It is from *him*.

Him, whom I can still feel inside me.

Who left me standing there!

Who I still hear whispering in my ear, "From now on, you play by my rules."

He, who I simply cannot get out of my head and just thinking about him gets me wet.

Like now.

He took off, leaving me completely dissatisfied — and totally confused.

Here I had thought it was only a one night stand with Mister fucking-hot Rush, though he seems to have other plans. I have to admit, but for the first time since Riley's father, I'm willing to spend more than one night with the same man. Though only because of the sex. He has that certain something that has me hooked. Thinking about him, I feel like I'm on cloud nine. My mouth is dry, my panties wet, and my knees weak as I reach for the packet and pull on the little tab. It opens and I'm confronted by a classy-looking black vibrator embedded in red velvet. I quickly close the packet and feel myself blushing.

A vibrator!

He gave me a vibrator!

Oh, my God!

Under the packaging is a folded sheet of paper. As usual, a message from him. I unfold it with trembling fingers.

"Entertain me, Miss Pierson!" is written in his beautiful handwriting and below it, "*But don't you dare come!*"

I giggle like a young excited schoolgirl who is using her parents' computer for the first time to look at what a porno is... I feel young, wild, and so damn naughty when I think about what he's asking of me. I'm supposed to entertain him, okay...um, how would he see it? Is he here? Somewhere?

The thought makes my heart beat faster until I can feel it in my jugular. I've forgotten about work. I've forgotten about *everything*!

I take the package and walk straight in to his office, turn on the light, and it's empty, no one here...

"Keaton?" I whisper timidly, like a complete imbecile because there's something wrong with me. I even look around, behind the door, and lastly under the desk, as if he would be sitting huddled in the leg space.

"You really have lost it this time, Olivia Pierson!" I mutter to myself, straighten up and stroke my neck, then puff out my cheeks before I let the air escape in one long breath.

I imagine him suddenly standing behind me and whispering in my neck with that sexy voice, "WHAT?"

But he does not appear like a vampire or ghost.

He is not here.

I'm alone.

Disappointed, I drop onto his chair and place the packaging with the vibrator in front of me. I pout as I swivel back and forth in his chair. I'd love to have a recap of what happened earlier on the staircase or, better yet, a whole damn seven-course session! Oh, yes, I really want to fill my stomach with his...a red blinking light catches my attention.

It is exactly opposite me...

The camera in the corner of the office is flashing... I tilt my head to one side and take a closer look at the thing.

Do these things record when they blink?

Is he watching me?

OH, it would explain so much!

Is he watching me here at work every night?

Is that the reason the camera starts to blink red when I enter a room?

Should it not confuse, perhaps, unsettle me? Should not the thought disgust me?

Should, should, should — poppycock... I hate that word, always have, even back in school when teachers said you shouldn't do this and you shouldn't do that. *Yeah, no shit, dumbasses, I know that, but I do it anyway, and just because you told me not to I'll do it now in spite of it*, I've always thought — which did not exactly help my popularity with my teachers or any other person of authority. Well, I was and always will be a little rebel, so? The system has enough lemmings! I have never been one and never will be. I was always stood out from the others...which is why I find the idea of Mr. Rush sitting somewhere in a dark room watching me...exciting, arousing...totally thrilling.

As I find everything regarding him.

His note said to entertain him with this dildo.

The camera is still flashing red...

He expects a show!

Well, if there's one thing I can do, it's put on a hot show!

I immediately take off everything that *should* and *must* be gone. I instantly become the woman that I am when I ignore all conventions, morality, and scruples. It feels so damn liberating!

So good!

I smile as I stand up... arch my back, then with elegant flowing steps and swaying hips, circle the table while pulling the ribbon out of my hair. I fan out my golden locks over my back...almost feel him grab them as he did when he was in my mouth, so hard, so ready to come...so unspeakably intoxicating!

I lean my butt against the desk, let my head fall back and slide my hands to the zipper of my hoodie, which I always wear when cleaning. I slowly pull the zipper down while looking directly into the camera, all the way down, and back up again, smiling ever wider. I'm naughty...knowing that he must be cursing right now...watching me. The idea turns me on so much that I would love to open my pants and massage my clit quickly. The impatient Liv craves quick salvation. But he wants a show — so he should get one!

Slowly, I let the hoodie slip off my shoulders...then take my top off. Thankfully I'm wearing a sexy black bra. My nipples are hard and strain the fabric — already. Sliding my fingers down, I open the button of my jeans and pull down the zipper — then oh-so-slowly reach in with one hand and stroke my pussy, which I notice is wet.

Still.

Wow...

If he is really watching me, then it should get him crazy now for I purposefully ignore the vibrator...to rile him, to lure him out of his hidey-hole (if that is even close by). I want to punish him a little for earlier when he left me hanging unsatisfied and do myself inside my pants where he can't see anything. I groan as I let my head fall back while my fingertips slide over my clit...

I'm ready to come, which he forbade me to do, but I'm playing with the idea of not giving a flying fuck.

Who does he think he is? My daddy?

Yuck! Wrong thought, Liv! I think, grin, then moan and quickly pause briefly or I would come for sure.

The guy makes me hot even when he isn't present!

He's a hot little bastard and I love that he is the way he is...

"What do you think you're doing?" I suddenly hear him ask from the direction of the door. I shriek and quickly pull my hand out of my pants. Thankfully, I was leaning against the table or I would have fallen. My head whips around and my hand goes to my racing heart when I see who is casually leaning against the doorjamb.

Mister *I fuck you, not letting you come, then gift you a vibrator and think I can order you around* Keaton.

There he is leaning in the doorway, in a black turtleneck sweater, with one hand casually in a jeans pocket, watching me from under one raised eyebrow.

FUCK!

He is here!

FUCK!

“You can close your mouth, Olivia. You won’t blow me now.” I close my mouth again, feel it immediately, want it immediately. Oh, God, I’ve never wanted anything as much as that man’s cock.

He pushes off and strolls casually towards me, elegantly, like a predator its prey. He’s playing with me — I love his games!

First, he goes to his record player and puts on music, *Corrupt* by *Depeche Mode*. It feels as if it’s OUR song.

Next, he strolls to the small bar in the corner and pours himself a drink while my eyes follow every self-assured move. Then he sits down on one of the two armchairs, puts an ankle on his knee and his prominent chin on the fist from the arm whose elbow is resting on the armrest, and says, “Do as the note says.”

“Have you been watching me through the camera?”

“Maybe.”

“Do you do that every night?”

“You seem to be misunderstanding something, Olivia, you are not the one asking questions. You follow my instructions. We both know what you want since you’ve tasted me earlier today, so when you do what I ask, later on you may get another one. So oblige.”

I narrow my eyes.

A million thoughts flash through my head.

There are two possibilities.

I enjoy whatever we have between us. I enjoy his game to the fullest — and willingly join in.

Or I throw the damn package that's holding the goddamn vibrator at his head, turn around and go.

But deep down I know I won't get another chance if I turn my back on this man a second time. He had no problem showing me what he thinks of me running away and even stated that he wouldn't accept it a second time.

So I say, "Okay!" shrug and...do it...

I simply let myself go.

I smile at him, his eyes twinkle with greed and controlled lust as I turn around and pull my jeans down. He hisses softly when he realizes my panties are drenched... I jiggle my buttocks — if I can do one thing, that's it! After all, that's what I have it for. As I look back at Keaton, I see a muscle in his cheek twitch and the fist on which his chin is resting is no longer relaxed either…oh, no.

His eyes are demanding.

And I will obey.

But that doesn't mean I cannot tease, provoke, toy with him...

I wink at him, his eyes narrow. Next, I sweep his neatly stacked papers off his desk. The muscle in his cheek twitches unmistakably. I sit on his desk and lie down on one side with my butt to him. I brush a hand down my side and over one buttock...

I slap it.

Now his gaze no longer sparkles, it glows.

I pull my panties aside provocatively.

He curses quietly... I let the fabric slide back over my shame.

Which is incredibly wet, by the way. I'm also turned on by this here.

Then I open the package...and run the classy black vibrator along my side...over my butt and back up... I arch my back, present my butt to him, and push my panties to the side. He has a perfect view of when I reach back and slide the cool silicone over my wetness. I close my eyes as the vibrations ignite each nerve within my body. Again and again, I stroke it over my slit and then position it at my entrance.

The vibrator is ripped out of my hand and thrown aside.

I gasp.

Suddenly Keaton is over me and grabs my hair, his gaze...oh, his gaze...WOW! I've never seen him so intense!

So full of passion.

Greed.

HUNGER.

Full of such barely restrained emotions.

"You like screwing up my plans!" he says and kisses me...

WOW!

I try to turn on my back when he slaps my ass, grabs and pulls me closer to the edge of the table so my ass almost hangs off it — just the right height for... Then without warning, he thrusts his huge hardness in me and I yell out his name, entirely unprepared for it.

"OH, GOD," I gasp as he pushes inside me.

He slaps my ass again.

"What's my name?" He pulls back.

"Keaton!" He thrusts in me again and I notice I'm already starting to twitch.

"Who do you belong to?" He pulls back again.

"TO YOU!"

"Say, I'm yours, Keaton Rush!" And he thrusts hard into me again.

Oh, God …

I whimper.

He pulls out of me.

I *hate* feeling empty!

"I'm yours, Keaton Rush. *Please*!" I plead. He thrusts into me again and finally lets himself go. At last, he gives up his beloved control. At least a little. He trusts in me in this position for a few times while holding my hair so I cannot move, which makes each thrust somehow even more intense. Then he pulls me on my back with a "God damn, Olivia!" and spreads my legs.

He holds my ankles and enters me again.

Deep.

So deep.

His teeth bite deeply into his lower lip and he looks completely focused as he's fucking me hard and fast. Then his thrusts slow...and his eyes dart from our crotches where he was looking up to my eyes. They're veiled and full of...sadistic joy.

"I'll be coming soon, Olivia," he announces.

"NO! DON'T! KEATON!" I shout and try to push him out of me only to make him laugh and moan at the same time.

He grabs my hair with one hand, pulls my head painfully back, and no longer pulls out of me, remaining deep inside me. His hot tongue glides over my bared throat up to my ear and he whispers, "Mouth or pussy?"

I curse him with all the expressions I can think up.

"You amuse me, babe!" he says, then out of nowhere circles my clit with two fingers, almost driving me insane. My muscles contract jerkily around him. He groans hoarsely, which sinks into my bones and marrow, making me even more lustful than I already am when he penetrates me seemingly even deeper and rotates his hips... "Lucky for you!" he whispers and rubs the throbbing little pleasure spot.

I'm going to explode.

It's too much.

My muscles are contracting so violently that now he too lets himself go and comes with me. I only see stars. The orgasm is so intense, like everything else between us.

This man will be my downfall.

But I will go down happily!

Oh, fuck yes!

25. *Intimacy*

Keaton

I love how you look at me right now, Olivia, with such absolute devotion and a spark of rebellious disbelief. It goes against your nature to relinquish control to a man. So far, you've always been the one who held the reigns. But with me all that changed.

I feel the same, baby.

All this is new territory for me too.

It's new territory for me to be fucking a woman on my office desk.

Or to desire you even more.

Or to want to know what's going through your head once I broke away from you and zipped up.

You dress without so much as looking at me.

Now I feel...*unsure.*

I'm not used to feeling uncertain. Usually, I'm in control and superior, but with you, I never know with who I'm dealing. Will you push me away and take off again?

I cannot stand the thought.

Again, I act rashly, like when you put on that performance and lured me out of hiding...I simply had to have you.

You're finish dressing and close your pants. I step up behind you, grab your arms, pull them back, and hold you tightly before I mumble in your ear, "You will never run away again." I'm not only talking about now; I want you to stay with me.

"I didn't mean to run away," you reply, panting, I loosen my grip and give you a little space, which I hate to do. However, I am rewarded for you turn and look at me tentatively. You lift your arms and put them around my neck. No woman ever dared do that. But then you're not like other women... You touch me in a way that I believed impossible. I'm not into tenderness. I like sex, fast rough sex. This here is actually not for me, still, I'm not pushing you away.

I cannot push you away.

Not when you're looking at me like that.

You are so beautiful, baby.

"Will this become a habit, Mr. Rush, where you attack me out of the blue to have hot sex?"

"Would you like that?" *What are you saying, idiot?*

Since when do you care whether she likes it or not? This here is about you.

And sure enough, you smile, your cheeks glow, and your eyes shine as you say, "To be honest, yes, which scares me."

"Why?" You play with the hairs on my neck and goose bumps trickle down my spine. It feels strange, but good...

"You are so intense, so consuming. With you, it feels like I cannot breathe yet, at the same time, as if I am doing it correctly for the first time in my life. It scares me." *Yes, you should be scared, baby,* I think, but merely say, "Why?"

You are about to say something when you stop yourself, step back from me, and stare at the ground...

"I don't even know you! Not really!" you say accusingly. I cannot help but grin slightly as I say, "So?" I think *I know you too well, I know all about you, babe.*

"You could be a mad psychopath!" you state, slightly horrified. Damn, you're so adorable when you're right. I laugh.

It makes you stare at me. Your look is dreamy. I'm beside myself and you are pissed off, mumbling, "What's so funny?" Honestly, you like it too much, when I laugh, when I fuck you, when we talk. But I have to admit, I like it too. Every word from your mouth is precious. Everything about you is precious.

Right then your stomach growls. I frown.

"When was the last time you ate?" I ask, mainly to be polite, for I actually know. Today, I watched you all day long — naturally. So, I know you only ate breakfast! You were too busy with Riley.

"I, um..." You wrinkle your nose, thinking. I raise an eyebrow, curious if you will lie.

You do not — lucky for you. "This morning," you admit. I march to my phone and push the stored number for Tony's pizza delivery service. Every time we stay late in the office, we call him. I'm sitting on my desk with my eyes on you as I order. "Hello, I'd like to order two cokes, one large tuna, and one salami pizza with extra cheese, corn, and olives." You look at me wide-eyed when I order your favorite pizza.

Oh, honey...

"And cheese filled crust," I add and watch her pretty face glow with absolute ecstasy.

Yes, you are a woman who still knows how to enjoy.

You especially enjoy eating.

Just like sex — what a lucky shit I am...

***

Olivia

Mister *I fuck your brains out on the desk,* has something about him that makes me feel like a teenager. I'm totally beside myself, my stomach full of butterflies as I hang on to his every word like an idiot. He does not even need to be undressed or talking to me, no, his presence alone will do it.

He's sitting in the chair next to the couch that I'm sitting on while we wait for the pizza. That he knew all the toppings I like I find a bit eerie. Although, my rational mind arrives at plausible explanations; either I mentioned it at some point or I just love popular American toppings. I think my mind will come up with explanations for just about everything he does, no matter how strange it first seems. I mean, every American loves a cheese-filled crust, corn, and olives, right?

He looks at me. One leg is resting on the other, one arm casually laying on the back of the chair... The corner of his mouth twitches.

"What?" I ask, sliding restlessly on the couch.

"You are nervous!"

"Of course I am. I'm not here to just sit on my ass!"

"God forbid!" he says amused. I roll my eyes.

"I'm here to work, but my crazy totally hot boss won't let me!"

"You're hungry!"

"I won't faint from starvation! Keaton, at least let me get the vacuuming done."

"Say my name again."

I roll my eyes but say "Keaton". I meant to sound bored, but merely pronouncing his stupid name makes my heart beat faster. He smiles, my heart turns into a circus artist who performs somersaults. Is that life threatening?

"I like it when you say my name."

"I've noticed that too," I say dryly, recalling how he ordered me to say his name during sex. I'm hot again.

"And you like it too," he notes hoarsely, even his gaze is dark and obvious.

He wants me again.

And I want him too.

He was hardly out of me when he wanted to get back in.

The man is addictive. I'm obsessed with him.

I look at his mouth, that perfect soft mouth — that says such nasty things to me and bite my lip. I quickly look away from him.

"Is there something you want to tell me, Miss Pierson?"

Yes, I want you.

Now.

Always…

Which I don't say, just smile and lean back. "No, Mr. Rush..." I cross my legs and see him following my movements. Perhaps he also imagines what it would be like to kneel in front of me now, to push inside me while my legs are wrapped around him?

He seems amused when he says, "Oh well."

"What else do you want me to tell you except that you annoy me, Mr. Rush?"

"I annoy you? You sounded quite different though." I blush beet red as he says it, clearly hinting at the little escapade on his desk. He appears utterly content.

"Let me do my cleaning, dammit! I don't like sitting idly around!"

"Because you have to focus on me then?"

"Yes."

"Am I really making you so nervous?" Yeah, right, like I'd ever answer that honestly! If only he knew...

The pizza delivery guy saves me from further embarrassment. He knows Keaton by name and gets quite a big tip. Not only did he bring cola, but also a bottle of wine. I raise an eyebrow as Keaton strolls back to me. On the way, he grabs two more glasses from the bar.

"What?" he asks amused.

"Alcohol at work, Mr. Rush? You allow that?"

"Yes, especially when my coworker becomes as adorable as you when you have a drink." Shit. He finds me adorable. I'm dead — kind of...at least I no longer know what to say.

With him, everything is so new.

So unfamiliar.

I meant to keep him at bay, but when he's so open, laid back, and funny like he is now, I can't keep up my barriers. I don't have a problem keeping my distance from the cool impersonal Mister Rush, but not when I'm facing Keaton. I think he knows that. He uncorks the wine and pours the wine. We sip it while gazing into each other's eyes.

There's static in the air.

Then we attack our pizzas.

Mine is delicious and I cannot refrain from moaning.

Keaton's cheek muscle twitches — I love it when it does that.

But he continues eating quietly like it's nothing...

I want to know more about him, so I lean back and ask, "Do you have siblings?"

"No."

"Parents?"

He looks at me like I'm an idiot. I giggle. The damn wine has already gone to my head.

"I mean, are your parents still alive, and, if so, where?"

"Is this turning into an interrogation, Miss Pierson?"

"No, a job interview?"

"And you're hiring me as what, your fucker?"

"Wow, Mr. Rush, you're so direct."

"As are you." Both of us grin...

"Good, then look at it as a job interview to be my fucker!" I have to laugh again and as soon as he refills my glass, I take a sip. He no longer seems so relaxed, more like...watchful.

"Where are you from?"

"Actually, from England, Miss Pierson."

"Oh, that's the sexy accent." He grins and I suddenly realize the brain-language barrier is gone. Dammit. I open my eyes and turn bright red.

"Sexy, Miss Pierson?" he teases gently. I roll my eyes and take another sip.

"Like no other woman ever said that!"

"Not like you do!"

"How do I do it?"

"Uniquely."

"Aren't we all in a way?"

"That's true. But you're special, you stand out from the crowd." I guess I can return the compliment for I too have never met a man like him. Honestly, never. His compliment feels good. He thinks I'm special. Isn't that what every woman wants? To meet a beautiful mysterious man? One who is absolutely great in bed and thinks of you as something special? All of it seems almost too good to be true, too perfect. But I cannot bring myself to end this here.

We spend two hours sitting and talking.

As if we had done it often.

As if we already knew each other...

At least with the heart.

26. Fallen for Mr. Rush

Olivia

I still cannot quite put my finger on how this man managed to turn my world upside down in no time. I mean, the day before yesterday, we had sex for the first time! And now?

I firmly believe there is no time in my life for romance, yet I still can't get away from him and his multifaceted nature, his aura, the way he makes me feel. I forgot how it's like to be regarded as a woman — as a respectable woman. The disgusting leers I received at the strip club do not compare to Keaton's looks that seem to go straight to my soul. His are full of fascination and adoration. He doesn't see only two tits and a pussy. He sees so much more in me and lets me feel it with every one of his touches — even if at first it feels quite rough. In secret, I neither can nor want to part ways with him and fall back into my old routine.

My life was...exhausting and drab, honestly, every day was trying. My only glimmer of hope was Riley – and Rosie – providing she didn't just drop a turd somewhere.

Then Keaton Rush entered my life and suddenly, I am full of joie de vivre.

He scares me because he makes me feel things no other human ever did. I am aware I could quickly become dependent on him, perhaps I already am a bit. Nevertheless, I ignore my instinct to flee for I'd much rather let myself go. Fall into his arms, into his bed, into his life, even though I'm completely aware it's wrong.

As we sit in his car, the soft leather seat seems to devour me. He insisted on driving me home, I didn't protest. The office has not been cleaned and I feel a little bad about that, although, when my boss says I shouldn't work, who am I to argue?

It is quiet in the car, only the purring of the engine is heard. The full moon shines as brightly as the street lamps. The streets are empty, traffic signs are leaning slightly with the wind. Out-of-towners might think a storm is approaching, but I'm used to the local weather. Here in Chicago, we regard this as a light breeze.

Everything smells of him, probably including myself. I still feel his big dominant hands on my body as well as hear his wonderful laugh in my ears.

"You're making a detour?" I look at him questioningly. His gaze remains focused on the road ahead. He appears relaxed with one hand casually resting on the steering wheel. Even sitting behind the wheel, he looks incredibly sexy and I would love nothing more than to pounce on him the next chance I get.

"What are you thinking?"

I clear my throat as I tug on the sleeve of my denim jacket. "I know you live all the way crosstown. You're going out of your way, which wasn't necessary."

He smiles and I feel like I missed the joke. "I should have taken you to my place?" It sounds tempting. It would have been nice to sleep in his soft bed, feel his strong arms around me and in the morning, jump into his huge shower. However, I cannot, I have to think of Riley. I don't mean in a way of him being a burden, rather, I'm afraid I'll miss something from him. I already work too many hours, it wouldn't be right spending my free time away from him. I don't want to be a neglectful mother.

"No."

"I wanted to drive you."

"I know."

Now he nods. "I always do what I want." I've noticed as much and I like it. A man who knows what he wants and takes it. Not a wimp. But not an aggressive degenerate. No, he's the right combination of gentleman and fucker and I love it. He certainly does not represent the norm. He's not a man who would pick a *normal* woman and I abhor being normal. I crave the extraordinary and love it. That kick, that rush that Keaton causes me to experience when I can be just Olivia and not Mom.

The car slows down and as Keaton shuts off the engine, I realize we arrived. It is dark, the buildings tower in the night-black sky. The abandoned house to my left looks ominous. I have no idea why a single family home that's been abandoned for years is still standing on an apartment block. It seems a bit scary with half its facade peeling, ivy growing up the walls, and dusty windows obscuring a peek inside. Besides, it stinks of garbage, I can tell without even opening the passenger door. The loitering junkies and bums are loud. I particularly hate raising Riley in this neighborhood, but I try to make the most of it.

"See you tomorrow," I say, but make no move to get out.

He nods. "Until tomorrow."

Is he upset? I cannot tell, but he has no reason, right? He unsettles me. I tentatively place my hand on the door handle when I feel him grab my other arm and pull me abruptly over to him. At first, I'm startled, but then I feel his soft hot lips on mine and instantly relax. More than that, I become putty. His hands are holding my face while his mouth massages mine with just the right pressure. I love how he touches me, love that I can feel how much he desires me, love the static between us. It hasn't been three seconds before I'm digging my hands in his hair while our tongues play with each other until we cannot breathe.

He pulls back, breathing heavily, then leans his forehead against mine. His wonderful fragrance is right at my nose and I keep inhaling it as junkies do lines of coke. Everything inside me is tingling as if I'm electrically charged. Goose bumps spread all over my body and I shudder. This here...is fucking great.

"I want you to work for me," he whispers, then pulls his head back and I immediately miss his closeness. I am drunk — on Mister Rush. How fitting.

"But...I already work for you," I say softly, somewhat confused, while trying to ignore my wildly beating heart. The rushing is back in my ears, I'm still not fully present.

He laughs softly, causing a shiver to run down my back. "I'll find someone new to do your job. I want you to be my personal assistant." His words register oh-so-slowly while I gaze into his miraculous eyes, whose color I still cannot properly define.

"But…why? I mean, I have no references for the job and..."

"You would have regular hours," he says. "You'd be home every afternoon at two — at the latest. Isn't that the dream of every human being, not having to work all day and late into the night?" He doesn't know about Riley, whom I think about immediately. It would be perfect for Riley. I could take care of him around the clock, without bothering Penny on a daily basis. I would have more time for him...and for me.

"Besides...," his finger brushes oh-so-lightly over the back of my hand, it's enough to make me quiver, "...these hands are too valuable to be handling cleaning detergents every day."

He causes me to laugh softly, though, it sounds a bit nervous. "Please...I'm used to it."

"Then we should change that habit." His beautiful lips form a smile, but I remain silent. I don't really want such a job only because I'm sleeping with the boss. Besides that, his job offer sounds more than tempting.

"You'd also make more," he argues. "Much more, significantly so."

"Sounds like you're trying to talk me into it."

"I don't have to, baby. I've already convinced you." He winks at me, I laugh.

"I'll consider it."

"Don't take too long."

"No way."

He smiles. "Goodnight," he says, I return his smile and finally manage to get out of the car on weak knees.

Like I'm in a trance.

He really shakes up my world. I walk to the front door as if on puffy pink clouds. Only once I'm inside, do I hear him start the engine and drive off.

I cannot help it and lean against the door, close my eyes, and scream. I even dance around with my arms and legs flailing around, a little freak out. Somehow, I have to let this feeling out, this...*happiness*. Shit, it's been a while since I've fallen for someone like that. Maybe even never...

27. Escalation

Olivia

My good mood and the feelings of butterflies in my stomach abruptly go up in smoke since I have to go up to Penny's to pick up Riley. Apparently, they went up to her apartment and I notice something is wrong as soon as she opens the door. More than that, she seems angry.

Only once she has the door closed behind me, do I speak to her while inadvertently stroking Rosie, who's greeting me exuberantly. "Is everything okay?" She walks past me into the living room. Her apartment has the same floor plan, though her furnishings are crass. I watch her turn off the TV and toss the remote on the couch. Riley always sleeps in Penny's bed. The room that is Riley's is her bedroom.

"I'm okay," she says dismissively. I frown. Regardless

of if you know her, anyone can tell Penny is pissed off. She is not one to hide such emotions well even if she tries. She speaks from the heart.

"You really want to play this game now, Penny?" I ask impatiently with my arms crossed in front of my chest. "Spit it out already."

She looks at me, her eyes flash. For a moment, she seems to struggle with herself, but from experience, I know she won't remain *quiet*. Sure enough, soon after, she lets off steam.

"You know, Liv, I really wish you all the luck in the world, but lately, I don't recognize you!" she says. "And that bugs me! I don't mean that bad, but you're my best friend and I cannot keep things from you!"

I am flabbergasted and bat my eyes repeatedly. I've never expected a fight, even if her behavior earlier in the hallway was clear, I never gave it another thought. Is she mad at me because I've met someone? Or what exactly is the problem?

"What do you mean by that?" I ask skeptically.

She snorts and shakes her head. "Riley is sick and you have nothing better to do than meet a guy for sex? And in the hallway where someone could have caught you at any time. And just now, you were again with this Rush guy, right? I thought you had to clean offices? But no, the gentleman even chauffeurs you home! How gentlemanly of him! When did you become so selfish, huh?"

I can barely believe my ears and stare at Penny wide eyed. I'm embarrassed she obviously noticed the hallway sex, but I'm also angry with her! I thought she was my girlfriend. I'm furious on the inside!

"What makes you so sure I had sex with him, huh?"

"Oh, please!" she says snippily. "The whole street heard you guys...or rather you!"

Okay, I'm officially embarrassed, especially since it has become clear to me that Riley could have heard or seen us just as easily, though that's another matter, it has nothing to do with this. "Why are you doing this, Penny?" I hiss. "Why are you making me feel so bad? You know I'm always a mother and a friend first, just because I had some fun – *once* – you make a big deal out of it? And yes, I do clean offices every fucking night! Only today, Keaton gave me a ride home, is that so tragic?"

She remains stubborn and shakes her head, causing her blonde perm to brush her cheeks. "That's not what this is about! It's about you dropping everything for this guy! The past few days, I've noticed you're changing and are often absent, but you're a mother who cannot afford that!"

Wow...I'm growing hotter and my hands start to shake with anger.

"I am also a woman, not only a mother! And I don't think you have the right to judge or tell me what I can and cannot do!" Meanwhile, my hands are clenched and I'm breathing faster. I love Penny and am grateful to her for all she does, but I think, right now, she's treating me unfairly!

Certainly not like a girlfriend!

She ignores what I said. "I don't trust that guy! He just shows up here and fucks you in the hallway? Who does that, that's not right! Something about him is...alarming!"

I would rather die than admit I had the same feeling about Keaton, just that I like him.

"Boohoo! A man meeting a woman for sex, who would have thought?" I shout sarcastically, Penny snorts, obviously unimpressed. Now, I'm simmering — shortly before the boiling point. "You know what I think, Penny? I think you're jealous because you haven't met Mister Right yet and are still single! And you blame ME for your life solely revolving around Riley and me, right? Actually, we are a burden to you, right? That's it! I CERTAINLY WON'T BE CHASTIZED FOR NOW AND THEN, ENJOYING MY FEMINE SIDE OVER CONSTANT MOTHERING! So, you should look for someone else to take your frustration out on!" Yes, I'm damn angry and regret the words as soon as they spill out my mouth, but I won't apologize because what Penny said was uncalled for.

She stares at me as if I hit her, which I might have on an emotional level. I regret it. But I won't admit it.

"Leave!" she says icily while pointing at the door. "After all we've seen together, I won't listen to shit like that!" I notice her voice trembling and ignore it, simply march by her and lift my sleeping son out of her bed. He no longer feels hot or feverish, but I'll still call him in sick at school tomorrow. I pick him up awkwardly as he seems so much heavier than before and gasp. It seems it was only yesterday when he was a baby and I could hold him in one arm.

Even though I'm having a hard time, I carry him pass Penny and out the door, while ordering Rosie to come along. I have no idea how an unexpected situation could escalate so quickly. But I leave it be and go.

* * *

Keaton

I've already written up your new contract, Olivia. Actually, I did it yesterday, after our first night together. That was when everything became crystal clear to me.

I know you will accept the job, I'm having fun stapling the pages together. Right now, you're at the diner to quit. Last night's argument with your best friend could not have come at a better time for it convinced you to accept my offer, right?

You are proud. I love how proud you are. And you'll do anything, though I'm sure you won't apologize to Penny even if you were pretty mean to her, baby. Sorry, but it needs to be said. Naturally, I listened in over your phone. The latest interception technology from Germany is a reliable gizmo that always keeps me informed about every little detail of your life. I had to force myself to stand up for Penny because I cannot stand her, Olivia. She might always be there for you – that's probably her only asset – but I don't like her. She is loud, always grumpy, and chews gum like a Russian prostitute. It seems with Penny, the natural feminine elegance that every woman possesses simply extinguished. But she never lets you down, which is the only reason I have not made her disappear from your life — in one way or another. I want you all to myself, Olivia. I'll only share you with Riley.

Soon, I will be able to watch you all day without cameras. You'll be tiptoeing in front of me in tight skirts, I put a stipulation in your contract that prohibits wearing jeans. I get hard just thinking about you not wearing panties and bending down to offer me the perfect view. We will have a good time together, Olivia. And you won't have to do any more work that's beneath you.

You didn't ask Penny to help today. She's currently busy with a client, talking her ear off about her boring life. She's jealous of you, Olivia. She doesn't understand you — nobody but me ever will, believe me.

I'm sitting in the office getting your contract ready and watching you at the diner on my cell phone. You're wearing those scuffed sneakers again, completely unaware I cloned the phone you hold in your hand. Riley is with you, still not fully recuperated.

Soon, you'll have more time for him, babe.

And for me.

God, I'm relieved, Olivia. You have no idea.

28. Superman vs. Mr. Rush

Olivia

It's Sunday night, Riley and I are on the bus heading downtown. Every two weeks, I have to clean offices like this one on the weekend.

He looks terribly tired, but he's brave and doesn't whine — as always. Soon, my shift at Keaton's office starts. Well, actually, it starts later, but since I took Riley along and he goes back to school tomorrow, I'm hoping to also leave earlier. I'm exhausted and nervous. Today, I have not heard from Mr. Rush and I was too busy to call or text him. Anyway, after the night we had yesterday, I cannot think of anything else but him. Thankfully, this causes the argument Penny and I had to fade away more and more.

I hardly slept, too busy thinking about everything when,

finally, I came to the conclusion that something had to change. Granted, I can't say that I've given much thought to the future lately, but I am aware that I cannot clean and waitress forever while Penny watches Riley. It may sound bitter, but it is the way I earn a living. Keaton's offer comes at just the right time. It's like an offer from heaven... It would be stupid to turn down the opportunity! Especially in my situation! I have no degree or higher degree and my job opportunities and pay rate is limited! His offer allows me to spend more time with Riley and make more money than I could anywhere else. That's why this afternoon, I forced myself to be courageous and quit my job at the diner.

I know Keaton is serious and know that after such short a time, I already depend a lot on him, more so than is good for me. However, my intuition tells me I can trust him, that he will keep his word and be there for me. Insane, right?

Of course, Jack didn't react well to my quitting, I know I always did my job well and attracted many customers. Regardless, my decision was final and everyone had to accept it.

I know I acted rashly, but since yesterday, I cannot think of anything other than how my life is progressing. How much I have to work – how little time I have – how little money – how few prospects. Naturally, I'm scared since I have no idea if I have what Keaton requires, but I know I'll do my best. I could wait a long time for another offer like his to come along.

I will talk with Keaton about it, but first, I have to get through this shift. My eyes fall shut, sitting in the bus driving along the hillside makes me tired.

Riley leans his head against my shoulder and closes his eyes. Naturally, he asked me several times about Aunt Penny and why he didn't stay with her. I made up the excuse that she had an important appointment. Riley loves Penny, I don't want to burden him with our quarrel.

Fortunately, we'll arrive at our destination soon, otherwise, I might fall asleep. I help Riley off the bus, though he helps with his crutches, then we walk over and enter the huge building. His tired eyes widen as he glances around.

"WOW!" he shouts and it echoes through the empty lobby.

I laugh. "Oh, yes, wow is right!" He follows me to the elevators. "Do you remember what I told you?" I ask as we get in and watch our reflections in the three mirrored walls of the elevator. Two tired figures who should actually be in bed! Luckily, Riley feels much better and can return to school tomorrow.

He nods eagerly and a few dark strands fall over his forehead. I brush them back. "Don't touch anything, don't mess anything up, be good!"

"That's it," I say and nod. "Or Mommy gets into trouble. Everything up there is confidential, understand?"

"Like with the FBI on TV?" he asks in astonishment. I laugh. Oh, how I would like to experience again his childlike lightheartedness. I wish Riley would never lose this trait. We grow up way too fast and are confronted overnight with duties and grown up stuff.

"Yes, just like that," I say. "Pretty cool, right?"

Again, he nods so vigorously, his hair flies around. "Supercool!" The elevator stops and we go to the office. I turn on all the lights. Today, I have to hurry. Rosie is alone at home since Penny and I are not talking. Rosie doesn't like to be left alone, usually revolts by dropping a turd here or there where they're not found right away, although the smell gives them away, oh, yeah!

I grab the cleaning supplies out of the room and notice Keaton left another item for me. Since I have no idea if it is something naughty, I don't open the large envelope at the moment, set my cleaning stuff aside, and return to Riley, who is standing at the reception counter, looking out of place. He is not used to such luxurious facilities.

"Look, baby, over there's a sofa!" I point to the waiting corner. "You can wait there. It won't take me long. Do you have your Game Boy with you?" The device, by the way, is almost as old as I am, but it works.

Riley immediately pulls it out of his backpack and places it demonstratively on the sofa. "HERE!"

"Good, baby. Do you want something to drink?"

He shakes his head. "I'm fine!"

He puts his crutches down and sits on the sofa.

I smile. He's such a little lion.

As soon as he's engrossed in his Game Boy, I reach for and open the envelope. The sound of paper tearing echoes in my ears and I swallow for I suspect what it is. My heart starts to race. Only now am I aware that I'm taking a big chance in my life. Okay, yes, it's good, but what if I fail? I don't even know Keaton's position here, after all, everything is top secret and kept under lock and key!

I barely perceive the sounds of Riley's Game Boy as I pull the stack of paper out of the envelope. *Employment contract* it says...intuition tells me I should first read each paragraph thoroughly.

* * *

Keaton

You don't trust me, Olivia. And you are afraid.

I watch you standing in your dressing room so Riley cannot see you reading the contract. You'll have to read it a few times, it's not conventional. I'm not angry with you. I love your skepticism as well as the way you overcome it every time. You consider if you should do something and know it won't be easy or, perhaps, even impossible, but do it anyway. Over and over again.

It's important for me to catch Riley alone and now seems a perfect opportunity. You haven't signed the contract — not yet. You set it aside – you're a bit pale – and begin cleaning. Good for me, for now I can intervene. I haven't seen Riley in a while. Our game became too hot. But now I have to talk to him before our little secret comes out and ruins everything.

I'm so nearby, Olivia. As always. Right now, I'm sitting in my car in the underground garage watching you over my phone. You filled the bucket and start with the first office. Now is my chance.

I get out and take the stairs because I cannot risk you hearing the elevator. Though I'm athletic, I would be lying if I said all the stairs did not faze me. By the time I get to the top, my back is sweaty and I'm breathing heavily. I take a few minutes to calm down, lean against the door, and breathe deeply. In the process, I inhale the fragrance I gave you and which you usually do not wear often — probably because it's expensive. But you knew I would be here or, at least, nearby, right? So, you wanted me to smell you. Believe me, baby, I even smell you when you're not around.

Before I enter, I glance at my phone. You're currently vacuuming my office and then you'll wipe the surfaces with a damp rag so that gives me seven minutes alone time with Riley — that'll do.

Silently, I enter and go straight to the couch corner where Riley sits playing with his Game Boy. He's wearing black jogging pants and a winter sweater even though summer is slowly approaching. You are too anxious, Olivia. Really. His butt hangs partially over the edge of the couch and his red tired eyes are glued to the device.

He doesn't notice me. I glance over my shoulder – you're still vacuuming – and I kneel down next to Riley.

"Hi," I say softly enough so you won't hear me over the vacuum cleaner.

Slowly, oh-so-slowly, he looks up from his Game Boy and into my face. The way he tilts his head, looks at me before recognition sets in, and his eyes widening is almost mesmerizing.

"Shush!" I warn him up front and he immediately gets it.

"John!" he whispers.

I smile. Shit, Olivia, I really grew fond of him! And I missed him. If I were his father, the father of *your* child, I would spoil him the way he deserves. He is too old for his age and has to understand too many things. More so than others his age. More than a child should have to understand.

"How are you?" I ask.

"I'm fine! Where have you been? I haven't seen you in so long!"

I shrug casually. "Busy with undercover spy work."

"Wow," he mumbles. I have to refrain from laughing, children are precious. He doesn't even question my presence here. Or why I am here. That's just like he is.

"I'm here for a reason, Riley." He listens carefully and nods, the Game Boy long forgotten. "You know how undercover spies work, right? They always have two identities, like Spiderman, Superman, and all the others." He nods again, his little hands resting calmly in his lap. He has your nose, Liv. And your lips. You may not see it, but I do. I see everything that involves you.

"My undercover spy identity is John. I protect the weak, you understand, right?"

The vacuum cleaner stops, the following silence makes me nervous. You're the only one who can make me nervous, Olivia.

"Are you okay over there?" You shout. I place my index finger on my mouth to signal Riley not to mention I'm here.

He looks at me, then calls in your direction, "Yes, Mommy!" I hear you dip the rag into the bucket of water. I don't have much time left.

"My real name is Keaton Rush. Can you repeat that?"

He repeats my words and follows my gaze. "You're Keaton Rush, but your undercover spy name is John!"

"Right. Now listen carefully, okay? Your mom doesn't know we know each other. And I'm her boss. I own all this here."

"Really?" he asks enthusiastically. I smile.

"Really. Your mom can't know that we already know each other, she won't understand. And she doesn't know about John either, understand?" He nods again. "I really really like your mom and want to protect her."

"Is my Mommy in danger?" His eyes grow panicky; I immediately want to take the fear away from him.

"No! And I'm here to make sure it stays that way. There are many bad people in this world, Riley. I like you and your mom! I want to protect you, understand? So, when your mom's around, I'm Keaton, okay?"

He nods again, though I'm doubtful. I'm serious about what I told Riley. I want to be there for you two, Olivia, that's something I've never wanted before. So, it's important Riley doesn't spill the beans. Not even by accident.

"What's my name?"

"Keaton Rush."

"Excuse me?"

"Keaton."

"Repeat that."

"Your name is Keaton," he says softly with shining eyes. "And you'll protect us."

29. Negotiations

Olivia

I hurry and finish faster than usual with Keaton's office. The largest of the offices is out of the way. Now the floor must be mopped and I'm done. I want to get home as soon as possible so Riley can go to sleep and Rosie isn't left unattended for too long.

I'm still thinking about the contract, at home I will go through it again — point by point. Because I still can't believe what I've read.

I grab the bucket and leave the office. As I turn around and look for Riley, I'm startled.

What the hell?

He's still sitting where I left him, laughing lightheartedly at the joke told by none other than Mr.

Keaton Rush, who's squatting next to my son.

FUCK!

I didn't want him to find out this way! What is he doing here anyway? And...why is he so cute and sexy when he's talking to Riley?

He's wearing black jeans and a black shirt with the sleeves rolled up. To talk to Riley face to face, he's squatting with his forearms leaning on the armrest of the couch. His back muscles and sinewy forearms bulge distinctly and I immediately feel my heart beating faster as he runs a hand through his hair, laughing.

"Keaton?"

Both glance in my direction and Keaton stands slowly. He looks at me smiling. "Hello, Olivia." I feel a cold shiver run down my spine. He's probably upset I didn't tell him about Riley, but I don't care! Riley was supposed to remain my secret. It's far too dangerous to introduce him to whomever!

But then Keaton doesn't look pissed off at all. "I didn't know you had a son," he says while casually leaning against the reception counter so his scent is now wonderfully in my nose.

"Um, eh…I didn't know I was obliged to tell you about him!" I immediately counter.

He laughs softly. "Relax, he's wonderful." His statement confuses me for I know from experience that most men are turned off by children. I'm nervous about him being here and talking to Riley, but then the situation seems totally innocent and it's only me who's spreading tension.

"We had a good talk." He winks at Riley. "Right, little man?"

Riley nods eagerly, his cheeks glowing. "Oh, yeah!"

"Sweetie, play for a while longer, Mommy's almost done," I call to Riley, then gesture for Keaton to follow me. He does so while his eyes twinkle totally amused. I grab the contract off the counter in passing and we step into the next open office.

I leave the door open so I can keep an eye on Riley. Keaton is standing expectantly in front of me with his hands in his pockets.

"How old is he?"

"Keaton!"

"He is cute."

"Keaton!"

"Why does he have crutches?"

"KEATON!"

"Where's his father?" I can see by his expression, he enjoys riling me.

"He's six! He is not cute, he's perfect! He's missing one lower leg! And his father is none of your business."

Unperturbed, he suddenly grabs my forearm and pulls me close to his body. His warm full lips are near my ear. "Wrong," he whispers and goose bumps travel down my arms, "everything involving you is my business. You've accepted you are mine, so are your affairs."

His words are so hot, they immediately cause a pulling sensation in my chest and stomach...but my mind is clear and I yank my arm back. “My son is not in *our* business, understand?”

“I didn’t mean to bring him in.”

“That’s better.”

“Where is his father?”

I moan annoyed. “Leave it alone, Keaton.”

He chuckles softly and I almost smiled. Almost! “Okay, but only because you look so desperate.” He reaches for the contract I’m holding and pulls it out of my hand. “Apparently, you haven’t signed yet. Is there something you want to discuss with me first?”

Okay, he finally succeeded in pushing me especially because of that amused expression he’s been watching me with the entire time! I shut the door – Riley is too engrossed in his game boy anyway – and throw my arms in the air.

“Miss Pierson is obliged to wear a skirt every day? And she is obliged to give a blowjob every day before she leaves? Miss Pierson is required to hand over her worn panties to Mr. Rush at the end of each shift? ARE YOU FOR REAL, KEATON?”

He shrugs and laughs. “I’ve heard that work should be fun. I thought it would be a few ways to have more fun at work.”

“You’re joking?” I ask, frustrated, because I can’t believe he’s serious, but his expression tells me otherwise. “Keaton!”

"You're welcome to negotiate, but I won't give up on those points!" He seems too relaxed and amused. I walk over to him, snatching the contract out of his hand, and stare at him.

"Point one," I read it out loud. "I don't even have that many skirts to wear one every day!"

"I'll outfit you."

"HA, HA!" I burst out cynically. "Like that's going to happen! I don't want that."

"I really don't care." God, the man is so obstinate.

"But much worse are the blowjobs!"

"That's nonnegotiable!"

"Keaton!"

"What?"

"I'm not your little whore, I want to work here!"

He smiles at me like he always does and the look he gives me once again makes me feel like I missed the joke. His voice is also exceptionally gentle as he says, "You *are* my little whore. And you *will* work. You'll be given whatever practical training, but I won't give up my points."

Wow, okay, I actually *should be* angry now and hit him with the papers. I should fight for women's rights, be emancipated, and in a totally cool way, tell him I won't be anyone's whore. Though, that's a problem, because I am turned on by what he just said. I actually want this, want it deep inside me. Besides, I can't stand feminists! So, I don't put up a fight.

"Once a week!"

"Four times!"

"Twice!"

"Three times!"

"Okay!"

Holy shit, did I just say *okay*?

Now it's too late.

He nods quite self- satisfied. "Okay." He takes a pen from his shirt pocket and hands it to me so I can make the necessary changes. "I'll print out a new copy."

It is better, I think, but say nothing. "My panties..."

"Not open to negotiation."

"Keaton."

"No."

"Heavens!"

"It is the way it is."

I sigh annoyed. "Miss Pierson will end every sentence with 'Mr. Rush'." This makes me smirk. "That's still fairly professional, Mr. Rush, sir!" I salute haphazardly. He tilts his head and shakes it.

"When Mr. Rush is around, only he is to be looked at, nothing else, unless, of course, Mr. Rush asks Miss Pierson to do something else." I look up at him and shake my head — he smiles complacently. "You have serious problems."

"As do you."

I snort and read on. "Miss Pierson may only appear at work completely shaved. This pertains to the genital area, armpits, and legs."

"Isn't that a given?" he asks, honestly confused.

"So why put it in the contract?"

"I cannot stand stubble."

"So you shave your scrotum every day?"

He gives me a deadly serious look. "Don't test me, Olivia."

"Yes, Mr. Rush, sir!"

I see the corners of his mouth twitch. "All that stays as is. The blowjob deal we can change!"

I shrug. "Miss Pierson will only use lipsticks provided by Mr. Rush. What if I don't like one or it isn't my style, huh?"

"You will like them because I'm familiar with your style."

My heart beats faster, but I pull myself together. I'm in important negotiation talks! "Miss Pierson is always available to Mr. Rush." I look at him challengingly. "What happens if I'm not?"

"Finish reading."

I do just that and realize I previously overlooked the small print clause underneath. "Otherwise she will have to bear the consequences — see page twelve. Page twelve?"

"Later." He smiles darkly. I swallow.

"Miss Pierson will only use the mode of transportation that Mr. Rush provides."

"Yep."

"No!"

"Why not?"

"You can't buy me a car, Keaton!" I state as I frantically turn to page twelve and turn pale. I see written: *Punishments, should points of the contract not be respected: You will not come. As a matter of fact, you will not come for as long as I see fit. Spanking. Being ambushed, like in your hallway. You won't be allowed to come again — for a very, very long time*.

I swallow. "What…"

"What?"

"Keaton, you..."

"We were at the car. Or where are we now?" He smiles mischievously and I shake my head to come to my senses.

"The car, right...but...you cannot just do that," I say autonomously.

"I can and I have!" He casually pulls a key on a ring out of his pocket while ignoring my flabbergast expression. I'm so puzzled, I cannot even make out the logo. "You're welcome."

The guy grins like damn Santa! On speed!

"Keaton, I won't accept this!" As if the key were pure acid, I jump and let it drop to the floor. "A car, new clothes, makeup...that won't work, I can't! I won't!" I'm at a loss for words. A first! Okay, regarding anyone else, but not Mister *I'm-totally-gaga* Rush sir!

"You can and you will," he says. "It's a company car, baby. So you must. But today, you won't drive it anyway; I already have someone else waiting for you downstairs." How naturally the *you* comes out of his mouth, as if it wasn't a problem whatsoever that I have a little cute 'ballast' with me... Fuck... FUCK, FUCK!

I can only shake my head as I consider if the man is a curse or a blessing. "This here is not normal, Keaton."

"Are we normal, Olivia?"

Okay, he has a point!

I sigh in resignation and set the contract aside. Once he changes the point regarding blowjobs, I will sign! Looking at him again, I become aware of what he just said.

"What do you mean; you have someone else waiting for us downstairs?"

He shrugs. "I happen to see it, that's why I won't be driving either. Go look for yourself. Oh, yeah – I'll have a parcel of clothes of whatever else you need put together for you. You officially start next month."

Now he does something totally atypical. He reaches for my chin, looks me in the eyes...and kisses me on the lips. Quite chaste and innocent like, not wild and hard. "I'm looking forward to your first day at work, Miss Pierson," he whispers directly at my mouth. I almost die.

I watch him while the kaleidoscope of butterflies in my stomach almost makes me throw up. Holy shit...Mr. Fucking Rush, you will be my demise.

30. Friend Stuff

Olivia

Penny is downstairs waiting for us, leaning against her parents' little silver Ford. I know how much she hates to ask her parents for something. And as soon as I see her, I've forgotten all about yesterday's stupid argument and I'm no longer angry. I'm simply a person who easily gets angry but just as quickly as I am riled up, my anger diminishes too. I'm grateful for my faithful best friend and want to hug her. But as Keaton steps out of the building behind me — carrying the sleeping Riley, Penny's expression darkens and I'm immediately angry again. Can't she simply let me enjoy the happy feeling I'm experiencing right now? I mean, what man would insist on carrying my sleeping child downstairs for me, which man (especially which boss!) would sit with my son the entire time I'm cleaning and entertain him or put a blanket over him once he falls asleep. Thus he is affirming that which was absolutely not supposed to happen, namely, that this affair will make me lose my heart.

Nevertheless, she's here waiting for me. And I'm tired of arguing. She went to her parents and borrowed their car to pick me up — that's really something because her parents are stingy about lending the car! She forces herself to smile as Keaton places Riley on the back seat and introduces himself.

"So, you must be the best girlfriend." Again he grins like he's all-knowing. I frown and wonder if I told him about her.

"So, you must the new boss!" Penny says and they shake hands, though the looks they exchange get me get ready to jump in between should someone starts strangling the other.

"Okay, let's go!" I shout to break the unbearable tension and the two break apart.

"See you, Olivia," Keaton says as he takes a step back and I get in, as does Penny. I turn to watch him as we drive away and for some reason, the grin on my lips vanishes. Suddenly, the contract in my handbag seems to weigh a ton. I consider what Penny would say about the points and decide not to tell her.

She would lose it.

Why am I not losing it?

Why have I practically signed it already?

Simply madness...

Are not normal, Olivia, I still hear Keaton's sexy voice in my head and grin again.

No, we are not — and that's a good thing, I telepathically agree with him.

***

After three minutes, the silence between us becomes intolerable and both of us make an effort at the same time, uttering exactly the same words.

"I didn't mean it like that!" We falter. Then we burst out laughing.

It's good to laugh away the tension.

I can always do that with Penny.

Immediately, we are our usual selves again as if the quarrel didn't happen, well, almost. I overcome myself and say, "I was angry. And I'm totally grateful for all that you do for us."

"I only said that because I am really worried about you, Olivia..."

"Probably more so now that you've met him," I murmur and she sighs.

"What can I say?"

"That he's absolutely hot?"

"Yeah, he really looks stunning, but don't you think he's somewhat…?"

"Hot?"

"More like scary! I get goose bumps just recalling the look he gave you when we were driving off."

"How so?"

"I don't know. Like he's obsessed."

Yes, *obsessed* is the right word, but it's more about how I feel when I think about him. Not the other way around or…?"

"Obsessed with me?" I ask with a grin since I don't believe it. Not a guy like Mister Fucking Hot Rush...who simply has to snap a finger and five women would kneel before him.

"Oh, yes, with you, sweetie! I mean...you have the absolute dream package, just look at your body." I roll my eyes. "And then there's your face, what guy wouldn't enjoy it?"

"I'm much more than a pretty face, Missy! I also have a perfect vagina!" Penny laughs. I grin stupidly and abruptly realize what I said – and in front of whom – when Riley sighs on the back seat.

Shit! Bbright red, I turn to see if he heard me. Thankfully, he's still sound asleep.

"Whatever. Something about that guy sets my alarm bells off, but you seem to know better."

"Yes."

"And? You're sure?" She needles, nosy as usual, but she would not be Penny if she acted differently. I sigh and massage my throbbing temples.

"He's everything I never dared wish for, Penny," I say softly. "And if I know one thing, I'm already in too deep. I'm no longer able to stay away from him. And I don't want to either."

I've fallen in love with Keaton Rush. Really damn bad in love.

That's the only thing I know, the rest...we'll see.

***

The next day, Keaton doesn't make an appearance as I'm cleaning, but he left behind a whorish red lipstick. I grin as I apply it before cleaning. But then I enjoy spending all that time with Riley, my God, when was the last time I was able to spend a whole day with him and not constantly be on the go?

The following day at work, I find a revealing, sexy housemaid uniform. I roll my eyes as I put it on, then exaggeratedly push my butt out while I clean, giving him a veritable show, wherever a camera is blinking red.

He also doesn't show up that day and I'm starting to get nervous.

Did he have a change of heart?

He no longer wants me?

Does he think: Fuck, why did I have to get involved with that poor lunatic?

And her child?

On the third day, I find high heels waiting for me and

put them on together with the uniform...

Again, he doesn't make an appearance.

On the fourth day, I'm totally unsettled.

The contract is at home safely tucked away on top of one of the cabinets where no one can get at it. I have not signed it yet since I actually want to talk to him about it again, go through it again point for point — to dispel whatever lingering doubts. But he doesn't give me an opportunity. His gifts are the only sign that he hasn't forgotten about me. All this wears me down. On so many levels. I also realize that I don't even have his phone number and can't contact him if I want to — and I want to. That much is clear.

When he doesn't make an appearance on the fourth day, I'm a total wreck. I actually miss him. I'm wondering why it is so painful missing someone I don't really know yet.

I want to share a pizza with him again in his office. Or spend the night with him in his bed. After this week, I'm finished cleaning here if I actually start next Monday as his secretary — and personal slave, to call it by its proper name.

I'm still not sure.

I need...maybe a little more distance.

And good advice from people who actually know me.

I haven't been home since that business with my ex, so at the end of my shift on the fourth day, I decide to spend the weekend with my parents, go home and — face my fears. I should finally come to terms with the past so I – maybe – start a new future.

It will be good for me.

Besides, it's been a while since I've seen my family.

Riley has not seen his aunts, uncles, and grandparents for quite some time!

I spontaneously book a train ticket in the middle of the night and decide we'll leave early the next morning after my cleaning shift!

***

Rosie is being taken care of by Penny and we head for the train station. I love riding a train — though getting Riley to climb on board with his crutches is not easy, not to mention the suitcase seems to weigh a ton. However, we eventually sit in our soft seats and Riley happily drinks his lemonade as I gaze out the window at the passing landscape.

Indiana is beautiful and I always feel safe, at home here, no matter that it's the place where I had my worst experience. When I was 16, I left home so I could be with Dexter —Riley's dad. The two of us stayed practically everywhere until we rented a small apartment downtown. It wasn't until Riley had his accident that I dared go back home to my parents' house. I did not have to listen to anything nor did we fight, instead, I was welcomed with open arms and comforted. Therefore, going home always provides me with a warm feeling. The last time I was here,

I had broken up with Dexter, though nowadays, I'm no longer afraid of him. Considering all the shit he pulled, he wouldn't dare come near me. I watch the passing green luscious landscape and feel more at ease the closer we get to Fort Wayne. Our city is quite small and clean. Cute single family homes with surrounding gardens line the streets. One front garden is more beautiful than the next. Even the playgrounds are kept clean, no dirt to be found, not like in the city where I live now. I miss my childhood home, honestly. But I've made a life for myself in Chicago and I'm not someone who will take advantage of their parents. I work, earn a living, and live within my means.

I'm looking forward to seeing my parents. They have no idea I'm coming and I can't wait to surprise them. I'm looking forward to seeing their happy faces – especially my mother's – and smile. But most of all, I look forward to seeing my father. I've always been his little darling, we have a special connection, even though he worked a lot and wasn't home much.

The train ride doesn't take long before it pulls into the small station, the sky shines a most beautiful blue. Though we don't have far to go — just down the street, hang a right, then maybe another five minutes on foot, I want to spare Riley the ordeal and call a taxi. As life progresses at a slower pace in this small idyllic town, I take my time, sit on a bench, and bask my face in the sun while Riley rummages in his pocket for chewing gum.

What might he be doing right now?

Is he perhaps thinking about me?

Why didn't he show all week?

I imagine his eyes staring lecherously at me, wanting me, and everything in me contracts almost painfully with desire.

God, how I miss him...

Someone honks and I am startled out of my daydream. The taxi has arrived — the driver is...DANNY! Danny, a former schoolmate that always looked good and I had a crush on, but he never paid attention to me because I was a young pimply teen with low self-esteem.

"Danny!" I exclaim when I see his blond mane. He obviously doesn't recognize me at first, takes a double take, then frowns and asks,

"Liv?"

I laugh as he looks at me like a donkey with four ears.

"Yes." I grin at him and walk toward him. Riley limps behind me while eyeing the stranger skeptically. Riley does not like other men in my life — except...STOP IT! Perhaps you can think of something else for a change?

Danny seems to awaken from a trance and quickly jumps into gear, grabbing my suitcase while babbling. "Gosh, you look so different without braces, I hardly recognize you, and you've, uh...grown up. Wow and who do we have here? Is this your son?" He bows to Riley, who looks back at him, bored. "Hello, little man."

"Hello," Riley says curtly, then looks away. I grin and stroke his locks.

"Yes, this is my son," I say proudly, ready for Danny's remark. A remark about the crutches and whatnot — but then he isn't stupid, never was, and I wonder if he's driving a taxi in his spare time. He bows and says, "Well, let us chauffeur the princess to her castle," and holds the door open for Riley.

I receive a text message from Penny as I sit in the taxi, asking if I we've arrived yet. I quickly text her back that I'm in town and on my way to my parents' house.

"And? Where did you end up?" Danny asks. I sigh.

"Chicago."

"Oh, the Windy City," he says. I nod.

"Yep. And you? What are you up to?"

"Well, driving a taxi, which is my second job, I work full-time as a machine operator in the beverage factory."

"Okay."

"And I have no girlfriend or wife if that's what you want to know!" He wiggles his eyebrows. I laugh. I consider telling him off right from the get go for that's what I usually do. But Danny looks so damn good! And he has an athletic body, a pretty face, is funny and easy to talk to, not like with...

STOP, LIV! Honestly!

"I also have no girlfriend or wife!" I reply. We laugh. God, it feels good! To have a totally innocent conversation with a man! "Or a boyfriend, if you must know."

"What about Keaton?" Riley pipes up from the back seat. I turn to face him and he looks really angry at me.

Dammit!

Children!

They simply blurt out *whatever*.

"Yes, Liv, what about Keaton?" Danny asks, pseudo-serious with a smile in his eyes.

I roll mine.

"The thing with Keaton is complicated..." I say to both.

"He likes you!" Riley says immediately with his eyes narrowed and arms crossed. God, he's too damn cute when he's mad! I'd like to hug him until he screams for me to stop!

"I like him too...but..." I fall silent as I'm in no mood to explain myself to my little son and an almost stranger.

"Well, there's always a but, right?" Danny says casually.

"Oh yeah!"

***

Keaton

I put my phone away and try to calm down.

You're in the car with a strange man.

You say you have no boyfriend. You're right, I'm not your fucking boyfriend.

You.

Are.

Mine!

And that it is complicated with me.

Oh, Olivia, I'll show you how damn complicated I can be!

So far, I've been tame — but that will change *now*.

31. Home, Crazy Home

Olivia

My mother answers the door and seeing me there, screams so loud the whole town can hear. She throws herself around my neck — damn the woman is strong, really... I smile and return the hug, regardless that my eardrums are almost bursting. I pat her back while I inhale her so familiar old-woman perfume. I like old-woman-perfume on my mom. Her hair is colored a chocolate brown and cut in a stylish short hairstyle. It is quite daring for this small town, but then that's all that's stylish about her. My mother is incredibly short, perhaps 4-foot-nine-inches, but cute. Since I'm the taller one now, I want to pinch her cheek and utter *tsk-tsk*. Regardless, the woman is strong despite her small size and delicate physique! All her life, she has worked in my father's workshop, always dealt with men, and used to being assertive. I'm glad I inherited that from her.

My dad approaches — attracted by her loud screaming and pauses as soon as he sees me. I feel my heart aching a bit when I see him. My father used to have dark hair, a full dark beard, and a strong stocky body. He had the stature of a man who could lift a car — at least it's what I imagined as a little girl. He has lost weight, his hair and beard white. However, the blue eyes behind the glasses still sparkle, just like the smile on his face, which once was round.

"My girl, what are you doing here?" he asks and I fly into his arms. I embrace him and take delight in being back home.

***

My mother babbles nonstop as we prepare the food, of course, half the neighborhood has been invited to welcome home the lost daughter — and we expect a mob. But it is still quiet. My father is showing Riley his workshop and machines. The little one can't stop grinning, which causes me to smile happily too. My mother is pumping me for information, but then I expected as much.

She inquires about my job, but she only knows about the one at the diner. *Good, Mom, everything is good.*

I'm not going to mention Keaton's offer — especially since I've come to the conclusion that it isn't serious.

How is Riley doing at school. *Great, Mom. He has only good grades...*

And how does it look man-wise? *Nothing new, Mom...*

Speaking of...

Instantly, my mind imagines that particular image of a man squatting on the floor in front of Riley, both are laughing.

Fuck...

***

We have a huge dining table since we have a big family, but also because we often have people over for dinner, like this evening, we have ten. Our neighbors, the Fellers, are among them. I always played with their kids when I was little and Danny came along. In her euphoria, my mother also invited him as well as a few people from the street. It is a large eclectic group. Dad reminisces about the fishing trips he took me on when I was a teenager. Telling everyone how I always felt bored and lolled around on deck tanning, how I always threw the fish back into the water as soon as he wasn't looking, and how he always wondered why the bucket was nearly empty despite the fish he caught. People drank and laughed. Riley is comfortable, like he always does at my parents. Here, you cannot but feel comfortable. Danny sits right next to me, he turns me on, which normally I would ignore. But since I'm angry, I allow myself this little flirtation and do not drive him away. He really is a sweet guy — if I were to consider getting involved with a man, he would make the cut. Until a few days ago, I actually thought that I had no room for a man in my life...

Then I met Keaton Rush.

The bell rings as the main course is served. Chicken, vegetables, potatoes, gravy – lots of gravy – oh my mouth is watering.

Riley's eyes are glowing as he stares at all the steaming dishes on the table and is about to reach for something when I pull his hand back and kiss it. "You have to wait a moment longer, sweetheart!" I tell him as I tickle his palm with my fingertips, making him giggle.

"So, what are your plans for tomorrow?" Danny asks, startling me. I've forgotten all about him, which is typical when I interact with my son.

"I don't know yet...I'll see."

"Would you be in the mood for a little trip to the lake?" I look into Danny's blue eyes and wish he was another man sitting by my side...

"I don't know..." I answer and Danny leans down to whisper in my ear.

"Come on, I won't bite!" My mom is coming back into the room. Her eyes shine like nuclear power plants. She looks at me with a wide, awe-inspiring grin and says, "Look who's here!" and steps aside for me to see who's standing there.

My expression pretty much drops as...*he* enters the room.

Keaton!

He's here!

HERE!

At my parents!

OH!

My!

Fucking!

God!

And he appears really, REALLY pissed off!

SHIT!

***

I jump up, blurting "Keaton!' as if a spring bit me in the ass and everyone is staring at me. Then at him. Then at me again. A few people grin, others whisper. He merely raises one eyebrow. "Olivia."

"Have a seat, Mr. Rush! Let me get you a plate and cutlery!" my mother sings happily and I feel the blood leaving my cheeks. What did he tell her? What is he doing here? He, in his expensive designer clothes, doesn't fit in here. In his perfectly fitting jeans and white V neck pullover, Rolex, and expensive shoes... He looks like a company mogul who walked into a pigsty... My father brings a chair for him while eyeing him suspiciously – GO, DADDY! – but Keaton doesn't sit where my father placed the chair. He takes it, comes around the table, and demonstratively places it between me and Danny — whom he ignores for Riley greets him euphorically and Keaton ruffles his hair, saying, "Hi buddy."

Then he sits next to me. Every single fiber of his perfect body is tense.

Dammit!

DAMN! DAMN!

I cannot breathe anymore. I cannot think anymore.

My head seems empty.

The talk and the clanking of plates and cutlery around the table falls silent since everyone was helping themselves. I'm afraid to look at him or anyone else. I know I have to pull myself together, but I'm not sure how.

What's he doing here?

How am I supposed to react?

"It's nice of you to make it after all, Mr. Rush. Liv, you should have told me that you have such a great friend! And here you say you have no news about men!" my mother sings happily, as always lacking as much as a spark of empathy.

"Luckily, my meeting was postponed and I couldn't pass up the chance to meet Olivia's family in person." Pointedly, he takes my hand on the table and squeezes it. I'm wondering if I should to pull it out of his grasp, but somehow...I'm afraid. I know he's angry.

Just not why?

All week, he never showed, just left me hanging! I'm angry too! Oh, yeah!

I pull my hand away and notice him stiffen.

“I have to go to the bathroom!” I say, get up, and literally storm out of the room in the direction of the bathroom. I’m completely overwhelmed — and have no idea what’s what.

32. Give Me Everything

Olivia

I don't make it far — but I didn't expect to. Halfway there, I feel him grab my arm and whirl me around. Before I can say anything or get upset, I have his hand on my mouth.

"Where's your room?" he asks, and now up close, I see how furious he actually is. His fascinating eyes are reminiscent of a stormy sea, more dark blue than green. Oh-so-deep and dangerous...

I nod upward. He grabs my arm tighter and tows me up the stairs behind him. I'm stomping so loud everyone downstairs must hear it and ask, "Who is this, Keaton!" We're upstairs and he pulls me into the first room, which happens to be mine, or rather, was. I simply need to vent my anger and am about to whirl around and yell at him when he silences me by shoving me onto my bed. Trapped like a damn beetle, I land on my back with him right on top of me — his huge hand still over my mouth. "Now you listen to me!" he growls as he pushes down with his body, holding me motionless and robbing me of my senses. He is so close to me and so rock hard, which I clearly feel through our pants. "You'll never again leave the city without telling me!"

"I would have told you if I had been able to reach you," I shout, but his hand is muffling my words and it comes out as a mumble. I don't think he cares about what I have to say.

"You'll never go anywhere without me knowing!" he continues unabashedly, then reaches down and opens his pants. My eyes widen and my heart races as everything inside me contracts. Getting ready.

He is here! And he wants me! I will get him! YES! I'm wearing a pretty blue dress, skimpy panties...he's rubbing his knuckles over my shame as he tears open his pants. I moan as I'm already overly sensitive and incredibly turned on. Just being close to him will do that.

"You will not flirt with other men! If they so much as breathe in your direction, you will tell me and I'll take care of things!"

He pushes my panties to the side and his heavy erection on my middle — I realize I'm totally flooded and ready for him.

Traitorous body!

My pelvis rises to meet his friction and I gasp his name.

It almost kills me that he is here, it means a great deal to me!

"You haven't been in touch!" I shout accusingly against his hand.

"Because you have not signed!" And he just thrusts into me, all the way. All the while, his hand is still covering my mouth. Now, I cannot breathe, cannot move, maybe I should stop enjoying and start panicking, but only now can I really let go and let him take control, do with me what he wants. It feels so good, so liberating! I almost forgot how much better equipped he is compared to many other men...and how skilled he is with his cock.

How lucky!

I enjoy every inch of him that I feel inside me.

"OH, GOD!" I gasp as he pulls back and pauses. My eyes are closed with delight, he growls, "Look at me, Olivia!" As I open my eyes, he thrusts into me and...there is no more stopping him.

He fucks me wild and hard, one hand muffles my screams while the other claws at my hip, grabs my knee, and holds it up so he can thrust even deeper. He is rough, unrestrained, simply a force of nature. And already, after a few thrusts, he comes on my mound.

"That stays there!" he orders as he lies on top of me panting and still covering my mouth. "You're mine, Olivia, do you finally understand that?" he asks more gently as he removes his hand from my mouth.

His eyes are calm now, no longer so upset and it's now that I am certain he's here, really here! In my little girl's room, in my parents' home!

"Why are you here?" I ask as I take delight that he has not yet pulled away, still feeling him on top of me, still having him so close to me. I raise my hands and cradle his face, hold it...he lets me.

His expression softens.

"Because you're here," he says hoarsely, leans forward and kisses me. Gently. Not hard. So damn soft.

My pulse feels like the beatings of butterfly wings. I too put all my emotions, my needs, my soul into the kiss. I open myself up to him like I have never done with anyone before. Not even when I was young and stupid — and involved with my ex. We pull apart a bit and he leans his forehead against mine.

"I'll always be where you are." Although it should be scary, it's reassuring. "How do you know where my parents live and that I would be here?"

He grins. "I tracked your phone!"

"Keaton!" I gasp indignantly.

"I won't apologize for it." He kisses me again and my protests stick in my throat. "Say yes, Olivia!"

"To what?"

"To me!"

"But I already have..."

"Only your body, babe." *My heart too, for a while now*...I want to answer but keep those words to myself. It would be too early, it would not be...normal.

But then what is normal?

33. Who Are You?

Keaton

You are still shivering, Olivia, even after we leave your childhood room. It's a pity your posters no longer adorn the walls and your mother turned it into a guestroom. I think you shared a room with one of your siblings. Six children don't sleep in one room, right? Somehow I knew this one had been yours for you didn't make a fuss when I dragged you into it, but rather took it as matter of fact. I hope I've made myself clear to you and that circus monkey down there. Who does he think he is? Since when are you into farmers? I mean, that's exactly how he acts, unsophisticated and stupid. Honestly, that stupid gaze of his, no matter how he presents himself. I've always had an extraordinary talent to look behind peoples' facades. But then I also have my own means for that.

I'm holding your hand as we leave the room, firmly, perhaps I even hurt you a little, but you don't complain. We stop at the top of the staircase before heading down. You look at me from under your endlessly long eyelashes and bite your lip. I want to hear it, Olivia, which you know perfectly well.

"You showing up wasn't right," you say instead. "I...wasn't ready yet..."

"Ready for what, Olivia?" I interrupt. I'm upset you don't see it. "You're mine, you gave yourself completely to me, besides, I told you I wouldn't just let you go anywhere. The last time you ran away, I thought I made it clear to you weren't to do that again, right?"

I love the way your eyebrows pull together as you glare at me. Like I could take your anger seriously when you are so beautiful. "You can't boss me around!" you hiss but don't let go of my hand. You're so conflicted, Olivia.

"I'm simply helping you along," I say. "You want me and I want you — more than anything else. Just give in to me — completely!"

"You didn't get in touch!" you hiss. "All week!"

I smile. "And? Did that bother you?"

"Naturally!"

"There you have it?"

"What?"

"Proof that you want me, that you're busy thinking of me, that you cannot bear my absence. Still, you can't admit that I'm the man with whom you can imagine more. You are too afraid if you open up you'll get hurt." I lean closer to you and your eyes wander to my lips. You want me to kiss you, Olivia, but not now. Later. "Do you think you're the only one with a shitty past who has to overcome themselves to get involved in a new relationship, Olivia? But when it feels right, it feels right." Now you look at my eyes again to see if they betray any doubt, fears, or whatever garbage men rarely show. Naturally, you won't find anything since I simply don't want you to. "Say it."

You swallow. "I..." Restless, you glance back and forth and I know you're not ready yet. Okay, Olivia. I'm a patient man.

"All right." I let it go. "There's plenty of time, we are here for the whole weekend." I start downstairs as I say these words and you're following since you still haven't let go of my hand.

But then you will always follow me. You merely don't know it yet.

* * *

I have to admit, Olivia, your family is charming. I've done my research, familiarized myself with your upbringing. You were the youngest of six siblings, Daddy's Darling, until the age of 16 when you met that son of a bitch your parents didn't like, rightly so, and ran away. But after Riley was born and you had the…accident – let's call it that – you came back to them. Your father owned a workshop and did well for himself. He sold it and now it's your parents' pension. Your mom was always helpful, stood by his side — she's a lioness you rarely see. Although you siblings are scattered all over America, on holidays, your parents' house is filled with people, children, and love. It has warmth, small and cozy. I like it, though it also overwhelms me. Don't worry, Olivia, you may have missed the previous years' Christmases because you simply refused to go back home, but this Christmas, in six months, we will spend it here as a small family.

We are sitting at the table. Danny boy has made some room since I'm still pushing between you. Obviously, he doesn't appreciate my closeness as much as he does yours. Fucker.

Plenty of neighbors show up, the table is full, people are eating, laughing, and talking. Your mother's food is delicious, Olivia, though simple. Of course, everyone unobtrusively checks me out and I'm aware that dressed the way I am, I hardly fit in with the others, though I make an effort to blend in. You love me the way I am and I know you're around, Olivia.

Your father hates me, which I fully understand. After all, considering your track record with men and the way I came here unannounced, he finds me rude and is afraid for his daughter. But he doesn't need to be. You've never been in better hands than mine, Olivia. Your mother is thrilled that you brought your *friend* home. She's probably worrying about you and the way you live all alone. And she's right, Olivia, before me, you were lonely, even with the many people you dealt with on a daily basis.

"It's such a pity your siblings couldn't make it," your mom says. You merely grunt in agreement while keeping your eyes fixed on your plate. Your pouting amuses me, Olivia. Now your mom is looking at me. "I have five other children," she informs me proudly. "Do you have siblings, Keaton?"

I give her my son-in-law smile. "I'm an only child."

"That's so sad!" she says and I can't help but actually like her. "Children need siblings."

"Not all, Mom!" you say and seem embarrassed, for which there is no need. You're part of this woman, meaning, I can only love her too, Olivia. She is warm and sweet. A mother like I always dreamed about when I was a lot younger.

"What do your parents do, Keaton?" your dad asks sullenly, probably expecting an answer that would only strengthen his already made up mind about me. Everyone else is busy, only your family – and this Danny fucker – are looking at me.

"My parents are dead, they died when I was twelve." It's not bad, really, Olivia. Please don't give me that look I feel coming from you. It was a long time ago and I've since made my peace with it. Things happen and they cannot be undone. There's no point dwelling on the past.

Your dad's face somewhat softens — maybe it's remorse, not like he could have known about it. "I'm sorry," he says in his deep voice.

Your mother gasps, startled. "Gosh, that's awful, Keaton! You were so young! I'm so sorry!"

I smile. "It's okay, I coped." Now I feel your hand on my thigh. I would have told you much earlier about my parents demise had I known how tame it makes you, Olivia. I put my hand over yours since I'm your man. Whenever you offer me your hand, I'll grab it.

"I grew up with my aunt in the US and went to school there. When I was old enough, I took over my uncle's former position at the FBI."

I can tell the other people around the table are relieved at the change of subject. That's how it is, Olivia, people don't like to talk about death and dying. You're still holding my hand and I still feel your eyes on me.

"You work at the FBI?" your dad asks.

"That's how I met Olivia." I change the subject again because I'm not allowed to talk about my job, as you know, Olivia. "She's my secretary now." Yes, you may have not yet signed the contract, but you will. And yes, I'm laying the foundation for an alibi because your parents don't need to know my actual intentions when it comes to you.

"That's fabulous!" your mom exclaims. "Olivia, what a wonderful opportunity for you!"

"She has regular working hours," I say and immediately feel you squeeze my hand in an attempt to signal me to stop.

But now Riley speaks up and your hands are tied. "Now Mom always pick me up from school!"

"That's right, little man!" I say with a smile.

"That's funny," Danny growls next to me. "You already seem to get along nicely with the kid." Of course, I didn't miss Riley's reaction when you and Danny first spoke, he made me proud.

"He does," you say and although I'm not looking at you, I clearly hear the smile in your voice.

"He already knows at an early age what's good for him," I say dryly and receive an angry glare from Danny. What, you bastard? Did you think you could simply ambush Olivia and slip her one? The thought drives me crazy and I tense a little, which you notice. You're squeezing my hand again and I exhale forcefully.

"So, you work for the FBI," the pisser starts again. "What are your duties? Making coffee?"

"As I mentioned previously, Olivia is my secretary, which should tell you that I'm in a position where I need help with my busy schedule. Needless to say, there's nothing wrong with making a pot of coffee, no major crime there. Anyone who treats a cleaning lady differently from the boss is worthless in my eyes."

"I'm a machine operator," he says, completely ignoring my last sentence and I make an effort not to burst out laughing.

"Admirable," I comment.

I believe you have had enough and I love how you speak up for me, Liv. "Keaton oversees the whole department. He's his own boss, if you will." You're wonderful, Olivia. Really. You definitely inherited your mother's heart of a lioness.

Now she's laughing delightfully. "I'm so happy for you! You two fit wonderfully together. And here Riley usually doesn't like strangers."

I wink at the kid like we're accomplices, which we kind of are, Olivia.

34. Who Are You? II

Olivia

Who are you, Keaton Rush? I wonder as we leave the house. We want to go for a walk. Keaton wants to see where I grew up. Meanwhile, Riley is helping his grandmother clean up the kitchen and Danny made himself scarce. I didn't like how he challenged Keaton at the table and simply had to get involved! And his condescending way! I did not look down on him because he drives a taxi. Everyone does what they need to do. Stupid putz.

We're strolling down Pinewood Street. It's the street I grew up on. It's warm, much warmer than Chicago even though the cities are pretty close to each other. I'm still wearing my blue summer dress, only had to brush my hair after Keaton's attack earlier. He has changed clothes and is now wearing dark jeans and a simple white shirt. Styled so simply, he looks incredible! I love how his tanned skin stands out and his dark hair shines in the blazing sun.

We walk hand in hand and I look at him. I cannot stop thinking about everything that he revealed. His parents died, he grew up with his aunt, and...he mentioned I wasn't the only one who had a shitty past. It makes me question how he even knows I had a shitty past.

He's aware I'm staring at him and sighs. "Later."

"What?" I ask.

"We'll talk about it later. Right now, I want to focus on our surroundings." He saw right through me! He already knows me better than I thought.

Everything still looks the way it used to. The asphalt glistens in the sun, front gardens are well tended, and now, with summer on the doorstep, buds start to sprout.

"What's up with that Danny guy?" he asks, annoyed, as if it was weighing on him the entire time. "Were you two a couple?"

"No," I say. "I had a crush on him, I admit, but as a teenager, I wasn't all that good looking, so I didn't have a boyfriend. It wasn't until I was 16 when I met Dexter..." I bite my tongue since I actually did not intend to talk about him! Again, I think about what Keaton said – that I want him and I am supposed to engage him, but I won't let it happen. Is he right? Yes, I want him! But I'm also afraid of him! I know there is another side of him, one I haven't yet seen...and I'm insecure about the intense feelings I have for him after such a short period. I want him, skin, hair, and all...no, that's not normal. But we are not normal. My feelings are not normal.

"Is that Riley's dad?" he asks, gesturing straight ahead.

"How would you know?"

"I'm assuming, I don't know for sure." From the side, he gives me a little smile and I melt away. He's incredible, but...before I open up to him, I have to get something off my chest.

"Keaton, you mentioned that I wasn't the only one who had a shitty past. How…do you know?"

He remains completely composed and looks at the neatly lined trees. "Riley is missing a leg. You became a mother at quite a young age, providing my calculation is correct. You're living more practically than comfortably. And you are terribly afraid of getting hurt, the reason you are not fully committed to me. It's not hard to imagine that you've been through some shit."

I swallow. Okay, that makes sense, it really is that obvious! "And...what did you have to go through?"

"We weren't talking about me, this is about you," he reminds me and raises an eyebrow. "So, what's with Dexter?"

I sigh. So far, I've only talked to my parents and Penny about it. What happened was rough and Riley still suffers from it. It shaped us. "He and I had ran away," I say as we walk by the small supermarket where we used to dare each other to go inside and steal things. Whoever made it out unnoticed with the most items was the winner. "I thought I was in love with him. I was only 16 and he was already in college." My gaze is directed on the road ahead and I feel Keaton's hand tightening. He's jealous and possessive, I've noticed that much already. However, for some weird reason, it doesn't bother me, even though such behavior usually annoys me! "My parents didn't approve of our relationship — especially my dad. So, Dexter and I ran away, which was pretty stupid! For a while, we had a wild carefree life, but then I became pregnant and Dexter panicked. He didn't want the child, even wanted me to have an abortion. He had a good future ahead and despite everything, and mind you I had dropped out of high school, he continued his studies. And then...well, I refused and decided to have Riley. From that point on, it got really...nasty. I even tried to get away from him several times, but even though he didn't want me or Riley, he wouldn't let us go. He said having the kid was messing up his future and he certainly would not let me run away!"

"He's a son of a bitch who can be happy he hasn't crossed my path."

I smile. "I'm not telling you this because I want to be protected; I'm telling you this so you know my story."

"But I can?"

"You may, but only because I've found you worthy."

It makes him laugh. I love the sound. He lifts our linked hands and breathes a kiss on the back of mine. "You're too kind."

"Shall I continue?" I ask with one eyebrow raised.

"Absolutely."

"Good, so, I have no idea how many years crept by, but eventually, I couldn't stand it any longer and planned to sneak away during the night. I made it out of the house with Riley – who cried loudly – and onto the street, thinking we were safe..." The memory causes pain. I can recall every second, still hear Riley's screams. My eyes well up. "I should have carried him, but I had my arms full and...and that's why I was holding Riley by the hand, dragging him behind me. Out of nowhere, Dexter came racing at us in the car. He had been drinking and was mad and headed straight at us without slowing down. I didn't react fast enough. It all happened so quickly... Riley's leg was smashed so badly..." Before I can finish speaking, Keaton stops, whirls me around, and squeezes me against his chest. His strong arms wrap around my back and I press my face into the crook of his neck. I'm crying as I relive the terrible incident, where I was unable to protect my son. And because right now, I feel so damn safe like never before. In the middle of the road, in the warm sun, in his arms... Maybe I do belong to him more so than initially suspected.

"You two are safe now," he mumbles into my hair. "Believe me, Olivia, I'm always around. More so than you know."

I'm clawing my way into his shirt and relish letting go of my responsibilities for a while. To drop the facade, not constantly having to be the strong mom, just Olivia, who went through a lot of crap.

* * *

A while later, we're sitting on the half-pipe where I spent my childhood summers. It's a warm pleasant day and I eat ice cream while Keaton watches me. A few teenagers are still skateboarding by the time the sun starts to set. I feel so good, so comfortable and at ease, I never thought it possible. I show Keaton the school I attended and we fooled around in the schoolyard like teenagers. I show him the parking lot in which I lost my virginity after attending the winter ball, to which he pushes me against some stranger's car and takes me. It's fascinating how I can dismiss the imminent danger of people catching us when he's with me and somehow mesmerizes me! Although the sex is quick, it is terrific!

We buy an ice cream at the ice cream parlor in which I worked two summers to earn pocket money so I could buy a new bicycle and now we're sitting at the skateboarding park.

"I like your town," he says.

"Yep." I leisurely lick my vanilla ice cream.

Dryly, Keaton remarks, "If you continue to lick that ice cream so longingly, I'll fuck you right here in front of that wannabe badass." I swallow wrong at his statement and gasp. Oh my God, only he can manage to make me blush beet red within a few seconds.

"How am I supposed to lick it?" I ask as I look at him, puzzled and bright red.

He grins. "You have a point, no matter how you lick it, it'll turn me on." He casually puts an arm around me. I continue enjoying my ice cream and feel so good, so good, I believe he's right — I am already opening up to him more.

"Now that I've told you about the worst chapter of my life," I cautiously start and nibble on my waffle cone.

"You want to know what about my past?"

"YES!"

He sighs and runs a hand through his hair, which no one but Mr. Rush can make look so sexy. "But one should leave the past alone."

"But I want to know!"

"But I don't want to talk about it," he informs me a bossy tone.

"Don't you trust me?" I ask, pouting.

"Do you trust me?"

"Obviously."

He stares at me for a while before he rolls his eyes. "Okay, what do you want to know?"

I ponder for a while because this is *the* opportunity to look behind his hard facade, the one he rarely drops. "How you grew up, what happened to your parents...any previous women."

"Obviously, previous women," he mumbles, smirking. Oh, yeah! I've often wondered how many he had before me and if there was one who managed to break his heart.

"As you already know..." his face is unreadable, which is okay, I listen for I know how it is to fight one's demons, "...my parents died when I was twelve. Before they died, my childhood was...well, it cannot be compared to yours. Back in England, we had a huge mansion and servants. My dad always drove the newest cars. Everything was quite..."

"Superficial and cold?"

He doesn't seem to mind that I interrupt him. "Correct. My mother was especially cold, whereas my dad shined with absence. They died in a fire when I was twelve."

"In a fire?" I ask wide-eyed for that and drowning, I consider the worst ways to leave this life. How horrible it must have been for young Keaton, how hurt and confused he must have felt! I would like to hold his hand, but I won't right now since it's the wrong time to show pity, I know that much by now. Instead, I throw the rest of my ice cream in the trash located next to the half-pipe and look at him. His mind seems far away while his eyes are fixed on a point off in the distance. He has suffered much and it made him the man he is now.

"I wanted to make hot chocolate. It was December, shortly before Christmas. We had an old gas stove. Since the milk always spilled, I left the kitchen towel near the stove to wipe the pot. Then a friend of mine showed up and insisted I come outside because he wanted to show me something. I was 12 and a pisser, immediately forgot about the stove, the kitchen towel, the hot chocolate, and went outside without telling anyone. Not 10 minutes later, the entire house was engulfed in flames." He falls silent for a moment. I feel like crying. Such a tragedy! Such torment! All that guilt he has to live with day in, day out, weighing him down. "I heard their screams, it all went so fast. I tried to go into the house but my buddy held me back. Then the firefighters arrived. I was in shock...my parents didn't make it out alive. The mansion went up in flames within a matter of minutes. They were in the bedroom and office on the third floor."

"Keaton," I whisper and reach for his hand whether he likes it or not. "That is...that is incredible." I hold his stiff fingers in mine while he avoids eye contact, not wanting me to see his weakness. Yes, we have similarities. I'm quite familiar with those sentiments: guilt, fear, pride, and blame. "It's not your fault, you know that, right?"

He laughs wryly. "Who's would it be? It was my stupidity that killed my parents."

"I can sympathize only too well. I've often blamed myself and questioned why I didn't end up under the car instead of him. Questioned why I didn't press charges instead of running away to another city. But it doesn't help. Like you said, you cannot change the past."

"I've come to terms with it," he says and looks at me. Directly into my eyes. He feels connected to me, like I am to him. We have similar pasts, albeit we suffered in different ways. "That's when I came to the US and grew up with my aunt and uncle. It was not easy with them — she was a bitch, he a former soldier. But I prevailed and still alive. They provided for me and drilled into me to strive for more than I am. They taught me discipline and to never give in to my emotions, no matter how bad they may be. I owe them a lot."

I try to cheer him up. "We should visit them."

A lazy smile dashed across his full beautiful lips. "Yes, we should."

I lean on his shoulder and we remain quiet for a while, only the sound of tires rolling on asphalt and the wind rustling the leaves is heard, while the setting sun shines through here and there.

Since I'm a simpleton, I blurt out the next thing on my mind: "So, what about other women?"

He laughs in my hair and I feel relieved to hear that sound again. It's so reassuring. So exhilarating. So wonderful. "There were many. Jeanette was the name of the one who took my virginity at fourteen. Then there was Mara, who I manage to persuade to give me a blowjob every other morning, or Paula and Janine with whom I had my first threesome. Later on, there were oh-so-many more women." I feel like backing away from him, considering how openly he talks about them without feeling ashamed, ha! But then he chuckles again and his breath touches my skin. "But none were like you. No one will ever be like you."

My heart makes a joyous leaps and I'm smiling on the inside. "That's good, mister."

35. State of Shock

Olivia

Keaton is quite easy going. We are all aware that he's used to much better things, yet he doesn't complain about the small kitchen or relatively narrow beds. Four-by-six is too small for someone like Mr. Rush.

Since we shared so much yesterday and he met my family, I feel even more comfortable by his side. It's so easy, so simple and straightforward. Granted, my father has a problem with him, probably because he's dating me. But my mom constantly mentions how great we fit together and Riley uses any opportunity to make contact with Keaton — be it in the garden or while watching TV or having breakfast. I love seeing how patient Keaton is with Riley and how he answers every one of his questions.

Keaton, have you ever seen a UFO?

No, little one.

Keaton, do elephants taste their boogers when they drink?

Keaton, why are you so tall?

Keaton, why, why, why?

It's wonderful to see Riley flourishing. My parents' place is a real kid's paradise. Again and again, I throw Keaton furtive glances while I dream of being alone with him all the time and feel, smell, and taste him. But seeing the healing influence he has on my son trumps all.

After dinner, we decide to check out the town fair. Every now and then, the townsfolk find a reason to celebrate, even if it's not the 4th of July or Christmas. My parents are tired, but Riley is excited to go with Keaton and me.

Since the evenings are still a bit cool, I bundle Riley up in a hoodie and myself in long thin black sweater and tights. And Keaton...I have to sigh when I look at him. He's wearing black jeans, a black shirt, and a leather jacket. His hair is slicked back and he looks like the devil in angelic form.

As I'm coming down the stairs with Riley, he smiles. "All ready?"

"ALL READY!" Riley shouts back. I'm sure he would have jumped down the last three steps, if he had two whole legs.

"Don't come home too late!" Mom calls from the kitchen like she did when I was a kid; my dad mumbles something I cannot make out.

We wish them a nice evening and step outside. The sun has already set, but in our little town, even the nights are idyllic. The crickets are chirping and the warm yellow glow of street lamps illuminates our path. There are hardly any cars are on the road at this time of day, not even on a Saturday night. Riley is walking on his crutches between us as we head toward the fair grounds and I marvel at how familiar it feels.

The fair is not comparable to the ones in Chicago, New York, or wherever, it's simply a small village affair, where teenagers make-out in dark corners, small children enjoy cotton candy, and adult couples complain about the uncouth youth. It only takes 10 minutes to take in all the sights. A Ferris wheel slowly turns and there are lots of stalls where you can win or pull cuddly toys out of glass-enclosed machines and many attractions where moderators loudly announce the starts of new rides over PA systems.

"I've never cared for this," Keaton says as he glances around.

I grin and wink at Riley. "That's because you've never been to a town fair with us!"

The aroma of roasted almonds hangs in the air and I smell cotton candy. Hearing the laughter makes me smile and I rest my cheek on Keaton's arm. Naturally, Riley heads directly for the target-shooting stall. Keaton follows him patiently and shows off his marksman skills, the little macho! Every one of his shots hits. Spectators are astonished. Keaton, however, only smiles confidently, the sexy bastard... Riley is taken by him and overly joyful when Keaton gets him a big plush Superman. Of course, I get stuck carrying it, not only because of Riley's crutches, but also because the little man has much better things to do.

We enjoy cotton candy, Riley and I. Mine is pink. Mr. Rush rolls his eyes and informs me how unhealthy it is and that I might as well pour sugar straight down my throat, all of which doesn't discourage me from rolling a bit on my finger and tapping it on the tip of his nose.

His eyes sparkle ominously and I grin sassily — what can he do in front of Riley? Punish me? Most unlikely!

It is a fantastic evening, really. I feel free and...like the three of us are a real small cotton candy family. I love the idea and don't want to think about the future, just enjoy the here and now.

Finally, Riley talks us into going on the Ferris wheel. The line is long and we might have to wait for a while before we get our tickets.

"Mom, I'm bored," Riley whines after 30 seconds of waiting.

"I thought you wanted to go on the Ferris wheel!"

"But I don't want to wait!"

I sigh. "So, you want something but are not willing to do something for it."

"The American dream," Keaton whispers, I laugh.

"Can I buy almonds over there?" he asks excitedly. I gauge the distance to the booth selling almonds and decide it is close enough. I'll have a clear view of Riley, besides, we're in Fort Wayne. All of us here practically grew up together.

"Okay," I say and Keaton pushes five bucks into the kid's hand.

"You want me to follow?" he asks as we watch Riley hobble on his crutches.

"No," I say. "It's good for him and it increases his self-confidence to be independent."

"Wow. You're one of those educating mothers. Mine was like that."

I roll my eyes. "No, I'm not!" To punish him for saying this, I put more cotton candy on his nose. I still haven't finished mine, although Riley has. I already know who will have a bellyache later, but that's not so bad. It's more important for him to have a good time!

"Yes you are and I think it's hot." He puts his index finger under my chin and slightly lifts it. My heart flutters as he leans closer in an attempt to kiss me. Keaton being lower now allows me to look over his shoulder and...I abruptly freeze. At first, Keaton doesn't notice anything, but I'm completely stiff as his lips brush over mine. It's not until I drop the plush superman as well as whatever is left of my cotton candy, Keaton notices something is wrong.

"Olivia?" he asks and grabs my shoulders. I'm staring past Keaton and he turns around to follow my gaze.

I'm staring at Riley with a kneeling Dexter in front of him, who's talking to him.

* * *

Keaton

It takes a few seconds until I've grasped the situation and I'm instantly furious on the inside. I know who that is from the research I've done about you, Olivia.

That ash-blond guy in a lumberjack shirt who is kneeling in front of Riley, talking to him stupidly, is Dexter, the mutt.

"It's him, right?" I growl, merely for you to confirm. And you manage to nod. I've never seen you like this before nor will I ever again, Olivia. You're trembling, pale, fear plainly in your eyes. From now on, you will never have to be afraid again.

I break away and start marching, leaving you standing there. I'm angry, downright furious, and ready to kill somebody. The anger pumping through my veins like poison becomes unbearable. Nevertheless, I won't lose control in front of Riley, scaring him. He shouldn't think all men are assholes like his father.

Riley knows who's kneeling in front of him. It didn't happen all that long ago for him to already have suppressed his dad. I see his fear-widened eyes and that he's as tense as you are. He's holding his crutches as if at any moment, he's about to slam them over the man's head.

I observe all this in the few seconds it takes me to get to Riley and clearly see the relief in his eyes when I am next to him, calming me. In one quick move, though carefully executed because of his crutches, I push him aside and place myself between him and his biological father.

"Hey, pal," I say to the jerk, who is slowly standing up. He is disgusting, Olivia. I cannot believe you associated with scum like him. He reeks of beer, has a potbelly hanging over the belt of his jeans, his face is barely visible with all that blond facial hair. His eyes resemble small buttons and his skin is unclean. Riley doesn't look anything like him and whoever says so, needs to have their eyesight checked. Talk about an insult.

"Who the hell are you, calling me pal?" he asks, chuckling. I forcefully exhale.

"Riley," I say without taking my eyes off the bum. "Go to your mom, I'll take care of this." I know he understands me. I'm John again, here to protect him. He knows that, Olivia, he's smart. He leaves and I watch him until he's with you, finally pulling you out of your trance. You fall to your knees and embrace him, tightly press him against you as if someone would come at any moment to take him away from you. But you are safe, so I turn my attention back to the scum.

He noticed me looking in your direction and immediately taunts me. "Lookie-here...you must be her new beau, eh? I knows she has a super pussy and all that, but you gonna end up with a cripple, man! No idea what that bitch told you, but she's a filthy slut!"

God, Olivia. If it weren't for Riley, I'd ram the bridge of his nose up into his brain. I know all the moves and techniques to take someone out within seconds. He deserves to be taken out. No, that would be too lenient. I'll take care of him later when I can punish him properly.

Not now.

Not in front of Riley.

Or in front of you.

"Listen up, you little degenerate bastard," I whispered close to his stinking greasy face, while jamming my gun through my leather jacket against his ribs. You may not know it, Olivia, but I'm always carrying. There are too many sick people in this world.

He feels the barrel and immediately blanches.

"If I hear you talk bad about Riley or Olivia again, make inquiries or stalk them, I will end your miserable existence." I look deep into his little piggy eyes and see fear in them while sweat drips down his temples. And, sure enough, he does the stupid thing and continues talking. But then stupid people like Danny or Penny talk a lot, Olivia.

"You're risking your life for *her*? Did she let you do her in the ass or what?"

Again, I forcefully poke the barrel against his waist, he gasps, and takes a couple of steps back. "I won't have to face repercussions, my friend. I'm an FBI agent and then some. I'll simply make you disappear, bones, teeth, and all, do you understand me?" He turns pale, squints, and glares at me, his manly pride hurt. "Take one wrong step or say the wrong word – I will know every move you make! – and you're history, you disgusting piece of shit." I shove him away, but...the guy has balls, Olivia, I have to give him that. He snorts, charges me like a wild bull, and takes a swing at me. However, I'm sober and faster and quickly ram my fist into his nose.

"KEATON, NO!" You shout, trying to interfere, but dammit, Olivia, stay out of it! Please! Now you're pulling on my arm and he's trying to get a hold of you — I free myself and knock the jerk unconscious.

Breathing heavily, I glance around.

The music stopped – so typical for a small town – and the people are staring at us as sirens approach. Wow, they are fast!

It doesn't worry me, Olivia, I merely want to see you two safe.

You're crying and Riley is looking over from the Ferris wheel, obviously frightened. "Are you okay?" I ask you, you nod and cry at the same time. I'm pumped up on adrenaline, Olivia, I'm sorry I'm so unsympathetic. My brain is set to practical mode at the moment.

"Come here," I say to Riley, he doesn't hesitate and makes me proud. He hobbles over and I take you both in my arms.

I don't give a damn.

All that matters is your well-being.

36. 100 Percent

Olivia

We are back at my parent's house and I'm glad they are asleep. Dad might grab his shotgun and immediately run off and Mom would start to weep while holding Riley, making him even more worried, were they to hear about the incident.

I'm carrying Riley's Superman and crutches while Keaton is carrying him. He fell asleep in his arms. We go quietly up the stairs to my old room and Keaton puts Riley in my old bed. I want him with me tonight since I was worried about him today. I don't want to sleep without feeling Riley. I gently take off his shoes and jeans and push Superman against his side before I cover him. I sit on the edge of the bed knowing Keaton is behind me. I can feel him and I am glad he showed up here today. Earlier, I actually witnessed how powerful he is. The police didn't even question him. He flashed his badge as soon as the two cocky policemen strutted over and they immediately fell in line, almost saluting him. Keaton simply explained in judicial gibberish what happened (I didn't understand any of it) — they politely said goodbye to Keaton and dragged Dexter to their patrol car.

My heart is finally beating less furiously as I brush my knuckles over Riley's cheek. He is so beautiful, so fragile. What would I do if someone to took him away from me? Or if Dexter had another tantrum and ended up hurting him? I would never be happy again. He already turned Riley's whole life upside down and changed it forever. I will not let that happen ever again. Not as long as I'm alive.

I feel the mattress give a little as Keaton sits behind me and places his chin on my shoulder. There are more and more incidences where he drops the emotional distance he puts between us and simply hugs me. He's gentle with me... I smell his scent and feel his breath while we watch Riley sleep.

"Thanks," I whisper and squeeze the hand that is wrapped around my stomach.

He kisses my neck. "Always."

I cling tightly to him and his closeness reassures me. It's so wonderful to have him here, to feel safe, and relaxed.

"I think now is a good time to tell you something," he whispers. The room is only illuminated by the moonlight, which makes Riley's face appear paler than it is.

I might joke around if I weren't so upset, perhaps now he'll finally admit a flaw because he is too perfect. I don't care if he's a contract killer or associated with the Russian mafia. I'll keep quiet.

"I did something for Riley without first informing you."

Now I stiffen a bit and try to break away to face him, but he holds me tighter, so I ask, "What is it?"

"There's a prestigious clinic in New York. It only accepts private patients. I explained Riley's situation and managed to get him a room. He'll be staying there during summer vacation. You can accompany him for the duration of his stay if you like or I can hire someone to look after Riley, whatever you wish. He could get a professional prosthesis, followed by physiotherapy and training so he can walk and do everyday things without limitation." Funny, but the first thing that comes to mind as he tells me this is that I have a sister in New York. Only then do I slowly catch the meaning of his words.

"Keaton, I cannot afford that!"

Now he finally lets me move to face him and I gaze into his soft beautiful eyes. He opens himself up to me — so who would I be if I were not to do likewise?

"I know, baby." He gently cups my chin and smiles. "That's why I'll take care of it. No protesting. You owe me nothing. I do this for Riley so he can do without the crutches and be a kid, if that's possible."

Suddenly, my eyes well up and my vision blurs. I sob for nobody has ever even hinted at doing this for me or Riley. Nobody has even paid us that much attention. And no one has ever shown so much interest in our well-being.

He continues wiping the tears from my cheeks while I swallow the lumps in my throat.

Now he laughs. "Does that mean you are okay with it?"

I only nod as a new barrage of tears roll down my cheeks and he kisses my wet lips.

"Thank you," I breathe shakily.

"Always."

And in that moment, I say it because it comes straight from my heart to my tongue. "I'm yours, Keaton Rush. One hundred percent."

He tilts his head with my face in his hands. "You're sure? I'm a bit psycho."

I have to laugh again. "Who said we're normal?"

His thumb strokes my lip. "Well, we certainly are not."

* * *

The next day after breakfast, we say goodbye to my parents. I feel a bit melancholy, but I remind myself of the circus with Dexter and quickly get over it. I promise Mom to call more often and Dad that I will take care of myself. Riley is showered with sweets, seemingly over yesterday's incident. This morning, when I asked him if he wanted to talk about it, he said no. Of course, I know I'll have address the incident at some point, I don't want him repressing things and bottling them up in his subconscious mind to later hinder him in everyday life.

As we're driving down the road in Keaton's car and the town sign grows increasingly smaller in the rearview mirror, I breathe a sigh of relief and he reaches for my hand. The way he sits behind the wheel of this luxurious car with his sunglasses on is so sexy! I squeeze the fingers that lie on mine before I look ahead.

Ahead to a whole new future for Keaton and me, far away from the old painful past.

See us as a small cotton candy family.

37. The Real You

Olivia

The trip was relatively uneventful. I've completely forgotten how nice it is to have my ass chauffeured around. To not be bound by departure times. To simply sit back and relax, assured that I'll make it home safely. It is...nice.

Like the whole weekend with Keaton Rush.

It's almost too good to be true.

I'm already a little scared of what will happen once we arrive home. Will the bubble around us suddenly burst and I'll land hard in reality? Will he distance himself from me again? And I from him?

Riley is still fast asleep when we reach Chicago in the late evening.

Every now and then, I think about Dexter, how helpless I felt, like being catapulted back into a past, which I hate. I turned into the old Liv, which I promised myself I'd never do, the one who stands idly by. He had not forgotten about me after all, which, honestly, scared the crap out of me. What if he gets it in his head that he actually wants us back? What if he comes to Chicago — and Keaton is not around?

"Here we are," he says far too early.

I don't want to part with him, but not only because I feel so safe with him. Also for other reasons — much, much more riling reasons.

"Yes." I know I should get out now — but I'm not moving an inch.

Neither does Keaton.

I swallow...it sounds unnaturally loud between us.

"So..." I say. He just looks at me with one eyebrow raised.

"Yes?" he asks with a gentle smile and turns my face toward him.

"I should go." He brushes his thumb over my lip while still holding my chin.

"You should," he whispers, leans forward, and kisses my neck, right under my ear where it drives me insane. I moan softly.

"But I don't want to!" I whimper like a schoolgirl and feel his grin on my skin.

"Why?" he teases, leans back, and looks me directly in the eyes so that I lose myself in his bottomless depths.

Dammit!

The man is already getting too much under my skin, it's like I'm obsessed with him — but I can't nor want to do anything about it. I don't feel like fighting anymore, I only want to let go for once in my life. I raise my hand and place it against his cheek. It's still unfamiliar to only touch him. At times, he exudes such danger, I think I'm stroking a wild lion, a hungry wild lion ready to pounce at the right opportunity. But Keaton doesn't attack and devour me. He doesn't move, only his gaze softens a bit. I cradle his cheek, stroke his silky hair, and let the strands run through my fingers. I love touching him... Then I gather all my courage and come out and ask, "Would you like to stay the night?" Fuck it! FUCK IT ALL!

I'm rewarded for being courageous because he turns his face, kisses my palm as he holds the hand in his, then takes a deep breath and looks at me damningly stirring from under his forbiddingly long eyelashes. He says, "Always!"

And that settles it.

***

He seems so out of place in my apartment, just as he did in my parents' dining room. He looks like he belongs in another world, though the picture of him carrying Riley into our apartment is just right. Keaton treats him so unspeakably sweet — even I cannot believe it at times.

Because usually he's direct, cool, and controlled, only with my son does he let his guard down and is downright loving, patient, and quite funny. I find men who are good with children incredibly attractive, but Keaton Rush takes it beyond normal limits. As he places Riley in bed and covers him, I feel like jumping him, but I restrain myself and continue leaning against the doorway, watching the gentle smile on his face. It makes it – as if it is possible – even more beautiful. He seems to feel my eyes on him and raises his, grins at me — again like a lion about to pounce. He walks over to me, buries his hands in my hair, and kissing me, pushes me out of the room against the wall beside my door.

"You have no idea how long I have wanted this!" he mumbles against my lips. I wonder what exactly he means by it.

Being close to me again?

Kissing me?

Being with me in my apartment?

Like a...family?

I couldn't even begin to hazard a guess, especially since he's kissing me senseless. Then, he suddenly pushes away and says, "I'll go get my things out of the car."

He leaves me standing there with swollen lips, completely dizzy — and a stupid grin on my face.

***

We eat microwave macaroni from plastic bowls while we sit on my little couch and watch TV, an episode of *How I Met Your Mother*, and drink cola directly from the can. I love that.

He's so easy-going — though at first glance, he seems quite unreadable and uptight. We talk about the weekend while avoiding the Dexter incident. He does not push me, except to fully engage with him. And I'm glad I did, I'm glad I let him into my world and opened up to him. And now I want to know EVERYTHING about him.

I think about how to phrase it and if I might be too demanding after just such short time, but then for us appearances are unimportant. We value other things... It is irrelevant how a normal relationship SHOULD function. We are not normal, as he already stated numerous times and I have to agree with him. At least, what I feel for him can't be considered normal.

I take my last bite — no longer interested in eating and set his bowl aside as soon as he's finished. He frowns as I sit sideways on his lap – which still requires lots of courage from me – and raises an eyebrow. But his arms snake naturally around me and hold me tight while I trace with my index finger through his thin sweater between his pectoral muscles.

"Keaton..." I mumble, making certain I keep my eyes on my finger and not his stirring eyes.

"Yes, Olivia?" he asks, amused as always.

Ass...

Hot ass.

My ass!

"This weekend I opened up for you, *completely*. I told you who I am, who I want to be, my desires, my dreams, and...I realize that I know pretty much nothing about you." His whole body stiffens and he doesn't say anything. He seems expectant and I force myself to look up — in his eyes. "I would like to know more about you. Who you are, the real you."

He remains silent.

He just looks at me.

A cheek twitches.

He doesn't like it.

Crap!

Have I ruined it all now, was I too hasty? Did I push him too hard?

"I told you all about my past, Olivia."

"Yet I feel I have merely scratched the surface."

He raises an eyebrow. I become SO nervous but keep on talking. "I feel like you're...playing a role. A perfect role, especially tailored for me, but no one can be that perfect. Everyone has skeletons in their closet, you know about mine. You know about my dark times and I have no idea about yours."

I know he *has* some. I can see it in his eyes right now. I was always feeling it. There's so much more that I need to find out about Keaton Rush.

"You really want that, Olivia?" he replies after a few

seconds of silence, sounding... uneasy. He swallows, his eyes are hard and relentless — but he does not turn from my gaze.

"Yes." I don't have to think any longer about it. I'm not scared. There's nothing the man could say that would drive me away and I already know deep down that I will hear some heavy stuff.

But I'm ready.

"Good," he finally says curtly and harshly. He doesn't like it. Not one bit. But he will open up to me — for me.

"Keaton..." I cradle his face in my palms as if it were something excessively precious.

"Huh?' he snorts, annoyed.

"You know you cannot drive me away."

"H'm..." He stares pass me.

"No matter what, I belong to you, one hundred percent, remember?" His looks at me, his gaze flickers. Right then, I would like to tell him what I REALLY feel. I would like to tell him that I've fallen in love with him, maybe even already love him. He has given me no other choice — you can only fall head over heels for a man like Keaton Rush. He is perfect. For me — and my son. He wants to give Riley a new future! Ever since he said that to me, I have one thing on my mind. I LOVE YOU, KEATON RUSH! Even my inner voice screams loudly in agreement. I have never been so sure about anything in the world. Nevertheless, I fight hard to keep myself restrained. He would really think I'd gone crazy! "And I love belonging to you," I say instead. It's a fairly acceptable, slightly modified version of the emotions currently raging inside me. Now his gaze actually clears – like clouds drifting away to reveal a bright blue sky – and he smiles.

"Say that again!" he demands and is no longer hard and aloof. Thank God.

I lean forward and oh-so-gently brush my lips over his. "I love being yours," I breathe in his mouth. His arms tighten around me...

"Again!" he orders and his breath is my breath...

"I love..." I don't get any farther because he whirls me around, bends over, and kisses me.

Kisses me with everything he has.

And I kiss him back with everything I have.

38. Dark Side

Keaton

I'm nervous, Olivia.

This was not how I planned it.

But when does a plan with you ever work out?

Since Riley has no school on Monday, I give us the day off and we spend it...well, like a family.

"Cotton candy family," you mumbled in your sleep today and I grin. Lying here, I watch you, bathing in the happiness that overcomes me every time you lie in front of me and smile softly, like just now. I could watch you for hours, Olivia. I don't think that will ever change.

I make pancakes for Riley and you — you love them. Of course you do because you love whatever I do for the little one. Afterward, we go for a stroll in the park with your drooling monster. I pick up Riley on my shoulders when I realize he's exhausted, you almost start to cry. But then you are a little crybaby, Olivia, though I wouldn't want it any other way. You are emotional, temperamental, and are full of fire.

The fire to my ice.

Riley could not be more proud when he suddenly is towering above everyone else and the other kids look up at him. We have lunch at the diner you used to work at — you miss your regulars and proudly introduce me to everyone as your friend. You regard me cautiously from the side the first time you do it, but when I only react, smiling amused, you turn a brilliant red and from that moment, glow like the sun in persona.

I'll do anything for that glow. I'm addicted to it.

You talk to your former patrons, the tottery old men that can't get enough of your ass, babe, but it'll be me who's going to spank it later on — and much more.

Thinking about our upcoming trip tonight makes me all tingly. I can hardly stand it, but then I'm not sure if you're ready yet. Yes, I know, you have a dark wicked side, Olivia. But there's a difference between darkness and absolute blackness.

I intend to lure you there.

Either it'll be a revelation for you.

Or you'll run away.

I've never been gone this far with a woman.

I've always had meaningless one-night stands without

even considering what a woman might think of my preferences. Or of my nightly undertakings, *my* blackest side. Would seeing what I'm really capable of, scare her?

But with you I consider it.

With you, I am nervous.

You make me feel like a little boy, Olivia.

I feel uncertain, quite unlike myself.

You throw me off course, baby. You have no idea how much.

When we're back in your home, I tell you to arrange for your terrible girlfriend to babysit Riley tonight and excuse myself. I still need to get a few things for you, you want to go with me, never want to be separated from me again — I can see it in your eyes.

But there are things a man has to do alone, Olivia.

Right now is one of them.

You accept it because you're already asking yourself if you want too much of me.

Olivia.

Even everything would not be too much.

I would marry you on the spot if you so desire.

I would give you five more children and fulfill your most secret dream of a big family if you so desire.

I'd move to the damn North Pole with you if you were to ask that of me — regardless that I cannot stand the cold.

For there is one thing I know as sure as the sun rises every day.

You are *everything* to me.

The one who touched my heart, the one who possesses it now — and I cannot do anything about it. But honestly, I no longer want to.

My heart belongs to you, Olivia.

And you can keep it — I have no need for it without you anyway.

***

Olivia

Riley is upstairs at Penny's. It's already dark — I'm waiting for Keaton to return to me.

He said he needs to show me who he really is.

That he cannot explain it to me.

What is he going to show me?

I'm so excited I cannot sit still, pacing back and forth in my apartment. I give the already sparkling kitchen another cleaning and drink a glass of water. Then I think it would be nice to talk to Penny about it — a serious talk. But I cannot do that because, for some reason, Penny really doesn't like Keaton. Earlier, when I told her that Keaton showed up at my parents unannounced and that we spent an incredible weekend together, she raised her eyebrows and her expression said it all. *He shows up uninvited? How does he know where you are? That's similar to stalking, right? Does he still give you room to breathe, Liv?* But she didn't say any of it, which I give her credit for. It's never been easy for Penny to keep her opinion to herself — but I love that about her. And I won't justify Keaton to her. I know it's right. I really don't care what everyone else thinks.

I know I want him and he too belongs to me just as I belong to him.

That's all that counts.

And yet I am a nervous wreck.

What will he do to me tonight?

Where will he take me?

I know he has a really dark fucked-up side to him, I just don't know to what extent.

I've read too many books!

Seen too many movies!

My vivid imagination does the rest.

During the day he's a shrewd FBI agent, by night an ice-cold hitman?

Is he like Fifty and has a game room?

Is he a member of a secret sect?

Is he a secret agent?

A freemason?

Damn Dan Brown! Honestly!

I called him three times in as many hours.

Call number one went like this.

"Olivia?"

"Keaton! Tell me where we're going!"

"Not a chance, babe!"

(I pouted) "Okay."

"Be patient."

"Yeah, yeah."

"You know what that means, Olivia."

"Well, you're not here to lick my ass."

"You'd like that."

"Yes, I would."

"You are a slut."

"And you love it."

"I do, baby. Now hang up. I have to go."

"Okay..." I did not hang up and continued to sulk until he struck a harsher tone.

"Olivia, I..."

"All right already!"

Then I hung up.

Just to call him back half an hour later.

"Olivia?"

"I have no idea what to wear!" It sounded more than reproachful and I could *almost feel* him rolling his eyes.

"Let me worry about that."

"But…"

"Olivia!"

"OKAY!" I hang up. The phone immediately rang and I answered guiltily, "Yes?"

"If you hang up on me again, Olivia Pierson, I'll put you over my knee first thing when I get back and that is not an empty threat!"

Oh, wow. Imagining it makes me wet.

"You're turned on right now, aren't you?" He sighs.

"Yes," I admitted. He laughs hoarsely and quietly, which

only turns me on more.

"OH, we fit well together."

"Do we?"

"Yes. You may hang up now."

"But…"

"HANG UP!"

I hang up...and called him back an hour later.

"Olivia?" Now he sounded slightly annoyed and out of breath. What was the man doing?

"When are you coming?"

"Soon."

"Soon means what?"

"Not much longer!"

"You're so cryptic!"

"And you're damn nosy!"

"Yeah, so!"

"Patience is a virtue, baby."

"Pff..."

"I'll be there in half an hour and you better be naked, shaved, and horny. See you soon."

That takes the wind out of my sails, but when I say something else, all I hear is static.

I am so shocked I do not call again.

***

I undress when the half hour is almost over — I actually wanted to rebel by putting on extra layers of winter clothes, but instinct tells me I should tease Keaton only slightly. My telephone terror must have accomplished that.

I sit completely naked on my couch — overcome by a strange feeling...and wait...

***

He has arrived at my place and seems changed. Like when I first met him.

Closed off.

Cool and distant.

"Hi," I say while keeping my naked body behind the door in case anyone walks down the hallway. He raises a brow.

"Hi," he says as he walks by me.

I don't dare touch him as he passes with his hair soaked from the rain and his wonderful scent hitting me. He's carrying a bag that he sets down on the coffee table, then he sits down on the couch and spreads his arms over the back like a king before his subjects.

He tilts his head and stares at me as I stand chewing my lip in front of the closed door, clueless what I should do next.

He's enjoying himself.

Making me nervous.

And he's hard — as I can clearly see.

It's the only visible reaction to my nudity.

"Put that on." He nods to the bag. I approach it slowly and pull out a...red trench coat that matches the red lipstick perfectly that he gave me recently. It looks beautiful and I can already tell it'll fit like a glove. The next item in the bag is a small package — containing a garter belt. I turn bright red as I look at him.

His gaze is challenging and betrays his impatience.

I double-check the bag to be sure, but yeah, these two items are it. "That's it?"

"Add the lipstick and high heels that I gave you recently."

FUCK!

"I don't have all night, Olivia!" he urges me relentlessly.

What happened to the sweet funny man who I just spoke with?

He has been replaced...

By Mister *I'm-so-hot-when-I'm-so-ice-cold* Rush.

I swallow and my heart pounds wildly as I do as ordered. Since I also want to break through his reserve, I place my foot on his knee and pull up the naughty dark stockings. Not one muscle twitches even though he can see perfectly between my legs how hot the situation is making me. Madness. And he hasn't even touched me yet!

I slip on the stockings and high heels. Then I traipse, ass swaying to the bathroom while happily noting his eyes are glued to my butt. I take my time putting on the red lipstick. I'm tempted to put on some other makeup, though I'm too chicken when he's in this kind of mood. So unpredictable. Yes, that's how he is right now.

I return and he still in the same position.

"Stand in front of me," he says and looks at my pussy. I do it... "Now turn around." I feel like a piece of meat when I do it and love it. Yes, I'm a whore, his whore! And I enjoy it fully.

"Good! Now put on the coat." I do as I'm told and cinch the belt around my waist.

"Come here," he orders and I think he wants to look at me again, but as soon as I'm within reach, he yanks me onto his lap and his eyes and face are close...so close.

"I give you one more chance to say no. But if you say no now, Olivia, then that is it." WHAT?

I didn't expect that. That's not fair!

"Yes, baby, I know it's not fair. Don't look at me like that!" He cups my face and strokes my cheek with his thumb. "But that's how I operate. All or nothing. One hundred percent, Olivia."

"One hundred percent!" I say oh-so-softly and timidly, which is quite unlike me, and shiver at the same time. I sense what I'm getting myself into, at least, deep down...and notice I'm a little scared. But who wouldn't be, right?

"So you'll trust me implicitly and do whatever I say?" He asks and I nod.

"Say it, Olivia. I have to hear it. Say, *I will trust you implicitly, Keaton Rush. And I'll do whatever you say*."

"I will trust you implicitly, Keaton Rush. And I will do whatever you say," I repeat breathlessly, feeling as if we were in front of the altar and I'm repeating the priest's words, though what he intends to do with me will be anything but holy. My outfit speaks volumes.

"In return, I promise to never ask anything of you for which you're not ready, Olivia Pierson. I promise to always respect and protect you even if at first, it may not appear so." This scares me more than anything else he has said so far. His gaze darkens as he leans forward and whispers in my ear,

"Yes, baby, you can be scared...actually, you should be. I love it." Cold, I shiver while, at the same time, his hand moves up and cups my pussy. Which is already wet thanks to our conversation. "I love that you're so courageous, Olivia..." He inserts two fingers inside me, bends them upward, and gently massages my G spot, making me gasp... I throw my head back and he kisses my throat. "Only those who are courageous get what they desire deep down, baby."

"God, Keaton!"

"I know what you want," he whispers near my ear and kisses underneath it. "I know how you need it. Just as I know where your personal abyss leads..." He fingers me harder. "I want you to let go, Olivia. I want you to crash. And that you fly and are free."

I nod and look him in the eye.

"And I want you to catch me."

"I will always do that!" He kisses me briefly and smears my lipstick, probably because he cannot stand it any longer either. However, unfortunately soon after, he pulls his fingers out – and here I was so close – and says that we're leaving now. I become even more excited and agitated, yet never in my life, do I feel closer to being me than right now.

Than this night.

39. L'obsession

Olivia

We drive forever away from the city. Along a deserted rainy country road lit only by streetlights

What is this?

I do not like it.

My instincts are on high alert.

I'm as tense as the string of a bow and slowly begin to regret having agreed to all this.

I mean, seriously.

How long have I known him?

How well do I know him?

He could be a crazy psychopath.

A murderer with an eerie cabin in the woods, who takes young pretty woman and slowly tortures them to death.

Fuck! Liv!

Not to mention, he is acting quite differently now than he did earlier today. He's no longer cute, sweet, or tender. He doesn't even so much as look at me even though he usually knows how I feel, so now he should also notice how damn nervous and unsettled I am. But he does nothing to reassure me...

As we drive along the unpaved pebbled road in complete darkness with only the headlights illuminating the way, the play of light and shadows in the trees seem eerie. The moon isn't even out to provide some light. It is increasingly raining heavier and the queasy feeling inside of me grows stronger and stronger.

I have Riley. I have responsibilities. What will become of him if I don't make it back... What will Penny think? Will she adopt him? I haven't even said goodbye to him! I haven't told him how much I love him and that he's the sun in my life.

I'm so stupid, so stupid, so... In front of us, out of nowhere, two huge dark iron gates appear, a camera zooms in on our license plate and they slide open.

We enter a narrow paved lane that seems to go on forever. We are no longer surrounded by forest — but a park?

Okay! It definitely doesn't look like a cabin, which is slowly revealed in the rain. It's...a designer mansion! One that is usually featured in magazines about the rich and beautiful! It is modern, has clean lines, and is huge! It is made entirely of black stone. And towers high in the sky... I'm so taken aback, I have no saliva. I really didn't expect this here in the middle of the forest!

"You may close your pretty mouth, Miss Pierson," Keaton teases me and gets out. A few seconds later, he opens the passenger door, offers me his hand, and helps me out. He hands the key to the valet, *a real valet* standing in the middle of the forest in the rain. He leads me up the marble stairs to the double doors of the huge mansion. My knees are already weak. But I close my mouth and follow him...

Two minutes later, my mouth falls open again because the interior of the house is even more impressive than the exterior. First, we enter a huge room occupied by a man in a tuxedo. He's manning a golden rope that is set up in front of a curtain as a barrier. The penguin in the tuxedo bows as soon as he recognizes Keaton and murmurs, "Good evening sir!" Keaton's coat is taken from him, but when another page comes to my aid, Keaton signals him not to and he withdraws.

Another penguin approaches with a tray with two pitch-black shot glasses that contain a clear liquid. Keaton hands me one and raises his. "Cheers!" He clinks glasses with me. His eyes have a hard unyielding glare — it makes me nervous and keeps me from commenting. Llike him, I quickly down the surely expensive schnapps. It burns in my throat — I instantly feel more relaxed. But not nearly enough...

Next, the head penguin hands Keaton a mask and says, “Have fun, sir”. It is reminiscent of a Venetian mask, but without any frills, just plain black, which goes perfectly with my red lips. Wordlessly, I turn around for Keaton so he can put it on me.

My heart beats faster and faster.

I hear the deep bass of some hot rhythmic, modern number coming from the other room and again am surprised for I had not expected it out here in the middle of the boonies. Especially not what I encounter as we step through the curtain. We find ourselves in a huge living room. Or should I say salon? The lights are dimmed but many different sized candles light the room. No matter where you look, everything is cast in a mysterious glow. Like Keaton, I notice everyone present is wearing evening attire... At least the men. All of whom are young, athletically built, and good looking...like him. The women — wear *nothing*. I’m the only woman wearing something and immediately feel strangely exposed. Because of it. How crazy is that. Various chaise lounges stand around, a fireplace provides warmth and a cozy atmosphere. Bouquets of red and black roses are tastefully arranged throughout the room. The carpets and furniture look as expensive and exclusive as the spotlighted, erotic paintings on the walls. A piano takes up one corner, a black marble pedestal the middle of the room. On it is a kind of altar — I stare at Keaton wide-eyed. He says nothing. Merely focuses. On me. Only on me. He looks at me and only me, is absorbing every single one of my emotions. As it slowly dawns on me what this place is and what he has in store for me.

My feet stop automatically and anchor themselves to the ground. Keaton stops and waits patiently, like he expected this response.

Before I can say anything, a woman steps into view, one who even takes my breath away. I'm certainly not a lesbian, but if I were, I would kneel and kiss her feet. She has flowing long red hair that matches her lips. Besides me, she's the only other woman with something on. She's wearing a tight-fitting leather dress; high heels make her already long legs seem endless. Her body is as curvy as that of a goddess. It's all natural, not silicone-enhanced that I immediately notice with a professional and quite envious look. She smiles at Keaton. "Hello, John," she chirps enticingly.

"Hello, Amber!" He grabs her under the chin, raises her face, and kisses her.

WHAT THE HELL!

Everything in front of my shocked eyes grows blurry, which abruptly focuses, blending everything else out.

Except their tongues shamelessly wrestling each other and I feel as if the rug has been pulled away from under my feet.

I did not expect this.

It hurts!

It is unacceptable! But then it's also sexy how Keaton's jaw moves during kissing...and how really well they seem to fit together, is what a very stupid part of me thinks, the trashy part in me, the part that I usually only show on stage. I'm trying to break away from him, but he simply keeps hold of my upper arm and me in place, while he continues kissing her. Then he lets go off her and grins devilishly and defiantly at me, and I realize that I'm getting to know a completely different Keaton Rush from the man I so far know.

He's a sadist, a conscienceless barbarian and animal.

He jerks me to him and whispers in my ear, "It was merely a little welcome kiss, Miss Pierson, that's all." Everything before my eyes grows blurry again before they sharply focus on his full lips.

"Fuck you!" I spit at him.

"No, I'm going to fuck you. Very soon."

"You can't just do that!"

"I can and I will," he says and tows me after him.

I'm pissed off.

And yes, I'm also aware that he likes it and that it makes him hard, thinking that's probably exactly what he wants.

Now I'm incredibly pissed off.

Out of sheer anger, I down the next offered glass of whatever he gets from one of the perfect, *nude* waitresses and almost instantly feel light-headed and my tension easing.

He sits down with me on one of the sofas in the middle

of the room. A few naked women are kissing while men play poker and smoke cigars. You don't look at me. Not one lecherous look glides over me...which surprises me. I'm not used to it. Usually men ogle me like I'm a piece of fresh meat because I'm blonde, have an ass, and tits. Keaton puts an arm around me and turns my face to him. "I kiss her, but I fuck you, Olivia. I too belong to you."

"Then you should not do something like that in the future! At least if your balls mean anything to you!" I hiss. He laughs softly as he brushes his nose over my temple. His scent envelops me and I close my eyes since I'm suddenly as horny as a bitch in heat... God, I want him! And just BECAUSE he just did that!

So much!

So crazy!

"Then I'll leave it be. Your wish is my command!" He kisses me, his lips moving so beguilingly on mine that I allow it — though at first, I try to fight him. However, I did not expect to be this aroused already for my insides are constantly contracting. I want him, right here and now. The atmosphere and music alone pull me under their spell and in a rush... The flickering candlelight conveys the feeling of intimacy as if only us the two of us are here. But at the same time, I'm painfully aware we are not because everything seems overly sensitive. My nerve endings are tense and I am tingly on the inside when I feel his tongue and soon after, his hand, which pushes under neckline of the coat and spoils my bare breast. My nipples are the treacherously hard. I open one eye and notice a couple of men actually staring. All of them are attractive and they only look, nothing else... They seem patient, expectant...as if they have all the time in the world, simply waiting for a secret sign. Alerting them to whatever.

Keaton uses one hand to spread my legs apart and slowly pushes up the fabric of my coat, exposing me while he continues to kiss me, driving me insane, and I let it happen. I eye the men challenging, even spread my legs more — because I want them to find me hot. As hot as I am right now. My clit pounds and pure lust rushes through my veins...as Keaton slowly opens the coat. I'm half-naked, actually completely naked — not so different than the way men have already seen me on stage. Now some open their mouths as their breathing becomes labored, one or two pupils dilate, but everyone stays put. Keaton's hand slips down my stomach, cups my wet pussy, and I push against his palm. I need him inside me. Now the men's eyes turn greedy, a few adjust their crotch and slide nervously on their seats. I smile contentedly.

Keaton glances at them and they quickly avert their gazes.

Wow.

What is that about?

"You like that, right?' he asks near my mouth, but I cannot reply as he slides two fingers inside me...the shameless dirty bastard. Yes, that's what he is. And I love it. I moan his name and let my head fall back. I let myself go as he leans forward, brushes my nipples with his lips and teeth, and sucks on them while leisurely fingering me. Everyone can see it, they *should* see me. Oh, yeah!

His breath is hot, he even breathes faster. When I glance at his crotch, I notice quite the tent in his pants.

I moan louder.

As my inner muscles contract around his fingers, I almost feel him inside me and want him to do it.

Now.

Keaton pulls the fingers out of me and brushes them between my labia. Upward. And back down. Back upward. And down again. It's quite tempting, yet not enough...

When I open my eyes, I only see him.

Only him and his intoxicating eyes, which currently resemble two dark lakes that are staring right into my soul.

"Do you want to go up on stage?" My eyes glide up to the pedestal...and I swallow as I glance back at him.

"What happens up there?"

"Everything you've ever dreamed of deep down inside you...and nothing you don't want." He puts one leg over mine and holds mine apart as I try to close my thighs.

Heavens!

"How would you know what I want?"

"I know you!" He pushes two fingers inside me, I gasp and I cling with both hands onto the upholstery below me while my pelvis raises and pushes toward him. Lust robs me of my mind though it's funny, I can still formulate clear sentences.

"I'll fuck you in front of everyone, Olivia. The way you wanted it back in the diner when you knelt in front of me, your eyes literally begging me to do you right there in front of the window," he whispers in my ear and uses his fingers to show me what he's talking about. "I'll give you endless pleasure, make you soar...baby."

"Oh, God!" I gasp as he rubs his boner against me. He rubs against me what I so desperately want inside me.

"It will be hard and ruthless. It will be exactly the way you imagine it when you are alone. All that can come true now."

I nod even before I've actually given it any thought. Because my insides scream *YES!*

Finally, he grins approvingly as his eyes sparkle with lust, life, and desire. He whispers, "I knew it!" and kisses me briefly. Although, it resembles a violent emotional outburst, at least for Keaton...

He gets up and pulls me up onto the stage. As soon as I step onto it, I feel all eyes on me. It's like they're now allowed to look and I feel the blood rising to my cheeks and other places.

"You can always say stop," Keaton whispers from behind my ear as he pulls down the trench coat so that I'm standing on the podium only in high heels and stockings, seemingly illuminated on all sides — at least that's how it seems to me. My head is spinning, everything inside me is throbbing. "You can stop it anytime. Or ask for more!" he clarifies and uses his crotch to push me forward. To a kind of altar made of black stone. Keaton helps me lie down on it. The stone below me is cool, he pulls me so far forward so my butt is on the edge while he pulls my arms up and holds them firmly in place against the stone while he leans over me and looks me in the eyes as two other men tie my arms. I feel stretched, helpless, instinct tells me to flee, but then I look into his calm dark eyes and know I'm safe.

As long as he's by my side, I will always be safe.

"So nice," he whispers as soon as I'm tied up and immobile. The other men disappear from the stage and I'm lying there...breathless...panting while everything feels so much more intense. I feel like the famous sacrificial lamb on the altar. His index finger travels from my ankle up over my leg, my pubis, my stomach, between my breasts, and up to my chin. He lightly nudges it so I look at him as he positions himself over my head. "Do you really want this?" he asks again. Soft, like my Keaton.

I swallow. And nod.

"No, baby, tell me."

"I want it, Keaton Rush." It comes out a little more than a whisper, though it is from the bottom and most corrupt part of my heart.

He smiles and leans forward, kisses me...and everything grows blurry again as I taste his lips. He touches me...kneads my breasts, moans into my mouth, my nipples stand out even more as his hands slide down to my stomach. I squirm as much as my bonds allow me. And moan in frustration as he steps away and walks around me...so sexy...so elegantly, his movements are like flowing water while his piercing look is only directed at me. He stands between my legs and slowly opens his pants.

Too slowly.

And stares at me.

I can hardly stand it and writhe.

There is only him and me.

Me and him.

That's all, no one else in this world.

I have never felt this intensity. Never experienced this.

It is amazing.

The moment he finally pushes inside me, I come and shatter into a thousand pieces, knowing full well — I'll never be the same again.

***

Suddenly, there are hands everywhere. Strong male hands. Solely created to give me pleasure. Because yes, I just had a really intense orgasm, but my body still craves more. They stroke my breasts, tweak my nipples, and slide between my legs. Leisurely, slowly, quietly. Not in a disgusting groping way. No, only for me and my satisfaction, they pay homage to me, honor me. I open my eyes and glance to the right because instinctively, I know *he's* there. He's sitting in a chair next to me, lighting up a cigar, his eyes locked with mine. His expression is dark and damned turned on. Especially when I moan loudly as another huge cock pushes inside me. I gasp and my muscles greedily contract around it. I look at the man, see only his abdominal muscles, how they move, his tattooed muscled arms, dark hair, and full lips, which come down and kiss my neck. The guy is hot. I want him to come inside me. I want to drive him as crazy as all the hands on me make me feel. As Keaton's look makes me feel. As I raise and push my pelvis against the stranger, Keaton moans...but doesn't touch himself. He seems completely composed and focused, though his gaze betrays him. He's fully aroused...like I am... Soon, I'm coming again...as is the man. He squirts into a condom...before the next guy pushes inside me. He's equally well-equipped, just as sexy — I wonder if anyone here *doesn't* know how to fuck like a god... Or is it just Keaton's presence that makes me so hot and carries me off?

Away from morality, from any conscience thought.

Into a world that is only ruled by lust and desire.

To which I succumb more and more and more while I repeatedly climax...

I submit fully to my animalistic side.

To lust.

To intoxication.

I don't know how many men are fucking me.

I've lost count of my orgasms.

When I finally emerge from of the waves of lust and the intoxication slowly fades, dawn is on the horizon.

***

Keaton

I love you just now, Olivia.

You have taught me what the word love means.

You have taught me what feelings mean.

How it is when someone else is more important than oneself.

I'm watching them fuck you, see how your hot body glistens with sweat, how you're coming, twitching and groaning. You only moan my name, you only look at me. Because you know that you belong to me and that this here is my gift to you. I'm fulfilling your deepest forbidden fantasies, baby.

I *set you free*.

When you only lie there, spent and unable to move, I come to you and stroke your face, brush the sweaty streaks out of your eyes and...you smile at me.

That's the moment I became lost.

Really lost.

For now and for all time.

40. I Love You

Olivia

I'm completely beside myself when Keaton helps me off the altar and puts my coat around me. I cannot walk in my high heels as my legs are simply too weak. As they give way, his arm is there and safely catches me. Without hesitation, he picks me up and carries me out in his arms into the fresh air. I rest my forehead against his chest and keep my eyes closed.

Slowly the fog clears, the fresh air clears my head and I suddenly realize what I just did.

With whom I did it with...and how shameless I behaved.

So…so…

“What's this place?’ I ask as we stop on the mansion's front porch and Keaton set me on my feet. I glance up at the facade while we wait for his car... The house appears even darker now, just like he was inside.

"That's L'Obsession. One of my countless establishments," he replies and eyes me cautiously. His words dawn on me slowly. "YOUR establishment?"

"Yes." Unreadable, he looks at me.

I stare at him while my mind replays everything that happened in there.

How he used me.

Quite unconscionable.

Without qualms.

Coldly and ruthlessly.

But most of all, how much I enjoyed it.

Then I really am mortified.

I'm a mother! I have pride and a conscience! Even I have a limit to my shame!

But inside that place, I behaved like a whore! A real whore!

Dammit! How could I have been so stupid! So…so…

"Hey..." he says softly and his forefinger raises my chin. "Don't be embarassed. We're taught to feel shame, it's not inherent in us. And it is absolutely uncalled for! Behind these walls we forget everything we've been taught. Every single one of us. We are just us. We feel what we want to feel. We don't think or *over*think things. This here is my world, which I couldn't simply tell you about because it would have scared you off. I had to show it to you, let you feel it. Now it has happened! What happened has happened and that's it. In the end, it's only one thing that matters: Did you like it?" I nod mechanically.

"Did you have fun?" I blush as I nod again.

"That's all you should care about. You should never be ashamed for doing something you love, Olivia," he repeats his sentence from back when and suddenly many things become clear to me...

About me.

About him.

Keaton Rush.

What happened inside that place was terrific. Absolutely mind-blowing.

Even though I climaxed numerous times and feel completely satisfied, I still feel a constant spark of arousal coursing through my veins. That cannot be normal.

"Why am I still aroused?"

"The drink contained a mild aphrodisiac, Olivia. To help us loosen up." Loose, oh yeah, I've definitely was that in there. "It didn't make you do anything you didn't actually want to do," he says seriously. And yes, he asked me a thousand times if I really wanted it and he kept a close eye on me the entire time. I knew he would stop it at the slightest sign that I was experiencing discomfort...and that I was safe...

But...something still bothers me.

Something I cannot put a finger on, something that gives this intoxicating unique experience a bad after taste... I simply can't grasp it right now because my head is still in a fog, like an out of body experience.

I frown. I have so many questions for him and view him in a different light now. Keaton Rush is not an upstanding businessman, not a man of the law, not a man who is made to protect and serve others, as I assumed. He also has a destructive and unscrupulous side. A side that is willing to share what belongs to him. Did he bring other women before me here and fucked them in front of others? Am I the first to do this with him? I'm afraid not.

But that is not what bugs me. That is not what is destroying me on the inside.

Honestly.

I thoroughly enjoyed what happened in there.

I trusted him.

And I love him, I love him so much like I've never loved a man...and right now, I have to get it off my chest, I cannot keep it to myself any longer.

"Keaton," I say quietly and the truth spills out of me. "I'm afraid of you, of what you make me feel." The car pulls up and he waves dismissively to the valet. Instead, he briefly cups my face with his hands and looks deep into my eyes.

"You're scared because you've never felt anything so intense and you only feel it because of me. I am challenging you because I know what you're capable of, what's behind the many walls you're obstinately trying to keep erect, just to prove something to others. I'm here so you get to know and love all sides of you. The darkest abysses and the brightest, most magical moments. I've already told you, with me it's all or nothing. If this is a bit too much for you to handle or you cannot or do not want to deal with it, tell me *now*. Then I'll drive you home and we'll never see each other again." Patiently, he watches me and I know if I say the wrong thing, it'll be over. The feelings I experience when I'm with him scare me, but at the same time, they excite me and I cannot see myself living the boring old life of a mother and housewife anymore.

He offers me so much, more than I could ever have wished for.

More than I could have ever imagined.

But most of all, he makes me learn new things about myself. I'm dealing with my darkest fetishes, my most secret secrets, and subconscious dreams. Yes, he's correct, he's helping me.

On the other hand, I have no idea what my limits are or how far I can go.

"Do you trust me?" he asks, my eyes betraying my confusion and uncertainty. There is only one answer.

I nod.

He smiles crookedly, leans forward, straight to my ear, and asks, "Do you love me?" My heart briefly stops as goose bumps spread across my body and every fiber of my being goes crazy. My inner voice speaks up and screams only one word. *YES!*

I swallow and close my eyes as he whispers, "I love you too."

And that's all that matters.

At least, for the moment.

Epilogue

You don't see me, but by now, you suspect I'm around.

I'm always around — no matter what you do. As usual.

No matter if you are the loving mother or my depraved whore. I protect you when you think there's no one there for you, I listen to you when you think no one is listening to you, and I see you when you would love to be invisible. I feel you when you rub your small hot body against me and when you wear your little costume and play my assistant.

I know what you think of yourself and who you would like to be. I know what you need and gave it to you.

Now you're mine.

And that will never change.

Because this game has just begun.

THE END (for now)

Excerpt from POSSESED

Ardor, Stalking, and Drooling Monsters

Keaton

I love it when you are too hot, Olivia.

You've been lying in your underwear on the floor of your living room for a good 20 minutes now surrounded by 20 fans. They are set on the highest speed, but you're still too hot.

I zoom in and see drops of sweat rolling down your neckline.

I know I could knock on your door anytime and have my way with you, but secretly watching you is special in itself. It's something that will probably never stop fascinating me.

You still haven't unpacked even one of the 20 packages I've sent you. They contain new shoes, new clothes, new makeup — it's because you're too proud to accept them, no, it's due to laziness.

Since we dropped off Riley at the clinic, you've grown quite lazy, Olivia. The sink is full of dirty dishes, at least a week's worth, every day you eat pasta with some sauce and you sleep on the sofa with Rosie, who left behind greasy footprints everywhere.

I've suggested that you sleep at my place, but again, you were too lazy to pack your things and come over. So, I always must visit you in that pigsty, where some day I'm sure I'll contract herpes.

You have no idea what you're doing to me, baby.

Considering everything, I honestly can't explain why you still turn me on. I'm curious to see if you'll show up at work on Monday since you are so lazy right now — and if you still have a clean blouse. Maybe that will push you to open a few of the packages from me. Some contain really pretty blouses in them, baby, all your taste, plus much nicer lingerie. According to *my* taste.

I'm tired of always seeing the same items on your hot body.

Really.

It's time again to bring some action into your lazy sloth life, Olivia. I grab my cell phone and call while I watch you. I see you flinch when you hear the ring tone you chose to announce my calls. Darth Vader — back then, you thought you were so funny, Olivia. You lie there for a few seconds, probably on purpose, making me wait to annoy me. I know you. For that, I should spank your ass. Eventually, you nudge your hairy monster with your nose and are kind enough to reach for your cell phone, which is still lying on the ground.

"Yeah," you answer and I smile because you're smiling.

"What are you doing right now, baby?"

"Oh, I'm having a stressful day," you sigh theatrically. "Busy cleaning and all that, plus Rosie made a mess again in the apartment, and Penny needs my help too... Oh, and I have to go through all the paperwork and rules of etiquette that you've sent me."

"Quite praiseworthy."

"Yes, I listen to what you tell me."

"You're a good girl," I whisper and take my time thinking about how to punish you. As always, when I adopt that certain tone with you...but I decide to let you sweat a while longer. "Do you remember when I told you that I have eyes and ears everywhere, that I'm always there, Olivia?" Instantly, you're on your feet and glance around in panic, you even stumble over your drool monster. It barks and you jump, almost fall onto the couch as you reach for your dressing gown. With a quick move, you put it on and look around again, this time with narrowed eyes. I cannot help but grin widely.

"Are you stalking me?" Your eyes are slits as you continue searching and I almost laugh.

"I would never think of stalking you, baby. Only mad people do that."

"Ha-ha!" you reply sarcastically...I think; *if only you knew.*

"Don't forget you have that final meeting with Mrs. Assface, as you refer to her, at 1 pm."

"Huh, how do *you* know that?" you ask suspiciously. Yes, Olivia, according to you, I only know that Riley will attend a new school that suits him better once he's released from the clinic. After all, I have great contacts and you've given me your blessing to find something more appropriate for him. It might not be exactly cheap, but you don't mind swallowing your pride when it concerns your son. But I love that about you too. You have no idea that I'm familiar with your entire schedule — and I'll keep it that way.

"I know everything there is to know about you, so get used to it already! *Now* turn back into a human being!" With that I hang up.

In a Rush with Mr. Rush

Olivia

"Seriously?" I continue glaring at my phone, long after hanging up. I'm *always* a human being, even when I'm *not*. Okay, I know I've gained a few pounds over the last few weeks and Keaton said it suited me! And yes, oftentimes, my hair is a bit greasy, probably enough to grease a pan with if I wanted to, I pretty much have let myself go a bit ever since Riley left and only do what I feel like doing. I've never had this luxury — and I'm enjoying it to the fullest.

Obviously, I miss Riley and make up for it by eating junk food, but I am certain he's in good hands and he will return to me a happier person. Now, I have money! Thanks to Keaton! The crazy man has already given me an advance on my salary! Five thousand dollars! For the first time in my life, I can enter a store and buy what I want. Or cancel my rent agreement and move into a nicer apartment. A red Mini Cooper is parked outside the building. It's a company car that Keaton forced on me. Okay, I admit, I kind of love the car. I named it Mathilda, she is only three months old. I've never had a new car, let alone a car. Two years ago, I used some of the money I made at the strip club to get a driving license, but I didn't get a car since I couldn't afford the upkeep, like taxes, insurance, fuel, and so on. Anyway, a lot has happened in the last few weeks I never thought possible. Riley spends his days at the clinic and nights with my sister, Louisa, since she lives in New York. Regardless that she is single and focused on her career, she's lovingly caring for him. But then she always had a weak spot for Riley, how could she not love him?

He's not like those usual little turds, he's an actual treasure.

Keaton also loves him almost as much as I do, I'm sure of it. That is one of the reasons that convinced me to get involved with him. Even though I didn't want a man in my life and most definitely not a relationship.

Since I have a meeting with Miss Assface, I should get ready slowly, though I really am not in the mood for her unsophisticated prissiness. She is chronically angry with me – and probably with the rest of the world – and believes I'm neglecting my child, that I'm a bad mother. I really have no idea why I even have to talk to such a person. And in the middle of the summer vacation, like one doesn't have better things to do. But she stated it was important...so I agreed to one final meeting, rolling my eyes.

First, I search for something clean to wear before Rosie and I get ready. Unfortunately, I have no clean clothes since I haven't done a load of laundry since Riley left. I have no choice but to open one of the thousand packages Keaton sent me knowing it contains shoes. It's not like he didn't tell me often enough that he could no longer stand looking at my tattered shoes and that he wants to see clothes on me that flatter my body. I glance at Rosie and mimic Keaton, "Your figure is too good for mass-produced items, Olivia, you cannot wear things off the rack, Olivia, you are too good for it, Olivia." Rosie tilts her head and a glob of drool drips to the ground. "You're too cute when you drool!" I cannot resist, squat down, and lightly pinch her cheek. Bored, Rosie looks at me with her glassy bug eyes.

I sigh and look at the stack of boxes with my fists on my hips, like some archenemy. Then I go through package after package to determine which contain clothes and which shoes. "Okay, Victoria's Secret, in here is probably nothing appropriate to wear for my meeting with the teacher." I throw the box behind me and devote myself to the next one. "Bloomingdales... You really want me to look like a broad from Fifth Avenue?" I glance at Rosie and murmur, "Yeah, don't look at me like that. I know he cannot see me." I devote myself to the next box. My eyes look like saucers as I read the inscription. "H & M!" I shout out like a prayer and rip open the box. In it is a little card on which says in bold letters: **I knew you would open this package first, Olivia. It might not be what I like to see on you, but it is what you're comfortable in.** I grin stupidly as I clutch the card to my chest.

God, I love, love, love this man!

Overcome with joy, I empty the clothes on the floor where Rosie's hair spreads all over and contemplate. Skinny jeans for 20 dollars, tops for 12, colorful summer dresses for 30 dollars...and pj's with the words: *I'm a donut.* It's Keaton's way of being humorous and I'm cracking up quietly like a crazy person.

I opt for an airy yellow summer dress with spaghetti straps. Yellow equals happiness, which is how I feel when I think about him.

Then I go into the bathroom and get ready.

***

I park my inconspicuous red mini in front of the school, put my sunglasses on, and get out. In my head, I'm humming the soundtrack to Rambo to get ready for my battle with Mrs. Assface. I climb the stairs to the building in my pretty, flat sandals and abruptly stop when I recognize who's already there holding the door open for me.

Holy shit.

What is he doing here?

He looks wonderful dressed in loose white chinos and tight dark blue polo shirt accentuating his muscular torso and biceps. Fuck...I'm melting... As usual, his dark hair is slicked back and I'm reminded of this morning, when I clawed at it as he was going down on me while I was sitting on the kitchen counter. He's smiling like he knows what I'm thinking, then takes off his sunglasses and hooks them into the neckline of his shirt.

"Keaton!" I bark.

He grins. "Olivia."

"What are you doing here?" I whisper as soon as I am in front of him, his scent causing befuddlement.

"I'd like to get to know Mrs. Tightass or whatever you call her."

"You can't just come to a parent-teacher meeting without prior notice, Keaton!"

"I showed up at your parents without prior notice, baby. So I damn well can and will, so let's go!" I would love to stomp my feet like a little brat, for him to just show up here, looking outrageously sexy and not at all interested in my opinion. But I know better than to start arguing with him when he's in this kind of mood, so I walk by him into the building and feel him behind me. This here will have consequences.

In front of the classroom, I take a deep breath before I knock. Somehow, I'm actually glad he showed up, which of course, I will never say. Purely on principle.

"Come in!" It croaks and I feel like throwing up as soon as I hear her disgusting voice.

As soon as I open the door a crack, she spews her venom. "It's nice to actually see you show up for a parent-teacher conference about your son." Before I can return a snide remark, Keaton walks into the room and approaches her, offering her his hand. "Hello, I'm Mr. Rush, nice to hear how involved you are, Mrs. Garvey." She stares at him for a few seconds. I roll my eyes. It's all it takes for her to be completely under his spell, though by now, I'm used to his effect on women. Surely, cum is already running down her legs since she has been celibate for two thousand years. I grin and force myself not to laugh. Funny, a moment ago, that little toad face with glasses on the tip of her nose was as hard as can be, but now after shaking Keaton's hand, she seems softer.

"What's your relation to Riley?" she asks.

"What's your relation to my wife that you take liberties and speak to her in that tone of yours?" Keaton immediately snaps back at her without batting an eye. His face is totally calm and relaxed, whereas my mouth drops open and I look from one to the other. Toad face audibly gasps and is apparently at a loss for words. I sympathize with her. Most become timid when Mr. Rush is in his element.

Yet the only thing on continuous replay for me is: *His wife!*

"I cannot recall ever using an improper tone with your wife, Mr. Rush! Let us first take a seat!" She's still a bit perplexed, but quickly catches herself and gestures to two chairs. My heart is still pounding as I'm still thinking about him calling me *his wife* — it sounds so nice. We sit and I'm glad I don't have to face the dragon lady alone. As a couple, a lot in this world is easier.

"I thought you were a single parent, Mrs. Pierson."

"Well, you thought wrong, but let's get down to business. What is the problem? Maybe I can help?" Keaton intervenes, sitting there with his arm casually on the back of my chair, his fingers playing with my hair, distracting me. He probably intends for me to relax, yet here he only makes me feel even more anxious so that I cannot focus on anything else.

"Well..." Mrs. Toad opens her student ledger and references her fussy notes. "It seems most of the time, Riley doesn't pay proper attention to the lessons. He prefers to stare outside the window and look at the birds outside rather than at the board in here. And every time I pass him, he's busy scribbling whatever superhero in his notepad."

Keaton's expression is relaxed. "I don't see a problem. First, he can learn more outside in nature than in here, where he is drilled like a soldier who is not allowed to move freely or be a child. Second, are you actually trying to tell me creativity is a negative aspect?" The toad is baffled. She didn't expect such a reply.

"This here is a school, Mr. Rush, not a activities club. If you think your stepson can learn more in nature, perhaps you can take him on weekend trips into nature or to a comic expo. Here, at school, children are supposed to learn the curriculum that prepares them for the future, which includes abiding by the rules."

"I've never had any use for the stuff I learned in physics or chemistry classes. I have no idea why it is required to dissect a frog in high school nor do I have an idea why you think children can sit there and pay attention for six hours when you talk monotonously so that even I want to fall asleep. If you consider Riley's behavior *unwarranted*, you should have been at the school I went to at that age. Children need to move and they are easily distracted, so perhaps you should make your lessons more interesting, maybe then more will pay attention."

All the excitement makes the toad's freckled décolleté break out in red spots and I have to force myself not to burst out laughing. "Well, I've never had to listen to anything like that and I've been with this school for 30 years! How rude!"

Keaton skillfully ignores her indignation and keeps on talking in a bored way as if she didn't say anything. "You summoned us here for a final talk to tell us the boy has ADHD and it's best to keep him sedated so the teachers have it easier, or why are we here?"

"You're not only here because of your son, but because of your *wife...*" she actually makes quotation marks in the air with her fingers, "...never attended one PTA meeting under the pretext that she had to work, but now I learn she is not even a single parent. To me, it seems you don't even care about how your child is doing in school." Keaton's cheek muscle twitches, which is never a good sign, for Mrs.

Toadface that is. I continue forcing myself not to burst out in laughter.

"Well, Riley only has A's, B's, and C's?" Keaton says proudly and continues speaking, though now he leans slightly forward, to which Toadface automatically recoils.

"Besides, my wife's private life is not your fucking business nor how she spends her spare time and work hours. You're paid to organize the lessons in a way that makes the children want to learn and then they come home well-balanced. That's all you have to care about. But just so you know; Riley is in great health, apart from his leg of course, he's a curious, bright and happy child. He's a *normal* kid, like millions of other kids. So, do your job and use your spare time for a hobby, that way you are also well-balanced and happy when you're at home in the evenings. Then you'll have no more need to get involved in the privacy of one of your student's parents. I don't want to hear any more complaints from my wife, so please, Google my name, Keaton J. Rush, check out the connections I have and let your imagination do the rest. Besides, we will be taking Riley out of this inept school and placing him in one where he can be himself. Olivia, we're leaving."

The entre time I haven't said a single word, I simply sat there and stared like a sheep at Keaton, who is standing and lets me go first.

Even the toad has gone completely pale and doesn't know what to say. She is staring silently after us as we exit the classroom. I cannot help myself and stick my head back in, smile and wave at her and then Keaton pulls me back out of the room with a jerk.

***

As soon as the door is closed, Keaton undergoes a personality change and vents his anger while running his fingers through his hair, "Fuck, I didn't mean to get that involved, I swear, Olivia, but hey, I'm sorry tha..." He abruptly chokes because I have him by the collar, pulling him to the bathroom. I kiss him and enjoy his hoarse groan as he digs his fingers in my buttocks, reciprocating my ambush.

He just came onto me.

And I want him.

Now.

We're stumbling backward into the restrooms for the teachers and enter the first convenient stall. Keaton kicks the door shut with his foot and pushes me against it.

"Miss Pierson, so naughty, what would Mrs. Garvey say about your attack?" he teases me hoarsely.

"This here might be something she's fantasized about..." I wildly brush through his hair as I leave a wet trail behind on his neck since I cannot get enough of him. "I can imagine what she would say about the attack? Probably, *oh my God, Mr. Rush, you are so manly and well-equipped...*"

He laughs softly, his breath tickling my cheek. "Oh, Miss Pierson, what am I going to do with you?"

"Just fuck me, Mr. Rush. Right here and now!"

"It'd be my greatest pleasure, Miss Pierson." He runs his hand under my skirt and immediately slides it into my panties. I'm holding my breath when I feel his fingertips on my most private area. He grins diabolically and slowly pushes two fingers inside me...

Oh my God, it feels so good.

Groaning, I throw my head back.

"But Margeret, I told you Madame Pussy can't have cheese!" The disgusting voice of the Toad suddenly penetrates my lust-Rush, I freeze and look up wide-eyed at Keaton.

His grin widens — and he indicates with a forefinger to my lips that I should be quiet. I bite my lip because he doesn't even think about pulling out his fingers or something. Meanwhile, the Madame Pussy show continues and soon after, we learn she apparently has diarrhea. *Madame Pussy, who the fuck is Madame Pussy?* We peek through the small gap between door and stall wall and I can see Miss Garvey pacing back and forth in front of the sink with her cell phone, screaming into it. She constantly pushes her glasses back up the bridge of her nose and looks worried. "My poor, poor pussy. Yeah, I think it's best if you make her a hot water bottle...and give her some cod liver oil."

I had to keep from bursting out laughing and quickly pressed my mouth against Keaton's shoulder. Fuck!

The woman truly is beyond help.

She ends her conversation, does her business in the stall

next to ours, and walks out of the bathroom without washing her hands.

I can't hold back any longer and start to giggle... Keaton smiles at me, looking so damn beautiful. Then he starts to move his fingers inside me and whispers, "Well, let's take care of *your* Madame Pussy."

The First Work Days are Shit

Olivia

The first work days are shit. You don't know anybody, yet everyone gives you a funny look, probably because eighty percent know you're the pretty blonde bimbo who's sleeping with the boss and got the job because of it. The women hate me anyway, whereas the men have nothing better to do than to stare at my tits and ass and not take me seriously.

Working in that strip club had been good for me. It made me realize that I'm a beautiful young woman and men are pigs. Most of them.

Despite all the shitty thoughts about my first day at work, I'm fully energized as I get ready at seven a.m. and slip into my pretty white blouse and pencil skirt. Like every morning, I talk with Riley over the phone while I eat breakfast and enjoy hearing the exuberance in his voice as he tells me about his latest progress. God, I miss him...

After I bring Rosie up to Penny and exchange a few words with her – lately we do not talk much since she's still leery about Keaton – I walk downstairs and get into my car. Keaton, as agreed, already sent me the information about where I have to go. Confused I frown since the navigation system shows a destination outside the city. *A street with no name. Yeah, that sounds trustworthy.*

Okay, maybe we're going meeting in a secret Mafia hideout or something... *I'm sure we won't have a quickie in my freshly ironed clothes or hunt criminals through the underbrush*, I think as I drive off.

Out of the city, heading straight toward nowhere...

At some point, I drive through a forest and my navigation system even loses the GPS signal. Is he pulling a fast one on me? I try calling him, but I there is no cell phone service either. How did I make it to the street with no name and now stand here in my pretty business suit and heels, in the middle of the forest? My bright red Mini most likely will attract all the bears in the vicinity.

I curse Keaton Rush, though eventually decide to follow the path. I know any normal person would be driving back to the street with no name, but since I know Keaton, I don't think I'm lost. After a good five minutes of driving through the boonies, during which my ass receives a massage from all the prehistoric potholes, I arrive at a clearing where I see

Keaton's black Maserati parked in front of an absolute dump. In most places, its facade has peeled, the garden and surrounding area is overgrown with weeds, some windows are broken, some not, and half the roof is missing.

Fucking crap, he's an assassin after all, I knew it! I think, but I still get out and walk toward the house instead of running away screaming.

"Keaton?" I call softly, then my heels sink into the mud and I'm cursing as I have to pull them out, again and again... I must make a miserable picture. Then I find myself on a path of broken cobblestones that runs to the house before I finally open a rotten wooden door. "Keaton?" I call softly, afraid too much noise might collapse the house on top of my head.

"I'm here, baby!" he shouts. I am relieved and follow his voice. He's standing in what must have been the living room – wearing an immaculate dark suit – examining his surroundings with his hands in his pockets. "Isn't it beautiful?" he asks dreamily, whereas I look around in disgust. I see an ancient rat-infested couch and small black eyes flash at me from up in the rafters. I scream. "EEEE, there's an opossum up there, Keaton!"

He doesn't even look at me when he replies, "That's Daisy, leave her alone, she's more afraid of you than you are of her."

"Okay, perhaps you and Daisy would like more privacy, I don't mind going outside."

"So now you're jealous of an opossum, Olivia?" he asks

when he finally faces me. One eyebrow is up and he appears amused, as he usually does when I act a little nutty.

Ass.

"What are we doing here, Keaton?"

"You have to let your imagination run free, baby!"

"Oh, please, we won't be having sex here!"

"Just imagine…" He steps up behind me, wraps his arms around my stomach, and places his chin on my shoulder, and continues, "…in Daisy's place hangs a chandelier, below it a chaise lounge...over there a bar, next to it a cozy fireplace. Here we could put up a St. Andrew's Cross, and over there a whirlpool..."

"What the hell, Keaton, are you high?"

"Well, how would you arrange it?"

"Arrange what?"

"The nightclub, baby."

"A nightclub?"

"Well, starting today, you're working for me, are you not?"

"Yeah," I reply timidly.

"That means you'll assist me in everything I do."

"Shouldn't I do that at the FBI too?" I ask, confused.

He laughs amused. "Oh, baby, I won't let you grow old and wither in that dry boring office, like all the other snobs. You have so much more potential, of which even you are still clueless."

I turn to face him. "Wait a minute, will this be one of your brothels and I'm supposed to do something here, prostitute myself or whatever?"

Now he's not at all amused. His eyes flash.

"*If* you prostitute for someone, it'll be me. I thought we were clear on that."

"So what was that number back then?"

"Simply a little test if you'd be up for what I intend to do with you."

"You had who knows how many men fuck me while you sat there, watching, what kind of strange test was that supposed to be?"

"There were four, Olivia, my best four, if you want to know. Bryan, James, Louis, Costa are their names, if interests you. It is apparent the incident still bothers you even though you said you never wanted to talk about it again."

I huff. "You know what, Keaton, you're an asshole!"

"And you're too cute when you're at a loss for words." He gently lifts my chin and kisses me. I know he only acts this way with me.

When he pulls away, I am feeling calmer. I make the hard Keaton Rush turn into a picture-book fairytale prince.

"So, what's this all about?"

"As you know, I own a few establishments."

"Yes, you're a pimp, Keaton," I interrupt dryly.

"In street lingo, perhaps."

I roll my eyes. "Come on, what's this all about, Mr. Pimp? Should I become your madam or what? If so, I want a leopard coat and gold rings." He laughs. I just love it when he does that.

"Anyway, I have a few establishments and plan to open a new one. I want you to arrange everything. I trust you because you already have inside knowledge of men's darkest desires as well as exquisite taste." With each word, my eyes grow a bit wider. "There is no limit to the budget. I set up a meeting with the site manager, as for the architect, I'm sure you'll get along nicely... You have free rein, though I'm going to assist with the important decisions. This is my way of showing that I trust you one hundred percent, Olivia, and that I see so much more in you."

I'm just staring at him.

And continue staring.

And staring.

"Okay, so I know about hooker crap because I was a stripper, right?" I hiss, knowing I'm exaggerating. Keaton pulls his phone out of his pocket and says, "Okay, no problem, I'll call Amber and do it with her! As usual."

I instantly snatch the cell phone from his hand and hiss, "You will not do anything with *Amber*!"

"Oh, so you're in after all?"

"Of course I'm in! What do you think?"

"Well. But remember, Olivia, if you play games with me, you'll come out the loser!"

"Who's this stupid Amber anyway, what was it she called you again?" I cannot recall it, but she certainly didn't call him Keaton...

"Amber is my partner in these projects."

"Aha. And what else?"

"I've fucked her a few times." He looks straight at me and once again, I'm reminded of his other side, the not so sweet loving one... he's no longer my fairytale prince, more like a monster out to get me.

"And why did you kiss her in front of me like that?"

"I wanted you to get mad, baby," he states as if that explanation is sufficient. There are times when the man is really not normal.

"Have you fucked her since we started our thing?"

"Of course not, I might be a bastard, but I don't cheat!" He says the right thing, thus saving himself. "You belong to me and I belong to you too, only to you. Basically, you decide who I'm going to fuck. If you want me to only fuck you, so be it. And if you want me to fuck somebody else, then I'll fuck somebody else."

I shake my head.

"It's only 8:45 and I'm already dizzy from all this talk about fucking."

"Oh, baby, you love it." He smiles at me again and cups my cheek with a hand. He's gentle again, he's my Keaton again. "So, are you in, Olivia? Yes or no?"

"Like you'd ever give me a choice, Keaton."

Note of thanks

I want to watch *You*, but damn Maria forces me to write the note of thanks now. And yes. Maria read the PRESENT TENSE book ages ago, and yes, we let it inspire us, though, as usual, we put our own spin to it. As you've just read, the story of Keaton and Olivia is not over yet, after all, we are OBSESSED. We've been sitting here like the two lunatics that we are and laughed, gasped, shared the thrill, and threw up at some things.

A few things still have not been addressed, like how Olivia will react when she finds out Keaton has been stalking her and that he is John. Speaking of John and Riley. We really grew fond of the little rascal, quite unexpectedly so, just like Rosie. But, in actuality, we celebrate Olivia the most because she is like us. She is a strong woman in a less than optimal situation. She is no Miss Perfect, but a normal woman who would go through fire for her family, which she is still to do — SPOILER ALERT.

Thanks to our team at buchuebersetzer.webs.com! Thanks to APP Verlag!

Thanks to the bloggers who support us!

Thanks to Nicole – just for being Nicole.

And of course, THANK YOU ALL!

We look forward to your feedback!

How do you like Keaton? How do you like Olivia? How do you like Riley? Are you as obsessed with Mr. Rush as we are? Would you like to know more about his dark side?

We sit here biting our nails in anticipation of your reviews because that's what an author LIVES for! <3

Your little shits, Don and Maria

Other books by Don Both and Maria O'Hara

Seducing Mr. O'Connor: (German, soon to be translated into English) https://amzn.to/2RMQ1Rs

SPECIAL PRICE!

Supposedly, forbidden fruits taste best.

From the first moment Mr. O'Connor steps foot into Annabelle Thompson's classroom and introduces himself as their new teacher, she knows she wants him.

Whether she wears clothes where the navel is exposed or bright red lips — Anna never misses an opportunity to turn his head and truly believes the saying: Though the mind is strong, the flesh is weak. And willing! Quite so!

She soon starts to play a forbidden game — a game where she plays with fire.

A game where boundaries between passion and lust get out of hand.

A game that turns into so much more than originally planned...

But at what price?

This is the first of two volumes.

Rejecting Mr. O'Connor: (German, soon to be translated into English) https://amzn.to/2D3SYFo

SPECIAL PRICE!

A new year begins. And with it a new life — at least that's what Anna thinks after Aiden O'Connor dumped her in the most despicable way. She didn't expect to see him again — especially not as her lecturer at the university.

And this time, Aiden turns the tables.

He wants to win back Annabelle more than anything else and comes up with the strangest, most seductive engagements, while Anna vehemently continues to resist him. After all, she won't let him break her heart a second time.

The two size each other up like two starving wolves ready to attack — until events become intertwined and there's no turning back.

But in which direction?

Are you able to forgive?

Are you able to forget?

But most of all; are you able to resist?

The second and last volume about Anna and Aiden.

Tempting Mrs. Waldorf: (German, soon to be translated into English) https://amzn.to/2RG111T

When Nathan Thompson sees his boss Sharon Waldorf for

the first time, he immediately knows she embodies everything he despises: haughtiness, inflexibility, and absolute dryness.

The typical cock-blocker.

That's why he has a great time trying to lure her out of her reserve, to provoke her, to push her beyond her limits, and to have the hottest verbal arguments with her.

He isn't even her type. But then why is it Sharon cannot think of anything else than the beautiful chaos? Why does that the rude pervert makes her feel like a woman for the first time, desire overwhelming her that she soon can no longer deny?

How much can you lose yourself in someone that you actually hate?

Provocation versus sense.

Hatred versus desire.

Love versus lust.

Who will come out the winner in the end? Or is this game doomed from the beginning?

This is a one volume story.

About Don Both

Don Both is 29 years old, born in Czechoslovakia, and currently living in Switzerland. She started writing stories at the age of 12 when it was a subject in school and she made an effort to hand in the best short story ever. She succeeded and discovered she had a talent for writing stories. During her school years and vocational training to become a nanny, she let her imagination run wild as a hobby author. Initially, she mainly focused on writing romance novels and humorous comedies. However, she also dabbled in drama, fantasy, and horror. Later on, she added more and more eroticism that quickly became her favorite genre. In 2010, she took the big step, daring to publish a few of her stories on the Fanfiction website for a larger audience. Her fear of them mocking her was utterly unfounded. She quickly amassed a large enthusiastic following with her provocative yet honest stories and won awards in several competitions. Encouraged by these successes, in 2013 she published her first successful novel *Always on Saturdays* and has since become one of the most widely read authors in the e-book market. Privately, she is committed to animal welfare, attempts to do a good deed each day while enjoying her life in tranquil Switzerland together with her cats and super sweet shepherd.

Recommended reads

Previous volumes – Under Your Skin – A series!

Under Your Skin: http://amzn.to/2kvnPBv Presently only available in German, soon to be translated into English

Always on Saturdays – The Unholy Book of Tristan Wrangler – series, Available in German and English

A review, if you want to learn more about Tristan, Mia, and Robbie:

"The story has been told a thousand times – he is young, sexy, athletic, and rich. She is smart, chubby, insecure, from a poor family... Actually, I never expected to be this engrossed – but we're talking about Tristan Wrangler...who is really hot! It quickly becomes apparent that his perfect outer facade is hiding a wonderful person. I really like the writing style of Don Both. She can write as dirty as Tristan grins!"

The Unholy Book of Tristan Wrangler – anthology for a special price: http://amzn.to/2c3VpKd

My Girl, book 2 – special price: https://www.amazon.de/Immer-wieder-Verf%C3%263-Werkelband-ebook/dp/B01C63HCWC/ref=asap_bc?ie=UTF8

Mine, book 3: https://www.amazon.de/Immer-wieder-Tristan-Mia-ebook/dp/B012AQ6FPK/ref=asap_bc?ie=UTF8

Yours, book 4: http://amzn.to/2cq2tT6

Available only in German, soon to be translated into English: Mia und Tristans Travel zum Glück: https://www.amazon.de/Tristans-Travel-Gl%C3%BCck-kuschel-ige-Weihnacht-ebook/dp/B01MYSERYR/ref=pd_sim_351_1?_encoding=UTF8&psc=1&refRID=VDKYHM3BY7S1TJGTR2WW

If you want to know more about Lilian Price and Vladimir Romanov:

Available only in German, soon to be translated into English:

Mad Love: http://amzn.to/2c3Xt4D

Bad Love: http://amzn.to/2cqdXpI

And especially, Ménage à trois: http://amzn.to/2c3XFkr (This is about Kristov's parents)

The Tower series also includes a part of Kera Jung, but not with the familiar characters: https://www.amazon.de/gp/product/B00LGUV7FK/ref=series_rw_dp_sw

If you want to know more about Luca Cavalli and his Isabella:

Isabella Parker is thirty-two years old and as a successful public prosecutor, has achieved all she can professionally. Her private life is quite different — she has no need for love, friends, or a family. She likes being a loner until she meets the charismatic Luca on her (forced) vacation, who shows her what it means to live.

On one hand, she has never met such an attentive,

charming, and attractive man, and on the other, he does have a dark side — one that could become a fatal attraction.

By the time she finds out it is already too late and she succumbs to the subtle seduction of the mysterious stranger.

This concludes the first move of his game.

A slightly different Don Both novel...

Completed romance/erotic/thriller

Available only in German, soon to be translated into English:

Corvo - Game of Love: http://amzn.to/2cqcmzY

About Maria O'Hara

Maria O'Hara was born in 1991 and lives in Baden-Württemberg. Writing for her is the equalizer to everyday life, balancing between reality and fantasy. With the right musicians, she can capture precise moments in her mind and after many cups of latte, it can happen that the night is abruptly over and three chapters have been written. In the foreground, Maria's stories are about drama, the more tangled and profound the better.

Published in German:

Wild Cherry, Sweet Cherry

Ride or die – Obsession, Ride or die – Black summer, Ride or die – Dark Paradise

Beautiful Mess

Rebels – Band eins, Rebels – Band zwei

Pretty in White – Emily, Pretty in Black – Emma, Pretty

in Red – Ami

Pure Sin:

Mit Emily Key:

The Plaza Manhattan:

1. Room 666
2. Diamondheart
3. Game of souls
4. White Satin

Una Palabra

Mit Don Both:

Seducing, Mr. O'Connor

Rejecting Mr. O'Connor

Tempting Mrs. Waldorf

Obsessed

Possessed

Run, Baby, Run

Cry, Baby, Cry

Stay, Baby, Stay

Garden of Sin

Garden of Evil

Garden of Demons

Garden of Eden

XX – My Rose, my Thorn

Mit Kera Jung:

14 Carat

20 Carat

24 Carat

Printed in Germany
by Amazon Distribution
GmbH, Leipzig

27618991R00206